TOBIN FOR HIRE is the ninth in one of the most phenomenally successful series of all times. Nearly 3,000,000 copies of the hilarious adventures of Russ Tobin, Super Stud, have been sold throughout the world.

Also by Stanley Morgan in
Mayflower Books

THE SEWING MACHINE MAN
THE DEBT COLLECTOR
THE COURIER
COME AGAIN COURIER
TOBIN TAKES OFF
TOBIN ON SAFARI
TOBIN IN PARADISE
TOBIN IN TROUBLE

OCTOPUS HILL
MISSION TO KATUMA
THE FLYBOYS

Tobin for Hire

Stanley Morgan

Mayflower

Granada Publishing Limited
First published in 1975 by Mayflower Books Ltd
Frogmore, St Albans, Herts AL2 2NF

A Mayflower Original

Made and printed in Great Britain by
Richard Clay (The Chaucer Press) Ltd
Bungay, Suffolk
Set in Linotype Times

CHAPTER ONE

'Pssssst!'

'Mmm ...?'

'Russ!'

'Mmmm ...?'

'Are you awake?'

'Mmm ...?'

Splot! An old tennis sock hit me in the mouth.

'Wake up, Santa, it's seven o'clock.'

I could've killed him – Buzz, I mean. He'd just shocked me out of the most wonderful dream I'd had in months. I was in New York, lying on Slinky Linka's fabulous vibro-bed, wallowing in unashamed titillation, and she was willowing into the room wearing nothing but a pair of gold thigh-boots and a smile full of promise when the swine did it on me.

'Malone,' I groaned, 'you have no *conception* of what you have just interrupted.'

'Sure I have,' he grinned, throwing back his sheets and swinging his feet to the floor. 'You were having it off with Miami Jo Dell.'

'Wrong. I was *about* to have it off with Slinky Linka – you didn't even let me get it in.'

'Tough titty. Come on – out of there, the kiddy-winkies are awaiting.'

I gave another heartfelt groan, remembering – and already wishing I'd never agreed to take the job. All of which must be causing certain mystification among those of you who don't know what I'm talking about, so I'd better explain.

Well, to put you ever-so-briefly in the picture, my name is Tobin – Russ Tobin, a six-foot-tall, twenty-six-year-old and financially-embarrassed Englishman, momentarily half-asleep and trying to find his slippers. And my sock-heaving mate in the next bed is a big blond Australian lump who goes by the name of Buzz Malone. More about him in a moment.

The circumstances of our meeting aboard the Miami–New York train three nights ago defy reasonable belief, but suffice it to say that Buzz and I shared a nightmare adventure with a bunch of diamond smugglers, both on the train and later in New York City, and only just made it to safety across the Canadian border by the skin of our proverbials.

And here we now are, ensconced in the King Edward Hotel in Toronto, Buzz heading for the bathroom and me trying to wake up and quench my recent disappointment regarding the luscious Slinky Linka, a Russian dolly at whose adventurous hands I suffered gladly in New York.

It is, incidentally, Christmas Eve – hence his crack about 'Santa', because in one hour's time I am due to report to Simpsons store toy department to take up the duties of Father Christmas, one day only, the need for such employment being already mentioned – because I'm broke.

Buzz, apart from being a handsome, muscular, loyal, good-hearted sort of bloke with an infinite capacity for lechery, is a professional tennis player, circuiting the world playing with his balls, and in two days time is destined to desert me for a minor tournament in Victoria on the west coast. And it's through Buzz – or more precisely through a Torontonian friend of his, Greg Douglas, who runs an odd-job agency called 'Hire-A-Guy' – that I have landed this temporary and totally uninviting job as Santa Claus.

I mean, really – can you honestly see me dressed up as Father Christmas, patting the little stinkers on the head and yo-ho-ho-ing all over the place? No, neither can I – unless I do the patting with a baseball bat. But needs must when the overdraft drives, and if I'm going to stay in Toronto for a couple of weeks, until Buzz gets back from Victoria, I'm going to have to take whatever Hire-A-Guy chooses to dish out.

Ah, well ... no good presupposing misery. Perhaps it won't be so bad after all. Ha!

'Ho-de-ay ... staaart the day ... riiigghhtt ...' he is sort of singing in the bathroom.

I got out of bed and approached the door, finding him hiding behind a mask of shaving soap.

'It's all right for you,' I said. 'You won't be having a couple of pillows shoved up your jacksy and cotton wool stuck all over your mush in an hour's time.'

'Ah, you'll have a wonderful time, Russell – all those dear little buggers crawling all over you, sticking their fingers up your nose and pulling your whiskers. After all – what is

Christmas without kids?'

'Heaven.'

'Put it down to experience – all part of your "investigating life" programme.'

'This, mate, sounds suspiciously more like investigating death! However, do not think I am ungrateful. I appreciate your effort in finding me employment, even though I didn't envisage anything *quite* so extreme. If, however, you should enter the room this evening and find a gibbering idiot with bloodstained hands, do not be too surprised. There's only one kind of child I enjoy and that's an extremely distant one.'

'You know I don't believe that, Tobin. I believe at heart you're a juvenile push-over. And I further believe you're going to have the time of your life today.'

'Oh, yeah? And while I'm having the time of my life, what, pray, will you be doing?'

He grinned lasciviously at me in the mirror. 'With a bit of luck – little Amy Singleton, freelance artist and all-time wonder lover. She's expecting me at eleven.'

'My heart bleeds for you, you bum. I shall picture you having a real lousy time while I am having all the fun . . . and hurry up, son, I'm going to be late for the gaiety.'

At ten to eight we emerged from the hotel into the teeth of a howling snowstorm, and froze to the marrow instantly – not surprising, considering we were clothed only in our Miami summer gear, there having been no time yet to buy any winter stuff.

'Jeezus . . .!' gasped Buzz, signalling a kerbed cab. 'First thing I do today is invest in a parka.'

'I'm going to get something at the store – provided I'm still living at the end of the day.'

The taxi slushed to a halt and we scrambled in.

'Huh!' I said, rubbing a hole in the steamed-up window. 'Looks like I'll be seeing as much of Toronto as I saw of New York – the inside of forty-seven cabs and a billion tons of snowflakes.'

'Still,' he grinned, 'there were compensations.'

'By golly, you're right, son. Find us two love-bugs like Slinky Linka and Fifi and you'll not hear another complaint out of Tobin . . . a few groans maybe, but no complaints.'

A few minutes later the cab drew up outside a giant department store, corner of King and Yonge streets, its huge windows gay with Christmas scenes.

'Well,' said Buzz, 'here you are, mate. Just tell them Hire-A-Guy sent you. Best of luck. See you back at the hotel when you're finished.'

'That's how I'll be when I get there – finished.'

'Me, too – with a bit of luck,' he chuckled.

I got out of the cab, up to my ankles in snow. 'So long, buddy. If I don't make it – write to my folks, there's a good chap. And you can have my shirts and after-shave.'

'Keep your pecker up, Russell – and I'll promise to do the same.'

'Bastard.'

I closed the door and he was away, waving tauntingly through the rear window. I sloshed through the snow and approached one of the glass doors, pushed on it and nearly broke my wrist. It was locked.

I peered inside, seeing frenzied staff activity as they prepared for the last frantic day before Christmas. I knocked on the glass, attracting the attention of a stout old bird with blue hair, standing about twenty feet away.

'We're not open yet!' she mouthed at me.

'I'm staff!' I mouthed back.

'Ugh ...?'

'I'm ... staff!' I repeated.

She came closer. 'What?'

'I'm working here!' I shouted. 'Toy department!'

'Oh! You'll have to go round the back – to the staff entrance!'

'Oh, f ...'

'Mm?'

'Nothing. O.K. – thanks!'

Hitching the collar of my summer suit around my tingling ears, I stepped out into the sub-zero wind and set off down the block. Four miles later I reached the corner. A right turn and on again, head down against the battering snow, shivering, teeth chattering, wondering what the hell I was *doing* in this crazy situation.

Unbelievable ... one minute I'm having a wonderful time, lying on a shimmering beach in Miami with no more to worry about than ordering the next cold beer, and the next minute I'm freezing to death in a city I never planned on being in anyway! Heck, I should've been having a royal rave-up in

New York right now, courtesy of SunTime holidays, and would've been if it wasn't for that smuggling mob and an unbelievable case of mistaken identity!

Still, there was no going back now – or going *anywhere* for that matter, not without money. So – it's nose to the grindstone, Tobin – or rather chin to the cotton-wool whiskers. And shut up moaning, for Godsake. If you've got to be Father Christmas for the day, be a good one and give the kids their money's worth. It is their time, you know.

Freshly resolute, though aching with cold, I reached the next corner and turned into an alleyway, finding the 'staff Only' door a short way along it.

I knocked on it and it was opened by a grizzled old guy in a brown overall.

'Yes?'

'Good morning, my name's Tobin. I've been sent by Hire-A-Guy to play Father Christmas.'

He gave me a suspicious look, up and down. 'Bit on the skinny side, ain't yuh?'

'I'm all they could rustle up on the spur of the moment. I believe the regular chap went down with the flu.'

'That's what they say. Personally, I reckon he had a nervous breakdown. Well, come on in or you'll be goin' down with pneumonia before you git started.'

I stepped into a furnace. The temperature must have been up around ninety in there.

'Phew!' I gasped.

'Central heatin's gone funny,' he explained, closing the door. 'The engineers are workin' on it now. Wait there, I'll ring the Toy Department, get someone down for yuh.'

He got someone down for me – a Mister Dudley, a bald, fussy, irritating little squirt I disliked on sight. He didn't seem so flaming keen on me, either.

'Ah ... Tobin,' he said tetchily, entering quickly with a bird-like strut, his lip curled with inexplicable annoyance as he looked me up and down. 'Yes ... well, I suppose it *is* an emergency. Come along, then, we haven't a moment to lose. The store will be opening in half an hour and you have to get dressed yet.'

Out he swept, charged along passages and up flights of stairs at a hell of lick, muttering to himself as he went. Disgusting ... *far* too much responsibility ... doing three people's jobs around here ...'

We burst through a door into the glittering toy department, raced around its perimeter, entered an Aladdin's Cave grotto, passed Santa's golden throne and entered a door marked 'Private – Staff Only'.

How quickly the glitter and glamour disappears beyond such doors. Plain brick walls replace the magical, mysterious cave and colourful decoration gives way to low-hanging heating pipes. Grey steel lockers stood sentinel around the walls and a dozen plain wood chairs surround a rickety table, laden with used paper coffee cups.

'In here,' Dudley directed, flinging back the curtain of a changing cubicle, one of three positioned along the left-hand wall. 'There's the costume ... you can start getting the trousers on yourself. Miss Long, your Fairy Helper, will be here in a moment to give you a hand with the rest.'

'My F ...?'

'I'm here, Mister Dudley!'

A cheery, child-like voice floated over the partition from cubicle number three. 'Is that the new Santa? I won't be a moment!'

'Very good, Miss Long,' Dudley replied stiffly, then again addressed me. 'Er, hm, yes, well all this is, of course, highly irregular. Normally we vet our Santa Claus *most* stringently ... highly responsible job ... calls for great patience and not a small amount of psychology. I trust you appreciate that the good name of the company might well rest on your shoulders? Have you ever done this job before, Tobin?'

'Oh, yes,' I lied.

'Ah. And you ... *like* children?'

'Adore them.'

'Splendid ... splendid. Well, I must go ... great deal to do. Miss Long will show you the ropes. I'll be keeping an eye on you, of course ... *highly* responsible job.' He turned to go, paused at the curtain, muttered, 'Amazing,' shook his head disbelievingly and disappeared.

'Good morning!' Miss Long called cheerily.

'Good morning!'

'Be with you in a moment. Can you manage the trousers?'

'Just about to try.'

I slipped off my coat, tie, shoes and pants, then took Santa's trousers off the hook and stepped into them. Blimey, they were enormous There was enough room in there for six more Santas and three or four reindeer!

Well, I was standing there in my Y-fronts, wondering how I was going to fill the trousers which were down round my knees, when suddenly the curtain flew back and there stood the most voluptuous Fairy Queen I've ever clapped eyes on. She was gorgeous! Take a blonde and blue-eyed Miss Universe weighing in at 40–22–36, dress her in white tights and a fairy frou-frou, add a silver crown to her long golden hair, place a twinkling silver wand in her right hand, and an astonished and *very* delighted smile on her lovely lips, and you'll get an idea of what I was gaping at right then.

'Wow!' I gasped, paralysed with delight.

'Ooh!' she cooed, equally surprised. 'You're ... *Santa*!'

'Yes, I'm afraid I am.'

'Oooh ... super!' She moved tentatively into the cubicle, wide-eyed. 'But ... you're so *young*!'

'Twenty-six, actually.'

'And *slim*!'

'My word, you *do* look nice ...'

'And so ...' she emitted a little squeak,' ... *dishy*!'

'Well, that's very nice ...'

'Oh!' she groaned, slapping her sides. '*Why* weren't you here two weeks ago?'

'Well, I ...'

'Oh, what a terrible waste of Christmas. God, the man I've been stuck with was *awful*!'

'He was, hm?'

'Terrible. No fun at all. Hey, what's your name?'

'Tobin. Russ Tobin.'

'Mine's Lily Long.' She gave a sexy giggle, 'Sometime's known as Lily Longlegs.'

'I can see why,' I laughed, giving them a going over. 'They're lovely.'

'You like my outfit?' she laughed, twirling a pirouette for me.

'Stupendous.'

'I cut the neck lower ... I don't believe in hiding my light under a bushel.'

'So I see. They're ... I mean, it's beautiful.'

'Well ...' she sighed, throwing the wand down and taking another good look at me, hands on hips and head cocked coquettishly on one side. 'Better late than never, I suppose, but, *boy*, I wish you'd turned up two weeks ago. I reckon life would have been a heck of a sight less dull around here with you.'

'You reckon?' I grinned.

'Mmm . . .' she mused, a devilish twinkle in her eye that started my motor running. 'Well, we'll just have to see if we can't make up for lost time, hm?'

By heaven, what had we got here! A right little raver! Tobin, I do believe you might have done yourself some good after all, son.

'Er . . .' I croaked.

'Well, we'd better get you into this ridiculous outfit or Dudley will be on your neck.' She moved to a big cardboard box by the wall and bent over it, offering me a stupendous flash of her little frilly knickers. Hauling out miles of padding, she said, 'O.K., here we go. I reckon you're going to need about a ton. Here . . . hold this end to your side.'

I did so and she began to circle me, giggling as she wrapped the damn stuff round and round my middle, pausing at one point to add a pillow to my belly, then continued.

'God, I'm going to be sweltered,' I gasped, the sweat already running down my face. 'Apparently there's something wrong with the heating.'

'How disappointing,' she pouted. 'I thought I was causing it.'

'You're certainly not helping matters.'

'What a lovely change to dress a nice slim guy instead of a big fat slob. Round . . . and round . . . and round,' she teased, trickling her fingers slowly over my stomach as she came round the front.

'Lily . . . don't do that.'

'Don't you like it?'

'I love it. Don't do it.'

'Why not, Santa?' she cooed innocently, widening her big blue eyes.

'Because Santa's only human, Fairy Helper . . . and if you persist . . .'

'Yes?'

'By the end of the day he'll be ignoring the kiddy-winkies and making a grab for the Mummies – to say nothing of his Fairy Helper!'

'*Su*-per!' she chuckled. 'Oh, *how* I wish you'd been here two weeks ago.'

'Well, all may not be lost, Lily. Try waving your wand and wishing very hard, you never know what Santa will bring you.'

'I'm already working on it,' she grinned. 'There have got to be *some* perks to this business.'

Now, at this point I think I ought to inject a little warning. There *may* be one or two of you inclined to view these proceedings with a degree of scepticism, possibly because it all sounds too good to be true, and I grant you it does sound just a touch like that. But let me assure you it really did happen, true as I'm writing this down.

Now whether it was Christmas spirit that caused it or the fact that through the greatest good fortune I happened to encounter four of the sexiest ladies in Canada, or the fact that *all* Canadian ladies possess a highly developed fondness for the other, I wouldn't know. But what I do know is that the events I now unfold finally sent me on my way not only in a state of bewildered and sublime exhaustion but also ensured my earliest possible return to investigate the distinct possibility of this national female trait so amply promised by, for starters, the voluptuous Lily Longlegs.

Well, there you are. Back to the story.

At last she had me padded up and a right berk I felt, too, all swollen out in front like a pregnant hippo and with great mounds of stuffing round my waist.

'My God, what we do for money,' I groaned, hitching up the voluminous trousers and securing them with a length of string.

'How come you got this job?' she asked, holding up the red Santa jacket. 'You sure don't seem the type.'

'Lily, it's a long and unbelievable story. I'm not even supposed to be in Canada today. Right now I should be on vacation in New York ... but a pal and I were chased over the border by a couple of hoods and ...'

'No kidding!' she gasped. 'You mean, *real* hoods!?'

'Frighteningly real.'

'For heaven's *sakes*! But ... why? ... how ...?'

'I'll tell you about it later. Dudley will be storming in here any minute ...'

'Oh, screw him. Gee, how exciting! Chased by real hoods.

Here, come and sit down and I'll put your whiskers on.'

I sat, with considerable difficulty, on a wooden chair. She took a set of white whiskers from the box and came up close, then very gently applied them, her tender touch making me shiver and go funny in the head. She was so very close, her thigh touching mine, her delectable boobs only inches from my mouth and her angle of inclination affording me a stupendous close-up of them.

'You ... smell awfully nice, Fairy Helper,' I croaked.

'Do I?' she chuckled.

'You ... really oughtn't to stand so close. You're driving Santa up the wall.'

Another chuckle.

'And if Fairy Helper doesn't move away very soon ... Santa is not going to be able to control himself.'

'Wonderful!'

Next thing she was on my knee, kissing me. A minute more and we were going at it like we'd missed breakfast and were taking an early lunch. Man, she was hungry. What a little sexpot, moaning and groaning, wriggling all over me, now and then leaving my lips for a quick bite of ear-lobe or a nibble at my neck, then back again for more.

My heart was thumping lumps out of my ribs and, now that he was over the initial shock of her unexpected attack, Hercules was rising stupendously to the challenge and poking me in the chest, just below shoulder level.

Even beneath all that padding she felt him blossom and this sent her into fresh paroxysms of delight, and if bloody old Dudders hadn't entered the outer room just then and announced his arrival with a cough, I reckon it would've been frou-frous away and a Merry Christmas all round.

'Er, herm ...'

Lily stopped what she was doing, stared wide-eyed at me, then shot off my knee and fumbled for my whiskers which were now round the back of my neck.

The curtain flew open. Dudley gave an irritated sniff. 'Nearly ready, Tobin? You only have three minutes.'

'Y ... yes, just the whiskers to put on, Mister Dudley. We ... had a little difficulty with my stomach.'

'Hurry along, then, hurry along.'

'Two minutes.'

As he exited, Lily burst into laughter and gave me a big hug from the rear. 'Who's a naughty Santa, then?'

'And who's a *very* sexy Fairy Helper? By heaven, Lily, you've got me in a right old mess. Any kid who sat on my knee right now would shoot across the store like it'd been fired from a cannon.'

'Oooh, let me try ...'

'Lily, now, no – we haven't got time.'

'How about lunchtime?' she whispered in my ear, then stuck her tongue in it.

'Eh! You're a very naughty girl.'

'I can't help it – I love it.'

'Well, I'm not totally unpartial to it myself ...'

'So I see. Well, that's a date then. Come on, let's get these stupid whiskers on.'

With the aid of elastic and a spot of spirit gum she got me smothered in fluff, eyebrows and all, then I pulled up the hood, slipped my feet into a pair of black wellington boots and finally encompassed my ridiculous girth in a wide black plastic belt.

'There – all ready,' she pronounced. 'Stand up and let me have a look at you.'

I did so – and promptly sat down again, toppled backwards by belly ballast. I stood up again and this time she slipped her arms around me and gave me a quick kiss, miraculously locating my mouth through four tons of crepe hair.

'Till lunchtime,' she growled.

'You're wicked – but I *do* like you.'

She wriggled against me and giggled. 'Come on – I'll introduce you to Albert, the old guy who chooses the presents for the kids. He's as deaf as a board, so you'll have to speak up.'

Taking my hand, she picked up her wand and urged me through the curtain, across the room and out into the corridor, then through another door marked 'Private', near the grotto.

Inside were racks of toys, packaged in gaily-coloured parcels, one rack marked 'Girls', then subdivided into various age groups, the other for boys.

Lily called out, 'Al ... bert!' and a death's-head face wearing no teeth and a hearing aid popped up behind one of the racks.

'Yesh?'

'Albert – this is our new Santa, Russ Tobin. Come and say hello!'

With a mutter to himself he hobbled round the rack, bent almost double, holding his back.

'Eh?' he said, adjusting the control on his hearing-aid, then giving the battery pack a bash. 'Thish damn thing's playin' again, Lily, you'll have to speak up!'

'Oh, God ...' she groaned, rolling her eyes at me. 'This happened two days ago and you should've seen the confusion. Albert ... this is Russ Tobin! Our new Santa!'

'Well, I can see he ain't Mother Goose! What happened to the other fella?'

'He's got flu!' she shouted.

'Hm!' he grunted. 'Well, I sure hope he can shout louder than the other one.'

Lily turned to me. 'You have to pass the message to Albert through that grille in the wall – tell him what age and sex the kid is, then he picks a suitable present and drops it down the chute. It comes out in the dragon's mouth by your throne.'

'Got it,' I nodded. 'Sounds easy enough.'

'It is – provided the deaf old bugger hears you.'

'Eh?' said Albert.

'All right, Albert,' she said, patting him on the shoulder, 'get ready to deliver. We're going on duty now!'

'Yers ...' he muttered and hobbled away.

'Arthritis?' I enquired compassionately.

'No,' she laughed. 'Yesterday he fell down the chute. Got so ratty he forgot to let go of the parcel. Come on, Santa ... your throne awaits.'

We went back into the corridor then out through another door into the grotto, finding Dudley marching towards us, eyeing his watch.

'Ah, there you are. Right, sit down quickly, the doors are open and they'll be upon us any minute.'

I took my place on the throne, and Lily stood at my side, wand at the ready.

'Now ...' said Dudley, casting an eye over my appearance, 'yes, not bad at all ... now, the children and their parents will approach from that direction, having seen the grotto, and when they come into sight give a couple of rings on your bell and a hearty chortle or two ...'

'Bell?' I said.

'Jesus – the bell!' exclaimed Lily. 'I forgot it!'

Off she scarpered, through the door we'd just come through.

'I *do* wish that young lady would control her language,' groaned Dudley. 'I'm afraid from time to time she does tend to forget she's Santa's Fairy Helper. Please remind her, Tobin.'

'Yuff,' I said, through a mouthful of beard. I pulled it away. 'My God ... goodness, it's hot down here.'

'Yes, I'm afraid the heating's gone wrong. Should be back to normal by midday, though. As I was saying, Tobin, ring your bell a couple of times and give the usual Father Christmas chortle, the kiddies expect that sort of thing, then take the child on your knee, ask its name, age and what it wants for Christmas, give a couple more chortles and repeat the name and age over your right shoulder into that hidden grille. Mister Segume will select an appropriate present and send it down the chute into the dragon's mouth. Fairy Helper will then pick it up, give it to the child and send it on its way with a cheery Christmas message. Got all that? It's simple enough, I'm sure.'

'Chryftal clear,' I said, spitting crepe.

At that moment Lily returned with the handbell.

'All set?' enquired Dudley.

'Yes, let 'em loose,' I grinned.

'Right, I'll leave you to it. Must get on ... frantically busy day.'

Off he shot, a very worried man.

'Phew!' I gasped, easing the beard away from my face. 'Jeezus, Lily, it must be a hundred and ninety down here. All right for you in your frou-frou ...'

'Ah, poor Santa,' she commiserated, stroking my face. 'Never mind, wait till lunch-time, then you can take it all off and lie down for an hour.'

'Eh? Lie down where?'

She giggled and prodded me on the nose. 'You'll find out.'

'Lily ... how can I possibly concentrate on my job when you continue to make salacious suggestions like that?'

'You want me to stop?'

'Certainly not. They give meaning to my life. Ho, if the lads could see me now, they'd still be laughing at New Year, and, Lily dear, you'd better stop stroking my face or I shall grab you where you stand and ... and ...'

'And what, Santa, dear?'

'And whisk you away to Aladdin's Cave for your Christmas prezzie.'

'Rub my lamp and I'll follow you anywhere,' she chuckled. 'Oh! Look out – here comes the first of the horrors ...'

She removed her hand from my thigh and came to attention in Fairy Helper pose, shoulders back and boobs pushed out, threatening to explode from her sequined vest.

'My my, you *are* a big Fairy Helper,' I side-mouthed to her. Ding ... ding ... ding! I rung, wincing at the excruciating racket. 'Ho ... ho ... ho!' and a 'Ho ... ho ... ho!' I chortled.

'Don't overdo it,' Lily muttered, 'you'll be exhausted by nine.'

'I'm exhausted now!' I gasped, wiping copious sweat from my face. 'Eh, up, here comes Little Lord Fauntleroy.'

He had that look about him, aloof, superior, walking coolly at his mother's side as though he was taking *her* to the grotto, a snide-looking little sod dressed in immaculate, long-trousered grey suit, sporting a precocious polka-dot bow-tie, hair plastered down and parted as though with an axe, aged about eight, going on forty-seven.

'Ho ... ho ...!' ding ... ding ... ding, 'and a Merry Christmas to you, my boy ... so you've come to see Father Christmas ... ?'

He stopped in front of me, his lip curled with acute cynicism, gave his fur-coated mother an upward glance indicating unadulterated boredom, then speared me with a glare of flat disgust.

'Certainly not, whatever-your-name-is. Just give me the present and let us get out of here.'

'Hm ...?'

He gave a wearied sigh. 'The inanity of the plastic and flashy exhibitionism entitled "A Magic Carpet Ride Through Aladdin's Cave" that we just endured being superseded only by your own ludicrous, childish and irritatingly insincere joviality, I suggest you hand over the present to which I am entitled so that we may remove ourselves from this idiotic environment this instant.'

Mother affected the ghost of an apologetic smile. 'I'm afraid he's rather too advanced for this sort of thing. He has an I.Q. of 146. This will be his last visit to a Christmas grotto.'

'No doubt to the undying relief of countless Father Christmases, madam. May I have the ... young gentleman's name and age?'

'His name is Frances ... and he's six.'

'Good Go ... my word, he is advanced. Did you hear that, Fairy Helper ... Frances is only *six*!' I emphasized, turning towards Lily and passing the information to Albert via the grille. 'Well, now, let's see what we can find in Santa's sack for *six*-year-old *Frances*!'

'Oh, Dragon Helper, kind and mild ...' recited Lily, waving her wand over the dragon's gob, 'Send down a gift for this happy ... child.'

Clatter ... clump ... thud. Down came a gaudily-wrapped parcel. Lily bent down, presenting me with another heart-stopping flash of her gorgeous bottom and retrieved it.

'There you are, Frances,' she beamed, passing her wand over his head. 'And a very Happy Christmas from all of us in Santaland.' I could see she was dying to ram it in his ear.

'Santaland,' he scoffed, taking the parcel. 'Mother, may we *please* leave this environment of abject puerility?'

'We're going right now, Frances. Thank you.' She nodded at me and off they went.

'Precocious little swine!' seethed Lily. 'Oooh, just give me two minutes alone with him and ...'

'Now, now, Lily,' I chided her. 'Remember you're Santa's Fairy Helper ...'

'Fuck Santa's Fairy Helper!'

I exploded with laughter. 'By golly, Lily, stap me if you ain't a mind-reader, too.'

That brought her back to good humour. She gave a laugh and kissed me on the nose. 'Santa is a dirty old man, isn't he?'

'I'll tell you what he also is, love – he's fed up with this bloody job already. Another brat like that one and I'll stuff my beard in his mouth and elope with you ... oh, my God, here they come again!'

Frances and momma were bearing down on us at a rate of irate knots, the kid waving a flaxen-haired doll at me as though intending to smash it over my head.

'What's this ... a *joke* or something!' he demanded, storming up and throwing the doll in my lap. 'Is this your idea of a joke!?'

'Er ... no. I ... suppose the name Frances confused my ... helpers back there ...' I stammered, nonplussed for the moment by the vehemence of his onslaught. 'I'll ... tell them …'

'Do that!' he rapped.

I turned to the grille. 'Er … is Santa's Helper there …?' No reply. 'I say … Santa's Helper …! ALBERT …!' A bit of a scuffle, then Albert's voice down the dragon's throat.

'What d'you want now?'

'Er … the last present you sent down … the one for six-year-old Frances …'

'Eh?'

'The last present … the one …'

'Hang on, my set's packed in again!' Thump … thump. 'Goddam cockamamie thing … keep shoutin' out there, I can't tell whether it's back on or not!'

'Albert, the last *present* you sent down … the one for *Frances* … six years old …'

'Ah! Caught a bit o' that! Comes and goes …' thump … thump … 'Keep talkin'!'

'Oh, this is bloody ridic …' I got off the throne, stepped into the dragon's mouth and shouted up its throat. 'The last present you sent down, the one for Frances, six years old …'

'Well, what about it?'

'You sent down a doll. This is a boy …!'

'Well, how in hell am *I* supposed to know! Frances … Francis – you'll have to give me a clue with the unisex names … hang on, this bloody machine's packed up again …' thump … thump. 'Of all the goddam times for it to … say something, will yuh?'

'Say what?'

'Eh?'

'Oh, for Chrissake, Albert, this is bloody *ridiculous* …!'

'Russ!' someone hissed in my ear.

It was Lily, tugging at my sleeve.

I turned to her. 'What, love?'

She jerked her head and muttered surreptitiously, 'Look behind you.'

I did so. Mister Perishing Dudley, plus three more mothers and five kids, was standing there, listening to every word.

'Oh,' I gulped. 'Er, … thank you, Santa's Helper!' I shouted up the dragon. 'Now if we could just have a present for a darling little *boy* aged *ten*, Santa would be most grateful …'

Thump!

Down dropped a heavy package, hurled with petulant force,

and hit me on the head. I staggered back, tripped over the dragon's teeth and fell on my ass, legs up in the air. The kids all collapsed with laughter.

Up rushed Dudders, caught me by the arm, seething, '*Mister* Tobin, what *do* you think you're *doing* ...!'

'It ... I ...'

'Get up ... get up!'

'I'm trying to!'

I finally managed it and the kids collapsed again because my bulging stomach was now a bulging crutch. My belt had broken and the whole lot had slipped down me trousers. In addition my beard was now hanging askew round my left ear and I had a lump of cotton wool on the end of my nose.

Dudley spun me round, away from the hooting public which now consisted of four mothers, seven kids, one father and a granny, with more coming up fast. He straightened my beard and removed the cotton wool while I was pulling three hundredweight of padding out of my pants.

'What *do* you think you're doing!?' he repeated, now puce with apoplexy. 'Kindly remember that this position calls for dedication ... decorum ... diplomacy! Crawling around on your hands and knees and bawling "this is bloody ridiculous!" is *not* in keeping with Simpsons traditional Christmas spirit and is *certainly* not the Santa image we had in mind when we hired you.'

'I'm sorry, Mister Dudley, but ...'

'Quickly – get back on your throne, you've got a *huge* backlog of children already. I'll talk to you later about this. Now, smile ... *smile,* Tobin! This is supposed to be a happy occasion.'

Fixing a plastic smile upon his own mug, he turned and pushed through the crowd, chuntering to himself beneath his breath.

Chortling to the crowd like an idiot, I wobbled back to the throne and plonked myself down. 'Ho ... ho ... ho, sorry to keep you all waiting, children, but Santa's Helper has just had a big delivery of toys from Fairyland and needed a few minutes to get them all sorted out ...'

'Yerk,' went Lily.

I turned to her and grinned. 'Now, Fairy Helper, where is that present for our dear friend Frances?'

Lily moved closer and murmured, 'The little bastard took

off a few minutes ago.'

'Thank God. Right, then ... now who is next?'

'I yam,' said a pretty little thing in pigtails.

'No, you're not,' insisted a red-haired thug aged five. 'I'm next!'

'You are not!'

'I yam so!'

'Now, now, children,' I chuckled. 'Perhaps we'd better let the lady go first, hm?'

'Why?' he snarled.

'Because ...' Because I fucking said so, son. '... because it's good manners, my boy.'

'I think it's soppy.'

I ignored him and reached for Little Pigtails. 'Rightee-ho, my dear, come and tell Santa your name and how old you are and what you'd like for Christmas. Would you like to sit on my knee?'

'No.'

'That's ... hm?'

'No.'

'Oh? And why not?'

' 'Cos mummy said to daddy that only dirty old men play Santa Claus so they can touch up little ...'

'Janice, *darling* ...' interjected mother, a hard-looking piece with curlers in her hair under a scarf. 'Just ... tell Santa how old you are and what you'd like for Christmas.'

'I yam seven years old and I want a dolly that wets its diapers and does poo-poos in its potty and ...'

'Er, no, Janice,' cut in mother, turning bright red, 'just wets its diapers, dear ...'

'But daddy said ...'

'Never *mind* what daddy said. Daddy's a foul-mou ... daddy, was only joking. Just tell Santa what I told you.'

The kid shrugged. 'O.K. – just wets its diapers ...'

'Fine.' I sneered.

'... though I'd rather have one that does poo-poos in its ...'

'Janice!'

I turned to Lily, who was shaking with laughter. 'Now, Fairy Helper, what d'you suppose we can find a little *girl* aged *seven*?'

'A little *girl* aged *seven*!' she repeated joyously, almost shrieking into the grille.

'Yuh don't have to shout!' bellowed Albert. 'My machine's O.K. now!'

Thud! A parcel shot down the chute.

Goodbye, Janice.

Next came Roy, the red-haired menace with a bad squint and four pounds of pig-iron on his teeth.

'Can I punch you in the belly?' he enquired.

'Er ... ho ... ho ... ho, now why would you want to punch Santa in the ... stomach, young fella?'

' 'Cos you've got a pillow stuck up there, I saw it.'

'Ho ... ho ... ho, that's not a pillow, my boy, it's ... it's to keep Santa warm.'

'You're warm already – the sweat's dripping off your nose.'

'Yes, well ... how old are you, Roy?'

'Six and seven-eighths.'

'And what would you like for Christmas?'

'A gun that shoots birds.'

That figured. 'I see ...'

'And a tank ...'

'Uh huh.' I turned to Lily. 'Well, Fairy H ...'

'I haven't finished yet!'

'Hm ...?'

'And an electric train set ... an' a building set ... an' a aeroplane ... an' a kite ... an' a pair of roller skates ... an' a bow an' arrow set ... an' a bicycle ...'

'Yes, well ...'

'I haven't finished yet! An' a football ... an' a dog ... an' a knife that kills birds ... an' a ...'

'Little *boy* aged *seven*!' Lily bawled into the grille.

Roy turned to his mother. 'She didn't let me finish!'

'Well, there are one or two other boys and girls waiting, dear ...'

'An' a tent ... an' a baseball bat ... an' a colouring book ... an' a ...'

Crunch! Down came the parcel.

'Here you are, Roy,' Lily smiled sweetly with a curl of her lip. 'And I do hope you get *all* you're asking for.'

Exit Roy, still rattling off his list.

The next few kids were really quite nice, some shy, some confident and one who wet himself with excitement, and the deliveries went off without a hitch. And suddenly ... we had a moment to ourselves.

'Phew!' I gasped, easing the whiskers off and mopping my streaming face. 'God Almighty, what a morning, Lily.'

'Morning!' she laughed. 'We've only been going half an hour.'

'Eh? Oh, Gawd, I thought it must be at least twelve o'clock. Honey, I don't think I'm going to last till six o'clock.'

'Six! I hate to break it to you, Russ, but tonight we close at eight!'

'Eight!'

'Never mind,' she smiled, taking my hanky and dabbing my face, 'there will be compensations. We get a long, lovely hour for lunch.'

'Right now that thought is the only thing keeping me going.'

'You're doing beautifully – and just think of the pleasure you'll be giving during the day.' She gave a chuckle. 'To the *kids*, as well!'

'Tell me, Lily, what do you do when you're not being Santa's Helper?'

She shrugged. 'Oh, this and that . . . photographic modelling, acting, TV commercials . . . have fun . . .'

'What . . . sort of fun?'

Her eyes crinkled wickedly. 'What other kind is there?'

My heart was at it again. Lunch time could not come fast enough.

A movement down the track distracted her attention and with an appalled start she groaned, 'Uh uh, here comes trouble.'

I turned and was mortified to see a tribe of some forty kids bearing down on us, shepherded by one harassed and obviously ineffectual young female guardian.

'School group,' murmured Lily in quiet desperation. 'The scourge of Christmas. Stand by for bother.' She turned to the grille. 'Albert!'

'Yus?'

'School group!'

'Oh, Christ. How many?'

'Thirty . . . forty.'

'Holy Mother – call the cops!'

'Too late . . . they're here!'

They were here. With a wild whoop, the leaders broke into a gallop. The corridor rang with shrieks and the thunder of boots and next instant they were all over us, climbing up the back of my throne, crawling under it, scrambling into the dragon's mouth and trying to get up the chute ...

'Boys and girls ...!' the teacher protested, 'now ... be *quiet,* all of you ...! Benjamin, get down from there ... Paul, *stop* that ...! oh! Mary Jane Bellamey, how *dare* you do that in public! Take your hand out of your ...'

Her words were lost in the uproar. Thump! A fist came over the back of the throne and whopped me on the head. 'Santa's a silly old bas ... tard!' the chant began.

'Hey, *stop* that! Get off there, you little b ...'

Thud!

Now the attack came from the front, opening with a boot on the shin.

'Ow!'

'Get off there ... get off!' Lily was fighting valiantly, bashing kids left and right.

'Santa's a silly old bas ... tard!'

Whop! a thump in the ear, then ... Splat! a spit-ball right in the eye.

'Madam ...!' I was on my feet, '... will you kindly ...'

A scraping noise behind me. I turned ... just in time to save my throne being carried off down the corridor. 'Leggo of that, you mad bug ...'

'Naughty Santa's swearing! Naughty Santa's swear ... ing!'

'I'll do more than swear, you heathens! Leggo ...! Gerroff ...!'

'Children ... children!' the teacher was bellowing. 'My *God,* they've gone berserk! Charles ...! Herman ...! OHHH!'

Whoosh! Suddenly my trousers were round my ankles, then the pillow fell out, then the padding fell down and I was standing in my Y-fronts, shackled to the spot. The kids were demented with laughter.

'Call the cops! Call the cops!' Lily was yelling into the grille. 'Albert, get Dudley down here!'

'Out ... OUT!' the teacher was screeching, hauling kids off the throne, hurling them away, yanking them out of the dragon's mouth, and Lily was in there helping, catching the odd kid a thump round the ear to help it along.

Then, bless him, down the chute came Albert, wielding a hefty cardboard roll. He landed on his back, feet in the air, struggled to get up, then pitched right in, whopping the brutes out of his grotto. 'Get outa here, you ... *var*mints!' Bop!

'Garn, scram!' Thud!

Like Comanches retreating from a ravaged wagon-train they ran, their dastardly deed accomplished, and as the last one disappeared, helped round the bend with a clip on the ear from the teacher, so a bellow of flagrant dismay rang out from behind us and up staggered a wide-eyed Dudley, quite beside himself with chagrin.

And who could blame him, for the scene he perceived before him was as far removed from gentile Christmasification as an opera from an orgy ... the throne reclining on its side, the dragon now toothless, cross-eyed and wearing crayoned spectacles, Lily's frou-frou in a state of bedraggled disarray, her wand bent like a limp lily – and Santa standing there in his underpants, his stomach round his ankles and his beard over his left shoulder.

Dudders approached, gaping like a beached goldfish. 'What ... on earth ... has been going *on*! Just *look* at this place! Tobin – for heaven's sake, man, pull your trousers up! And get your stomach back on, there are children coming through any minute. Well, *really* ... the very *least* I expected from Hire-A-Guy was simple competence!'

'It wasn't his fault!' rapped Lily, adjusting her frou-frou. 'It was that same wild Scarborough bunch that smashed those Ali Baba pots last year. You ought to complain to the school – ban them from the store!'

'That will do, Miss Long, that will do,' he sniffed. 'Get this place tidied up and try to maintain a *semblance* of Christmas dignity, for heaven's sake! And, Miss Long, you've ... laddered your tights. Kindly change them at lunch-time. *Never*, in all the years I've worked here, have I witnessed ...'

Off he stalked, obviously convinced we'd smashed the place up ourselves, seen off the premises with a rude gesture from Lily.

'Silly old twit. This is the last year I play Fairy Helper.'

'You were here last year, hm?' I grunted, trying to get the binding tied round the pillow.

'I was. Huh, you got off lightly. Last year one of those brats had a catapult – got Santa in the eye with a grape. Thank heaven it was seedless.'

'Bunch a mad animals,' Albert was chunnering, heading for the door. 'Just look at that dragon! I'll have to try an' glue its teeth back in at lunch-time.'

With my belly back, more or less, in position, I righted the throne, sat down, and allowed Lily to tweak my beard into place. She smiled down at me, sexily, fully restored to flirtuosity.

'I must say,' she cooed, trickling her finger round my ear, 'you looked *very* super standing there in your little briefs.'

'I did?'

'Huh huh. Santa's quite a big boy, isn't he?'

'Well, I . . .'

'Did Santa know his flies are open right now?'

'Eh?' I glanced down. By God, she was right. I made a move.

'No!' she insisted, stopping my hand. 'Let Fairy Helper do it.'

Oh, boy.

Staring me fixedly in the eye she lowered both hands to my lap and started fumbling with the zip, then suddenly, with a devilish murmur, she was inside for a right old handful.

'Hey!' I gasped.

'Ohhh,' she growled, gritting her teeth, her eyes going droopy and hot. 'Ohh, he is *beaut*iful. He's so warm . . . and he's coming alive!'

'Lily . . .' I croaked, helplessly.

And then – voices behind us! Out shot her hand. I quickly zipped up, crossed my legs, winced, uncrossed them. Then once again the hordes were upon us.

Well, the morning didn't go too badly after that – I think. How should I know? My mind was far too full of the antics of the nymph on my right to know what was going on. I couldn't keep my eyes off her, couldn't wait to get that ridiculous frou-frou off and . . .

Time dragged by. We had a ten-minute break at eleven for coffee and spent it grinning at each other like a couple of randy cats, touching each other behind Albert's back, and getting each other worked up into a right old state. Then it was back to the job, asking the same questions over and over again and ho-ho-ho-ing until I was sick of my own merry chortle. Maybe the obnoxious Frances had been right at that.

Finally the hands crept around to one o'clock and on the very stroke Dudley steamed round the corner.

'Right – lunch-time. Be back at two sharp. And, Tobin – my advice is to take a rest, this afternoon's stint will be a long, gruelling one.'

'I'll have a lie down,' I told him and Lily giggled.

We shut up shop and joined Albert in the staff room.

'You brought sandwiches?' he enquired.

'No,' answered Lily, linking my arm. 'Russ and I have made ... other arrangements. We're going out for lunch.'

'Dressed like that?'

'No,' she grinned, 'we're ... taking these off. See you later, Albert.'

We walked at leisurely pace from the room, but once inside the changing room made a bee-line for the cubicles and I ripped off the costume in one-tenth the time it took me to get it on. I was about to tie my tie when the curtain parted and there she stood, looking all fluffy and adorable in a light-coloured fur coat.

'Oh!' I said '*Are* we going out?'

'No. And never mind the tie, come as you are.'

She took my arm and gave it a squeeze. 'I'm having a *super* day ... how about you?'

'I'm having a ball,' I grinned.

'I'm so glad they sent you.'

'Me, too.'

We waved bye-bye to Albert, who was reading a comic, went out into the corridor, turned right and entered another long corridor. Half-way along this Lily stopped suddenly at a door, checked that the coast was clear, then took a key from her pocket and unlocked it.

'Quickly!' she whispered.

I was inside in a flash, finding myself in a dimly-lit store-room, a huge room piled high with mattresses, cellophane-wrapped blankets, carpets, rugs, all sorts of things. A metallic click behind me told me Lily had relocked the door ... and bolted it.

'Now no one can get in,' she grinned, holding out her hand. 'Come on – this way!'

We crept along an aisle formed by towering banks of mattresses, then jigged about a bit, finally coming upon a small 'clearing' of carpets, a great bed of them three feet high.

'Here we are!' she whispered excitedly, stepping up on to them. 'No one will find us in here.'

'Doesn't anyone come in here?' I asked, my heart thumping riotously.

'Very seldom. This is the "seconds" storeroom. All the imperfect stuff is stored in here until the January sales ... so ...' grinning fiendishly, she held out her arms to me, 'it's all ours.'

'Lily, you're incorrigible ...'

'Does that mean sexy?'

'Yes.'

She came close, wrapped her arms around me and hugged me. 'Then I admit it.' She half-smiled, her eyes lazy, smouldering, her voice a low, tremulous whisper. 'I'm terribly sexy ... always have been. I just love doing it. How about you?'

'Adore it,' I croaked.

'Wonderful. Kiss me.'

The first contact with her soft, eager mouth was a match to touchpaper. I exploded. She exploded. She thrust her belly hard into me, searching for Herc and finding him.

'Oh ... God, that's beautiful ...'

Her right hand snaked to grab him, squeeze him, then with a deft flick my zip was down and she was inside, holding him in her little warm hand.

'God, he's so hard!' she gasped. 'I want to see him!'

A fumble with my belt and my trousers went. Lily backed away, breathing hard, stared fixedly at him like a child with a new bike, then suddenly dropped to her knees in an attitude of supplication.

'God ...!' she gasped, 'how many pairs of shorts do you burst in a week?'

I laughed. 'Six or seven.'

'Ohhh ...!' she groaned, moving closer, now laying him against her cheek, her eyes closed ecstatically. 'He's so *warm* ... so hard ...!' She began to kiss him, frantically, with little tender, fleeting pecks ... down ... and around ... cooing and clucking to herself like a mother gentling a baby. And then, with sudden aggressive passion, she opened her hot mouth very wide and swallowed him.

'Ohh, Lily ...!' I groaned. 'Oh, love, that is ... stupendous.'

'You like that?' she said, with difficulty.

'Ha!'

She continued doing some delightful and *very* expert things with her dear little tongue for two or three minutes, then suddenly she was on her feet and smothering me with kisses.

'Russ ...' she groaned, plaintively.

'Yes, love?' I croaked.

'Take my coat off.'

My hands crept round to the front, my fingers locating three buttons ... plip ... plop ... ploop. The coat fell open. Holding me in a teasing, white-hot smile she stepped away and opened it wide, inviting inspection. I gazed down ... and bloody near passed out with excitement.

She was starkers.

Her body was perfect ... slender, long-legged, her handsome breasts high and firm, their large pink nipples standing out like .303 bullets, and a thick inviting mass of light-brown hair pointing the way to heaven.

'Ohhh ... Lily ...'

With a slow, delighted smile she dropped the coat from her shoulders, took a step forward and began attacking my shirt buttons. In a trice we were locked in each other's arms, devouring each other.

'Play with me,' she pleaded, her voice a choked whisper. 'We have almost an hour. Make it last.'

'I'll ... do my best, Lily ... but you've got me pretty excited.'

'Kiss me ...'

'Yes.'

'All over.'

'Yes.'

'I love that.'

'You do?'

'Adore it.'

She broke away, stooped for her fur coat and spread it out over the rugs, the fur side uppermost. Then she lay down on it and held out her arms to me, smiling joyously. 'Come here, you ...'

I went.

By *heaven*, what a lunch break. The bird was a glutton ... ravenous! She lapped up everything I gave her and held out her bowl for more, laughing and chuckling and urging me on to greater heights with each successive position, tirelessly energetic and endlessly inventive.

We did it standing, sitting, lying ... forwards, sideways, backwards and innumerable positions in between. Then suddenly time was running out and we were in the closing minutes of the second half with no extra time for injuries.

She came to her knees, eyes aglow, panting hard, and

gasped, 'Russ, dear ... we must go.'
'I know.'
'Just ... one more time?'
'O.K.,' I grinned. 'How?'
'The best way of all!'
'You're on!'
She spun around and buried her face in the fur. 'Take me!'
I took her.
'Oh, my God ...!' she gasped. 'Ohhh, that's so beautiful! Go, Russ, *go*! Hard! Hurt me! Fill me ... fill me!'
Well, one thing I've learned while travelling the world investigating life – and that is that it's not only ill-mannered but extremely unwise to refuse a lady anything while locked in the throes of love. And this time was no exception.
'Ohhhhh ...!' she cried. 'Ohhh, that's beautiful ... *beautiful* ...!'
'Ooooh ...! Ahhh ...! Eeeeh!' I was gasping, driving hard, fingers sunk into her voluptuous hips, then, with a great shudder, lunch was over.
'Oh ... Oh ... Ohhh,' she was panting, open-mouthed, eyes closed. 'Oh, you beautiful ... beautiful Santa ... what a wonderful, peachy Christmas present. You really filled *my* stocking ...!'
'Well, Christmas *is* the season for giving, Lily – and receiving, of course.'
'Boy, I certainly received, you devil. Ohh, that was heaven.' She opened one eye and squinted upwards at me, breaking into a cat-who-just-swallowed-the-cream grin. 'You gonna stay there all day?'
'Don't mind if I do.'
'You're a *very* sexy fella, you know that?'
'Nope.'
'You've never been told that before?'
I grinned. 'Nope.'
'You're also a terrible liar. Well ...' she sighed, 'I suppose we'd better return to the other fray. Easy how you go now ... oops! ... aaaw ...!'
Laughing, I helped her to her feet and hugged her.
'Thank you, Santa.'
'And thank you, Fairy Helper. You're more than welcome – anytime.'
'Then ... how about tonight?' she chuckled.

'Mmm?' I looked at her. 'You mean it?'

'Sure I mean it. What are you doing tonight?'

I shrugged. 'Nothing. I'd sort of arranged to have dinner with a pal, but ...'

'Well, I don't mean to sound pushy, but if you'd like, I'll cook you a terrific steak.'

'Steak? Where ...? You mean your place?'

'Sure. I've got a little pad – up on Yonge Street.'

'Lily, wild horses could not stop me. I'll bring the booze.'

She chuckled and snuggled in. 'You reckon we'll find time for drinking?'

'Are you all that hopeful of eating?'

'Not if I can help it.'

CHAPTER TWO

The afternoon passed quickly, my mind being too full of Lily and the evening to come, to be irritated by the four thousand nine hundred kids who sat on my knee, pulled my whiskers and generally made more noise than peas in a drum.

Even Dudders seemed agreeably delighted with my demeanour. He popped around several times, keeping a beady eye on things, and towards the end of the day even managed a smile.

'Everything all right, Tobin?'

'Everything is positively beautiful, Mister Dudley,' I said, slipping Lily a wink.

'Mmm ...' he went, frowning suspiciously, as though he thought I'd been on the prune juice during lunch. 'Well ... after an, hm, inauspicious start, you seem to have settled down extremely well. I shall, of course, report the same to Hire-A-Guy – credit where credit is due, I always say ...'

'That's very kind.'

'Not at all. I shall be around with your money later.'

'Thank you. I need it to buy a winter coat. Will I have time to buy one here?'

'Certainly. Pop up to the men's department as soon as you've finished. And I don't see why we can't arrange for a little staff discount. I'll give you a note.'

'Well, thanks very much.'

As he toddled off, I said to Lily, 'By heaven, things *are* looking up. Seems like my lucky day after all.'

She came in close and pecked me on the nose. 'To say nothing of the night.'

'No, to say nothing of that. Hey, what are you doing for Christmas?'

'I'm going home.'

'Oh. And where's home?'

'London.'

'Eh?'

She laughed. 'London, Ontario. I'm going down by train tomorrow morning.'

'Oh.'

'But not *too* early.'

'Oh,' I said, brightening.

'What will you do Christmas Day?'

I shrugged. 'Don't know really. I'll more than likely spend it with my pal, Buzz, but how and where I've no idea. Probably at the hotel.'

'How exciting.'

'Yeah,' I grinned. 'Still, he's a good lad.'

'*How* exciting.'

'Anyway, I should worry. I'll probably be in bed by nine – exhausted.'

She grinned outrageously. 'If I've got anything to do with it.'

The grotto closed down at seven, not at eight, all the kiddies presumably being tucked up in bed by then; and after we changed from our costumes Lily and I did a bit of shopping around the store.

I bought her a string of hippy beads with a dingle-dangle on the end that had the word 'LOVE' engraved on it, and hung it around her neck, receiving a kiss in return. Then I found Buzz a little something – a penknife to replace the one he'd broken trying to unpick the lock in Professor Kokheimer's Gothic tomb in New York, where we'd been incarcerated by the crooks. And finally I bought myself a dark-blue parka to keep out the Canadian winter. Not exactly Savile Row but extremely effective.

'Right,' I said, 'now I can face the elements. I look like

Scott of the Antarctic, but it's better than resembling a frozen corpse. Now – just one phone call to Buzz to tell him what's happening and I'm all yours.'

'I like the sound of that,' she smiled. 'The phones are over there.'

I got through to the hotel and they rang the room. Buzz answered too quickly to have been anywhere else but in or on the bed.

'Hello.' He sounded shagged.

'Hello – would that be Knickers, Knickers and G-String – growers of lovers' nuts?'

'Ha!' he laughed, coming alive. ' 'Ello, mate, how'd it go?'

'Un ... believable. Shot three, strangled four and winged at least another dozen.'

'Rather you than me. I've been thinking about you all day ... yo-ho-ho-ing and suffering eighteen kinds of agony.'

'Yeah, I'll just bet you have, you bum. How was darling Amy, the freelance artist and all-time wonder lover?'

'More wonderful than ever. Man, I am *dead*.'

'Serves you right. Me ...? I feel radiant ... energized, as only a man can feel after an honest day's toil. What are you doing right now?'

'Resting up a spell. Russ ... buddy ... I hate to break this to you but ... about tonight ...'

'Don't tell me – you've got a playmate.'

'How did you know?'

'Come on, Malone, this is Tobin.'

'Aw, I feel badly about it, Russ – you being alone and ...'

'Buzz, man, think nothing of it. You go ahead and enjoy yourself ... and try not to think of me tramping the frozen streets, eating a lonely sandwich in some desolate snack-bar, choking with ennui on every bite.'

'Tobin, will you cut that out ...!'

'Have a ball, Buzz, you deserve it after such a hard day. I'll see you sometime tomorrow morning?'

'Mm ...? Well, I don't know if my luck'll be *that* good ...'

'I wasn't referring to yours, son, I was thinking of mine.'

'Mm ...? What? You mean ...?'

'Sure, I mean. What d'you take me for – Santa Claus or something?'

He exploded a laugh in my ear. 'Boy, I might have known. You crafty basket. Who is she – a salesgirl?'

'Well, she's sold me all right, but, no – she's Santa's Fairy Helper.'

'Sounds mighty promising.'

'Believe it. Have a luvly time, Buzz.'

'Toodle-oo, mate. Come and help me crack my egg at breakfast – I won't have the strength.'

'Sure – but who's going to crack mine? Tarra.'

I came out of the box, grinning.

'What's funny?' Lily asked, taking my arm.

'Buzz is. The randy devil's got himself a girl for tonight.'

'So what else have you two got in common?' she grinned. 'Come on, let's go home, I'm ravenous. We may even get around to that steak, too.'

CHAPTER THREE

Miraculously we found a cab almost immediately, thanks, I was sure, to Lily, who looked adorable huddled in her fur coat, her pale hair fluffed around her ears. The driver ignored me, but gave her an approving wink and even opened the door for us.

She gave him a number on Yonge Street, told him it was near St. Clair, and we started off. Lily brushed snow from my hair, kissed my nose, then snuggled up, smelling deliciously, and for a while we looked out of the windows at the glittering shops, admiring the displays and listening to the recorded carols, enjoying the bubbling Christmasy feeling they evoked.

'Lovely time – Christmas,' she sighed, 'I adore it. You're a long way from home, hm?'

'Three thousand miles, but I don't mind. I'm having a great time right here.'

'Won't you feel lonesome tomorrow?'

'Not at all. I'll be home in a fortnight. No, Buzz and I will cook something up tomorrow. He's got friends in Toronto.'

She raised a brow. 'Obviously – and all female, I presume.'

'And how about the lads down in London, Ontario? Got anybody back there?'

'Mmm ...' she nodded. 'Seven or eight.'

'You know I believe you.'

'But, damn it, *you've* spoilt it. How can I possibly be impressed after you?'

'Flattery, madam, will get you ...'

'Get me what?' she grinned.

'I refuse to be drawn. I'll surprise you.'

'Promise?'

'You're a devil.'

'Then ... let's be evil.'

'Truly?'

'*Really*,' she chuckled.

'Right,' I laughed, 'you're on.'

Dammit, my heart was at it again.

It wasn't far to St. Clair, and within minutes we were entering a small modern block of flats. We climbed stairs to the first floor and Lily opened the door of number eight with a key, bowed me in, closed the door, then led the way down a narrow hall.

'Bathroom,' she said, pointing left as she opened a door on the right. It was the lounge, fairly small but nicely furnished, very cosy.

A deep floral sofa faced a fireplace filled with logs, and there was a dining-table and the usual fitments, though I wasn't paying them too much attention. I was watching Lily as she peeled off her fur coat and headed for another door on the right, which presumably led to the bedroom.

'How d'you fancy a real fire?' she asked. 'There's a gas poker over there. Just light it and stick it under the logs if you like.'

'I'd like very much. It's been a long time since I saw a log fire.'

I found the poker and lit it and was watching the flames lick round the logs when she came out of the bedroom draped in a pale-blue satin negligee that hid absolutely nothing at all.

'Manage?'

'Perfectly.'

'I'm going to take a shower.'

'Need any help?'

She laughed. 'I think you'd better stay out, otherwise ...'

Minutes later I heard her splashing about, humming happily to herself, so I knocked on the door and put a stop to it.

'Anything I can do for you?'

'Yes! You can find some booze in the kitchen cupboard, the one by the stove, and make some drinks.'

'The booze! I was going to buy some!'

'It's all right, Tobin, I'm used to pikers. Thought you avoided it very smoothly, though. There's some scotch, gin and vodka, help yourself. I'll have a vodka tonic, lots of ice, easy on the tonic!'

'I might have known – that's my drink.'

'Something *else* we have in common!'

'Oh?' I laughed. 'What else have we got, lady?'

'Passion!' she bellowed, and I laughed.

'That's what I like – subtlety! Drink coming up!'

While I was making them I heard the water cease and as I carried them into the lounge out she came, wreathed in steamy soap-perfume and looking radiant.

'Boy, that feels better. I couldn't wait to wash Fairy Helper down the plug-hole.'

'You look terrific ... here, with just a smidgin of tonic.'

She took the drink, sipped it, pulled an agonized face. 'Wow!'

'More tonic?'

'Over my dead body.'

'Could I have a shower, d'you think?'

'Help yourself – it's unisex. Would you like a robe?'

I raised a brow at her. 'A man's robe?'

'What else – unless you fancy one trimmed with lace.'

'No, thanks.'

'Go and start your shower, I'll bring it in.'

I was down to my Y-fronts when she opened the door and slung the towelling robe at me. 'Here – compliments of my brother and I don't care if you *don't* believe it ...' she broke off, pulling an amused expression as she gazed once more at my shorts, then, with a yearning sigh, about-turned and went out. 'Don't be long, hm? ... momma's waiting.'

Ten minutes later, feeling twelve pounds lighter and ten years younger, I emerged to find her curled on the sofa, gazing into a flourishing fire.

She looked up and inclined her head approvingly. 'Hmm ... not a bad-looking fella really.'

'Your brother must be a big guy – the shoulders are half-way down my arms.'

'Fortunately shoulders are not everything. Come and sit

down.'

I relaxed into the sofa, sipped my drink and lit a fag. 'Oh, boy, that feels better. I sent Santa after Fairy Helper at a fast crawl.'

'Feeling a million dollars, hm?' she smiled.

'Fit for anything.'

'Really. Are you hungry yet?'

'Nope.'

'But you had no lunch ... I mean ... nothing to eat ... oh, hell, you know what I mean.'

I laughed with her. 'I'm still not hungry. Maybe later. Right now I'm enjoying this drink, and this fire, and this girl.'

She snuggled closer, under my arm, 'I'm very glad, I think this is super. I'd like to spend all Christmas right here.'

'Do you have to go down to London?'

'Yes ... my folks are there, mother and brother, they'd be very disappointed.'

'Sure. When will you be coming back?'

'In a month.'

'A month!'

'Mm,' she nodded. 'I'm staying home for a while, I do it every year. Since my father died, Mom likes me to stay for a while.'

'Sure. Well, there's timing for you – I meet you on your last day in town.'

'Never mind.' She snuggled closer and pecked me on the cheek. 'I'm not rushing off tonight.'

'No. It could've been a lot worse.'

'Infinitely,' she agreed, placing her hand in my lap.

We lapsed into a little silence, stared at the flames licking at the logs and watched the sparks fly up the chimney, then, suddenly, I was aware of her hand moving against my thigh, no, not merely moving but touching, stroking, caressing, her fingers tracing idle, mischievous circles in the general area of Herc. I said nothing, choosing to imagine, with thudding heart, what she was thinking about and what she would do.

Try as I might I could not control the brute and against all control he came to life, reached urgently for the caress of her lazy fingers and in a moment was making a spectacle of himself and a tent out of the robe.

With her face lowered, hidden behind a swathe of hair, she began to chuckle, to shake against me.

'What's funny?' I demanded.

'He is. You are. Men are.'

'Huh.'

'Just look at him grow . . . and I didn't even touch him.'

'You didn't have to. You willed him awake.'

'Yes,' she chuckled. 'I talked to him. Arise, Sir Richard, I said. Come to momma, she wants to kiss you . . .' And with that she gently peeled the gown away. 'Isn't he beautiful?' she whispered. 'So strong . . . so hard . . .'

I jumped as she touched him, ran her finger and thumb fleetingly from tip to base and back again, lost in wonderment.

'It really isn't fair,' she pouted playfully. 'Men have so much and women have so little.'

'It's . . . what the psychiatrists term "penis envy",' I croaked, jumping again as she found the spot and gave it a tickle. 'Lily, don't do that . . .'

'Russ . . .' she looked up at me, her eyes fervent, 'lie down by the fire . . . take your robe off.'

As I said before, in these circumstances a gentleman does not refuse a lady anything. I shed the robe and lay down. She moved close, stood over me, then slipped the gown from her shoulders and dropped it to the floor, her flame-licked nakedness stopping my breath.

She smiled down at me, very relaxed, not the slightest bit inhibited, proud of her body and sure of me.

'What do you see from down there?' she asked.

'I see a *very* lovely girl . . . bathed in firelight . . . utterly desirable.'

'You desire me?'

'Like my teeth ache.'

She smiled a little amused smile, stepped between my parted legs, then descended very slowly to her knees, sucked in a startled breath as she enveloped me and finally came to rest against my thighs.

'Ohhh . . .' she gasped, her mouth pursed in wonderment. 'Oh, Russ that is fan*tas*tic!'

'It is,' I gulped, my heart thudding wildly. 'I . . . think you'd better sit very still for a moment . . .'

'Russ, I can't . . .'

'You must.'

'I can't! Russ . . . oh, my God . . . I think I'm coming!'

'Already!?'

'Yes ... yes! Ohhh ... ohh, Russ, I can't help it ... it's coming! It's ... ohh, Jeezus ...!'

With barely a movement of her body she went into a tight, curled spasm, eyes shut tight and teeth gritted in seven kinds of anguish. Once ... twice ... three times she shuddered, her hands clenched into fierce fists, then with a great, exultant gasp she relaxed, face lowered, hands dropping limply to her thighs.

'Oh, Russ that was wonderful,' she panted. 'My God, that was delicious.'

I grinned up at her. 'Well, there's more where that came from.'

'You are a lovely lover. Can you hold on a bit longer? I'm enjoying him so much.'

'I think so,' I chuckled.

'Wonderful.'

She dropped forward and kissed me on the lips, a warm, loose-mouthed kiss of a very sexy woman, then, with a naughty smile, she sat erect and once more took Herc to the hilt, closing her eyes in ecstasy as he travelled endlessly home.

'Ohhh ... Russ,' she said, heaving a vastly contented sigh, 'if only you knew how this feels to a woman. It really is the most *fab*ulous sensation.' She opened her eyes and smiled down at me. 'I pity you poor fellas. You may have it all to show, but you'll never know the heaven of having it like this.'

'Oh, we do all right, miss. It ain't exactly pure misery down here, you know.'

'I guess it would be nice to be able to change places just once, hm? – to get to know just how the other sex feels. It might cure a lot of sex problems.'

I laughed. 'What are they?'

She shook her head. 'I'm sure I don't know ... I've just heard about them. I hear of some women who find it impossible to have an orgasm ... well, by golly, I reckon they'd soon get over that one sitting where I'm sitting right now.' She gave a laugh. 'Hey, now there's a job for you – practical help for sex-troubled females. You ought to set up a company – call it "Orgasms Inc." or "The Friendly Stud Company".'

'Not a bad idea,' I laughed, 'provided all my customers looked like you. But then I doubt if too many girls like you *have* sex problems. And if they do, I reckon they can always find plenty of fellas to help them get over them ... Lily ... is anything the matter?'

A curious distant look had entered her eyes and her breathing was going potty again. Her breasts began to rise and fall quickly and now her lower lip was trapped between her teeth.

'It's ... you,' she groaned, beginning to sway, to rock. 'You ... and him! This great thing you've got stuck up inside me ... ohhh, Russ ...'

'Again?'

'*Yes*, again. Russ, I can't get enough of him ... Damn it, I'm coming ...! Oh, baby this is a big one ... this is a great ... fat ... fabulous ... ohh ...! Ohhh ...! OHHHHH ...!'

With a jubilant cry she was over the top, face tilted to the ceiling and eyes shut tight.

'WooooooOOWW!' she bellowed, breasts heaving frantically. '*God* ... that was something!'

With an exultant roar she collapsed upon me, panting hard, shaking her head. 'Ohh, Tobin, you are going to do me ... a terrible mischief, I just know ...!'

'Why?' I laughed.

'Because I've got the sneakiest feeling this is gonna go on for the rest of the night ... and at this rate of orgasm I shall, by tomorrow morning, have had one thousand six hundred and forty-two and instead of getting on that train I'll be carted off in a hearse – or whatever they *find* of me will be carted off in a hearse – and I'm lovin' every minute of it and if you *dare* stop for a second I shall scream the building down and have you arrested for rape!'

'I promise I shall not stop ... not even for a second.'

'Ohhh ...' she groaned, 'I don't know which is worse ... the prospect of you stopping or the prospect of you not stopping. But I'll take my chances and silently suffer anything and everything that comes my way.'

'Silently!' I laughed. 'You really let fly on that last one. I'm surprised we're not getting thumps of protest on the ceiling.'

'They're away for Christmas.'

'Just as well. If that last one was anything to go by, things might get a little rowdy around here. I'd hate them to call in the cops thinking you were being murdered.'

'I *am* being murdered. I'm being speared ...' she gave a sexy wriggle, 'by this terrible thing.'

'I can take it out, if you ...'

'You do and I'll snap it off.'

She sat erect again, grimacing as once again she settled into position. 'Jeez, that's agony ... would you like a drink? I certainly need one.'

'I'd love one.'

She reached behind her and returned with the glass, wincing again. 'Have you fellas any *conception* of what we girls suffer?' She handed me down my drink, took a sip of hers, smiling at me. 'Cheers, lover.'

'Cheers, angel.'

'I've never had a happier Christmas Eve.'

'Me, neither.'

'Just shows you – it doesn't necessarily cost a fortune to have a fabulous time.' She took my glass, set them both down. 'I think maybe it's a good thing I'm going away tomorrow ... two weeks of this and we'd both be dead. As it is I may not be able to walk tomorrow.'

'Hire a wheel-chair. I'd offer to carry you, but I fear I may well be in desperate straits myself.'

She narrow-eyed me threateningly. 'Oh, don't worry, Tobin, your turn's coming. In a few minutes we shall pause for station identification, consume a quick steak for sustenance ... and then I'm gonna start on *you*.'

'Oh, really?'

'Yes, really. Are you feeling hungry yet?'

I shrugged. 'So-so.'

'Which means you're starved. All right – we eat. Steady now ... ohhh ... ohhh, baby ... wow ...!' She got to her feet, glanced down at me and shook her head wonderingly. 'Incredible. Now, will you please hide it while I cook that steak ... otherwise we won't be eating tonight!'

We never did eat those steaks. Oh, she got them under the grill all right and even cooked one side, but then, with no more motivation than our inability to resist touching each other, we were suddenly in each other's arms and tearing at each other's robes.

'The steaks ...' I croaked plaintively.

'Screw the steaks,' she gasped.

And that was the end of dinner.

CHAPTER FOUR

We slept the sleep of the dead, waking around eight the next morning, still locked in each other's arms all snug and bed-warm and wickedly languid. She gave me a lazy lover-smile, kissed me lightly on the lips then squirmed into me with a contented mew, both of us relishing the contact of sizzling flesh and allowing sensuality free rein.

'Mmm, you feel so good,' she murmured, running her hand over my body. 'So warm ...'

'How do you feel, Lily?'

'Wonderful.'

'Lily, don't do that.'

'Why not?'

'Because you know very well why not.'

'Don't you *ever* go limp?'

'Not with a hot-blooded, silky-skinned naughty like you squirming all over me ... rubbing her fabulous naked body up against me ... and doing ...' I jumped, '... *that* to me!'

'Russ ... do you think there's something wrong with me?'

'Eh?' I looked down at her. '*Wrong* with you?'

She nodded.

'Why should there be anything wrong with you?'

'Because ... I want you again. I can't stop wanting you. Do you think I'm ... a nymphomaniac or something?'

I laughed aloud. 'Don't be daft. The dictionary definition of nymphomania is "a *morbid* and uncontrollable sexual desire in women". There's nothing morbid about yours, love. You thoroughly enjoy yourself. I think it's lovely.'

'But are you sure so *much* sex is good for a person?'

'Well ...' I laughed, 'I can only speak personally – and personally speaking I never felt better in my life. I feel terrific ... fantastic ... and, Lily, you really mustn't *do* that ...'

'It's awful, the way it gets you, isn't it? I don't want to move from here all day. Now I can understand all those jokes about honeymoon couples staying in bed for two whole weeks. Russ ... I don't want to catch that train. I don't want to go home. I just want to snuggle up to you and screw you all day ... then sleep a bit and screw you some more. I'm *sure* I'm a nymphomaniac.'

'You're a very sexy woman, I know that.'

'I sometimes feel I'm the sexiest woman in the world. I just love doing it ... *adore* it! And look what's happening to you.'

'Huh!'

'Ohhh ...' she groaned and slid right over me, wriggling hard into me and flattening her big squashy breasts against my chest. Then, with a neat, slick tuck of her hips she located Herc and sat him to the hilt.

'Ohhh ...' She sighed wistfully. 'Oh, God, that's beautiful ...'

'Happy now?' I grinned.

'Much better. I feel only half a woman without him in there. What am I going to do when it's time to go?'

I laughed. 'Well, I could come with you.'

'Like this!'

'Sure – we could make out we're practising for an outdoor dance championship ... the tango, maybe. Da ... *rum* ... dum ... dum ... dum ... darara ... *rum* ... dum ... dum ... dum ...'

'Ooooh!' she giggled. 'That's gorgeous!'

'Yes, I'm pretty good at the tango.'

'Russ ...' She became suddenly serious.

'Yes, love?'

'I *will* have to go very soon.'

'Yes, I know.'

'Will you ... do something for me?'

'Sure, what is it?'

'Just roll me over ... right now ... and do me *very* hard!'

Incredible – the adaptability of the human spirit, one moment languid, the next a fury of passion. The aggressiveness of her demand whipped me from playful dalliance into ruthless determination in the space of a wink and before you could say 'whoops!' we were going at it like we'd just discovered it.

Thank heaven the people upstairs were away for Christmas, because without doubt her cries and shrieks would have had the cops breaking down the door before she was half-way through. She was a tiger, a tornado, and when she hit her final stupendous climax she let out a bellow I'm certain Buzz must've heard back at the hotel.

'OHHHHH ... *GOD*!' she roared, taking everything with savage hunger and desperate for more. Then ... 'OHHHHHH!' an appalled, open-mouthed, wonder-filled gasp quickly followed by total collapse. 'OHHHH ... *RUSS*!'

'My God,' I panted, desperate for air. 'Lily, love ... that time you really surpassed yourself.'

'I surpassed *my*self!' She shook her head. 'Well ... *if* I'm a nymphomaniac I don't damn-well care! Oh, Russ, you really go.' She gave a weak, helpless laugh and flopped her hand against my back. 'Happy *Christmas* everybody! Guess what I've got! I've got good old sexy Santa Claus all to myself ... an' he's just given me the nicest Christmas present ever.'

I laughed at her, wearily, drunk with exhaustion, and snuggled into her. 'Lily ... mind if I stay here for a month and recover?'

'Who's got the strength to move you? Ohh, Tobin, you've really done it to me. I feel ... all floaty ... weightless ... so sleepy.'

'Then sleep.'

'Can't ... got to catch a train.'

'At what time?'

'Eleven.'

'It's only eight-thirty ... sleep.'

She shook her head exhaustedly. 'Can't ... never wake up ... ohh, I feel all ... all ...'

We fell into silence, fighting sleep for the sake of her train, but finally losing ... and woke again with a terrible start an hour later.

'Hm!' she grunted, jerking me from a stupor, then gasped, 'Russ! What time is it?'

With pounding heart I peered at my watch on the bedside table, then relaxed. 'Oh ... it's all right, love, it's only nine-thirty. Boy, I went out like a light.'

She gave a chuckle and kissed me. 'Now I *must* go.'

'Yes, I know.'

She smiled at me, regretfully. 'I'm going to miss you. I'm going to be wishing like mad that you were with me in London. Thank you for a wonderful Christmas.'

I stroked her hair, her face. 'And I thank you, Lily. I didn't expect you in my stocking. It's been fabulous, that's all.'

'Come on ... let's take a shower. I think we're *reasonably* safe now ...' She cocked her head on one side and peered at me suspiciously. 'Damn it, on second thoughts I'm not at all sure.'

I shrugged. 'Well, we *have* had an hour's sleep.'

She raised her eyes and gasped, 'Jeezus!' and shot off the bed.

At the station we barely had time for a hug and a kiss before she had to climb aboard, then the train pulled out. I waved her out of sight then turned for the barrier, suddenly aware that a great deal of warmth had just gone out of my life.

'Wrong sorta day to be seein' your girl off,' commented the guard at the barrier.

'Lousy,' I agreed.

'Though I daresay *any* day is the wrong kinda day for seein' a lovely girl like that off.'

'You said it.'

'Well, if it ain't an impossibility – Happy Christmas.'

'Thanks,' I grinned. 'And to you.'

He gave a wry laugh. 'Me? I'm havin' a ball right here.'

'You don't mind working Christmas Day?'

'Ha! Man, I *volunteered* for it! It's the only place I'm guaranteed a bit of peace an' goodwill!'

I left him doing a little soft-shoe shuffle to keep the circulation going and headed out to the taxi rank and back to the hotel.

CHAPTER FIVE

I found Malone in bed, flat on his back and snoring like a buzz-saw, looking for all the world like a guy recuperating from in-depth exhaustion, dirty sod.

Up till now I'd been feeling pretty perky, but the sight of him strewn in blissful vacuum suddenly auto-suggested that I, too, really ought to be feeling shattered and a great wave of languor swept over me. So, with that luxurious clarity of conscience regarding sloth and idleness that holidays permit, I ripped off my clothes and took a header into my own bed, determined to fully restore the batteries for the evening –

whatever *that* was destined to bring.

'Oh ... *boy*, that felt good – a deep, soft, comfortable bed and all the time in the world to wallow in it. Ho ho, I yawned, eyelids closing, not a bad life at all really ... actually pretty damn good. Sleep ... sleep ... beautiful sleep ... and cocooned in rosy contentment I slept.

For all of fifteen minutes.

'Hey!'

A wallop on the arse shattered me awake. 'Hm ...? Wha ...? Who ...?'

'Wake up! Happy Christmas!'

It was bloody Buzz, standing behind me. I rolled over, got him into focus, checked my watch and gave him an ear-to-ear sneer.

'And a Happy Bleedin' Christmas to you, you bum. Do you realize I've only just this minute got to bed! Fifteen minutes' sleep I've had all night ...!'

'Serves you right,' he grinned. 'Come on – get up, you've got a date.'

'Eh?' I uttered a heart-felt groan. 'No, not with a bird, mate, I couldn't ...'

'Not *a* bird, son – about twenty of 'em. We've been invited out to Greg Douglas's place for lunch. He's throwing a buffet ice-skating party. Lots of dollies. Should be terrific.'

'Yes?' I came alive, convincing myself that I'd had my full quota of sleep at Lily's place. 'What time are we due there?'

'Twelve thirty-ish. It's not far. It's in Forrest Hill – very swish.'

'Lovely. Ohh ... got something for you.' I skipped out of bed and searched in my coat pockets, finding his present. 'Happy Christmas, son.'

'For me?'

'No, your father, you twit. Open it.'

He did so, a grin of remembrance spreading across his face as he unwrapped the knife. 'Hey ... that's terrific, Russ. Heck, fancy you thinking of that. Very nice, mate, appreciate it. Every time I use it I shall think of us locked up in Kokheimer's tower.' He moved to the bed and fished a parcel from under his pillow and threw it to me. 'Happy Christmas to you, too.'

'You lovely fella,' I grinned. 'Hey, I'm not sure I like all this niceness. I feel better when you're insulting me.'

'We can start again tomorrow.'

I unwrapped the parcel. It was a pair of fur-lined gloves, with a note 'Keep 'em warm, son, you never know where they get to.'

'Ah, Buzz, they're fabulous, thanks very much. Just what I needed.'

'Well, I figured you wouldn't remember to buy any – and if you're going to be skating this afternoon ...'

'Me – skate! I've never ice-skated in my life.'

'Good, now's your chance to learn. I see you bought yourself a parka.'

'Got it at Simpsons.'

'Hey – I haven't asked you – how was the job? Any scars ... bruises?'

I grinned obscenely. 'Not from the kids.'

'Yeah, what was this "Santa's Fairy Helper" bit? Who was she?'

'Precisely that – Santa's Fairy Helper.'

'And did she?'

'Unbelievably.'

'Good on you. Well, what about today – you plan to see her?'

I shook my head. 'Nope. I saw her off to London – the Ontario one – on the train at eleven this morning. She's going home for Christmas. Buzz, man, you would not *believe* ...'

'Yes, I would, you randy bugger.'

'Ha! And how, precisely, did you spend *your* evening, Malone? Sticking stamps in her album?'

'Well, for Godsake, how did *you* know?'

I grinned at him. 'How're you feeling – shattered?'

He groaned a big one. 'Man, I just dare not think about that tournament coming up in two days. I'll be lucky to get the ball into the air, never mind ace-serve it. But, hell, let that take care of itself, I'll sleep on the plane. But ... *today*!' He slapped his hands together, deafening me. 'Today is Christmas and I fully intend to have a very good time. A bit of crackling and a little stuffing – *that's* what Christmas is all about. So a quick scrape with the razor, Russell, and let us sally forth in search.'

'You could fancy another bird ...!' I groaned, 'after the dollop *you've* just had?'

'Well, certainly,' he frowned, pausing at the bathroom door. 'Good God, man – that was *yesterday*!'

We left the hotel just after twelve, caught a cab outside and rode up Yonge Street to the district of Forrest Hill, which is every bit as affluent and beautiful as it sounds.

Greg Douglas's place was a stunner – a magnificent, rambling, ranch-style bungalow set in several acres of landscaped gardens, a monument to the profitability of Hire-A-Guy.

As we drew into the long, sweeping drive and caught first sight of the house, set back a good way from the road on a slight rise, I gave a whistle of amazement and drew a grin from Buzz.

'Some place, hm?'

'Wow! How old is Greg Douglas, Buzz?'

'Would you believe twenty-eight?'

'Good God. Tobin, what have you been doing with your life? Is he a millionaire?'

'Near as dammit.'

'Married?'

'Not officially. Greg prefers a harem. The twenty birds I mentioned are probably all his – but he's a very generous fella. He'll gladly lend us a couple.'

'Hey, just look at that pool!'

'Ah, yes, that's just the outdoor one, of course. He also has an indoor one ... *and* riding stables at the back ... *and* a shooting gallery, and a gymnasium, and a games room, and a small private cinema, and a ...'

'Stop! Buzz ...' I sighed, 'do you ever get the feeling you've been wasting your time so far? How did he make all the money? Rich daddy?'

'Nope. His daddy was a drunken bum – deserted the family when Greg was four. He's done all this by himself.'

'From Hire-A-Guy?'

'Some – but not all. He's into everything – real estate, insurance, gambling. Greg's a very smart fella.'

'And don't it show? Well, good for him. Jeez, this place is beautiful.'

'Wait till you see the inside!'

We drew up to a porticoed front door of panelled oak, paid the driver and got out, and before we could ring the bell the door opened and a diminutive Oriental gentleman, dressed in an immaculate white jacket, bowed us welcome.

'Mister Malone!' he beamed. 'So nice to see you again.'

'Thank you, Song, how've you bin?'

'Top hole, sir, thank you.'

'This is Russ Tobin, Song. Russell – meet Song Lin, the sexiest butler in the western hemisphere.'

'So kind,' grinned Song and bowed to me. 'Welcome, Mister Tobin, please come in.'

We entered.

I wonder if you've ever, literally, been breathtaken by the interior of a house – I mean, truly rooted to the spot, overwhelmed by its size, splendour, elegance, colour – and by the obvious cost of the whole operation?

We were standing at the head of a short, curved staircase and looking down into a huge and very beautiful sunken lounge, as unique and impressive an introduction to a home as you could encounter. The walls of the lounge were stone-built; its furnishings, in silk, leather, glass and chrome, a comfortable compromise between classic and ultra-modern, the entire room being covered wall-to-wall in deep-piled mushroom carpeting that looked luxuriant enough to dive into without fear of injury.

Designed in open-plan, other rooms led off through wide archways, giving a feeling of flamboyant space and indicating that it was the home of a sensualist, a man who just had to have plenty of elbow-room from which to conquer the world.

'What d'you think?' murmured Buzz.

'I think I've been wasting my time.'

'I know what you mean.'

'Please come this way, gentlemen ...'

We followed Song Lin down the stairs and into the lounge, and as its left-hand annex came into sight, so did a spectacular view of the landscaped gardens and an ice-rink filled with skaters.

'Man, just look at that,' I murmured to Buzz. 'The house goes on for ever!'

'I got lost here once – couldn't find my bedroom.'

'How many are there?'

'Twelve.'

'Huh!'

Song Lin led us through a glass door and out on to a paved patio the size of Wyoming, then took us across to a long glassed-in extension in which all the non-skating activity appeared to be taking place.

As we approached, I began to take closer note of the other

guests, both skaters and non-skaters, realizing that we were in the company of very beautiful people. They were all of an age, mid-twenties to mid-thirties, the men exuding the unmistakable aura of money, and the women great style, beauty and elegance.

We might well have been in St. Moritz.

As we passed close to the ice-rink I stopped to watch one gorgeous piece of crumpet in a bright-red outfit trimmed in white execute a splendid spin, come out of it with a graceful swoop and flash off across the ice backwards on one foot, missing the wooden barrier by the width of a bee's knee and curving back around the perimeter again, not with ostentation but with a truckload of talent.

Then I saw other skaters, men and women, doing similar spins and turns, and the standard of all their performances suddenly appalled me.

'Hey ... Buzz ...!'

He stopped and came back to me. 'Yes, mate?'

'Have you ... *seen* these people skate?'

'What about them?'

'Well, just look at them! I mean, they're terrific! Everyone of them!'

'Russell,' he sighed, 'you happen to be in Canada – not Ilford High Street. Everybody skates like this over here – they're born on 'em.'

'And you expect *me* to get out there with *them*?'

He grinned. 'You can carry a Union Jack, they'll understand.'

'No chance.'

'Aw, you've got to have a go, mate. I'm going to.'

'You are?'

'Sure. After all, it is a skating party ... it's only manners.'

'Yeah, I suppose so. But ... can you skate?'

He grinned again. 'Superbly.'

'Bastard.'

'Come on, I can see Greg inside.'

The glassed-in extension had a hunting-lodge feel to it – a roaring log fire and animal heads mounted around the stone walls – the atmosphere very 'après-ski', or more accurately 'après-skate'. The guests, dressed in colourful sweaters and ski-type pants, stood around in happy clumps, drinking and chatting, eyeing each other, being very gay and witty, the eyes of most women locking on to Buzz and me as we crossed the room, automatically interested in all male newcomers.

Song Lin led us through the appreciable crowd to a group standing near the open fireplace, heading specifically for a tall, handsome, dark-haired fellow in a white sweater and immaculate black slacks. At our approach he glanced at Song Lin, then at me, finally at Buzz and broke into a delighted grin as he recognized him.

'Buzz, old buddy! How are yuh? Nice to see you again.'

They shoook hands heartily.

'Greg ... this is Russ Tobin.'

'Ah, yes, Santa Claus,' he grinned, offering a strong, tanned hand. 'Nice to meet you, Russ. Say, I heard some good things about the way you handled that job. Hear it went well.'

'After a somewhat indifferent start,' I smiled. 'We ran into heavy flak for the first hour, but it smoothed out after that.'

'Well, Dudley reported very favourably, anyway. I like to check out the guys working for me. Sorry I had to hand you such a dog to start with. Maybe we can improve on the next one – provided you *want* a next one.'

'Well, yes, I'd be very grateful. As Buzz explained to you on the phone I'll be here for another two weeks – until he gets back from Victoria – so anything you think might suit I'll have a crack at.'

'Good man. O.K., I'll check the files day after tomorrow and call you at the hotel if I come up with something.'

'Thanks very much.'

'And now – forget business and have yourselves a good time. You'll find skates in the changing room through there ... or if you don't feel energetic, grab yourself a drink from the bar and mingle, the natives are quite friendly. I'll catch up with you later.'

We thanked him and as we broke away, he returned to the group ... to talk business.

'Come on,' said Buzz, taking my arm, 'Let's get you some skates.'

'Aw, Buzz ...'

'Nuts – it's all fun. Nobody gives a damn. I reckon you're a natural, anyway.'

'Mm, natural cunt,' I grinned. 'Well, I should worry – making an idiot of myself is nothing new. O.K. – lead on, MacDuff, and let's get it over with.'

Five minutes later, my feet encased in tightly-bound skate-boots, I stood up ... and promptly fell down again.

'No,' Buzz said patiently, in a tone you'd employ on a thick four-year-old, 'that's not *quite* the idea, Tobin. The object is to stand upright on the blades ... like this.'

'Oh! Like that!'

He caught me under the arm and pulled me up off the floor. 'Right, come on, I'll help you out.'

'Buzz ...'

'Shut up ... look at *that*! You're doing fine ... no, stand on the *blades*, Russell, not your ankles ... up ... up! Beautiful. Whoops! You'll soon get the hang of it. Come on, slowly does it ... left ... right ... left ... right ...'

'Buzz, as preposterous as it may seem, I do know how to walk ... ooh, Jeezus, hey, not so fast, man ...'

Like a motherless drunk I weaved, wobbled and wavered all the way to the door, gripping his arm with a desperation close to panic, my legs behaving like the bones had just been removed, everything disjointed, disco-ordinated and diskumknockerated.

'Never ... ouch ... again ... oops! ... will I criticize ice-skating on ... cor! ... the telly. I'd give the poor devils sixes right across the board for just standing up.'

'Russell, another five minutes and you'll be dashing around on them like you've been doing it all your life. See! You've reached the door.'

'Fantastic – now let's go back and take them off.'

'Ho, no you don't ... come on – outside.'

He slid the door open and guided me through, me clutching at everything in sight for support. Out we went, on to the length of coconut matting that was laid across the stone patio to the rink, and then we began the thirty-yard dash that took all of five minutes.

Finally, and unbelievably, we reached the wooden barrier and there, to my horror, I saw in gruesome close-up the five-hundred-mile stretch of open, virgin ice.

'Buzz, I can't ...!'

'You can.'

'I won't!'

'You bloody will. I'm going to take you round.'

'What! Right out *there* ...!'

'It's easier than on this matting, believe me.'

'I don't. No, Buzz, I'll spoil your fun. It's like being lumbered with a crutch-case.'

'There'll be plenty of time for the fancy stuff. Come on, step through ... careful ... *careful* ...!'

Sssssszzzz! As I stepped on to the ice my legs divided and shot away from each other. I slammed into the barrier, half-supported by Buzz, grabbed for the rail and hung there like I'd been shot.

'Bring ... your feet back,' he grunted, taking the strain. 'Go on – pull 'em in!'

I tried ... and finished up doing a very good impression of a Russian Cossack doing a knee dance. Ta ... ta ta ta ... tata ... ta ... ta.

'Come on, up ... up ...!' Buzz was gasping.

Finally everything stopped slithering and *very* gingerly I stood upright, legs shaking like metronomes gone berserk. 'Buzz, don't leave me!' I pleaded.

'Are you kidding? Your hand is grafted to my arm, cock. O.K., now, nice 'n easy ... let's *jurst* have a quiet little walk round the barrier to get the feel of things ...'

'I've got the feel of things, now – disaster!'

'Bollocks. Easy does it ... try and keep the blades upright ... left ... right ... kinda push into it, make like you're actually trying to go somewhere ... left ... right ... hey, that's terrific!'

'You're such an unconvincing liar, Malone. Do you realize I'm the only learner-idiot on the entire rink? Just look at those guys go ...!'

'Never mind them, they had to learn sometime. They were all as bad ... I mean ... as insecure as you at first. You're doing fine. Look at that – we made ten yards already!'

'Terrific – and all in only an hour and a quarter. Look, will you do me a favour? Will you let me mess about by myself for a bit – get used to it in my own time? I'd feel better if you went and had a good skate.'

'Ah, man ...'

'No, really, Buzz.'

He frowned uncertainly. 'You sure ...?'

'Positive. Go on, you head out.'

'Well, if you'd rather. I'll keep an eye on you ...'

'No, please don't. I'll manage.'

'O.K. – see you in five minutes.'

Sssshhhooossshhh! Away he went, generating unbelievable speed with nothing more than a wiggle of his feet, scything backwards to the centre of the ice, then changing direction in a graceful curve and shishing away to be lost among the other skaters.

And me ...? With an envious sigh and clutching the barrier with the desperation of a man dangling over a thousand-foot cliff, I started off on a laborious plod towards the far-distant end, managing barely more than a faultering walk, legs braced like iron girders and ankles as rigid as a couple of milk puddings.

About four days later I reached the end and hung there to catch my breath and congratulate myself on the accomplishment, feeling a bit like Hillary reaching the top of Everest.

Enviously I watched the other skaters, astounded at their skill as they zoomed across the ice, executing jumps, splits, turns and spins, flashing towards the barrier, and in the last split-second coolly curving away and repeating it all again.

Then, out of nowhere ... ssshhiisshh! 'How's it going!' Buzz flashed by, grinning and waving.

'Fantastic!' I called.

'Good man!' He was gone.

Right, I thought – time for the second leg. I started off, suddenly feeling just that *leetle* bit more confident. Left ... right ... left ... right ... and *then*, by God, I free-wheeled! Actually glided ... skated! No more than two feet, mind you, but definitely a skate!

Ha ha! Right – we'll try that again. Left ... right ... left ... right ... whheeeee! At least *three* feet that time. By George, he's got it! I think he's got it!

Aaanndd ... one more time ... left ... right ... left ... right ... hands away and ... wwwhhheeeee!

Suddenly my feet were thrashing like a demented batter-beater, my arms were whirling like a windmill in a hurricane and everything was hurtling backwards and downward in a horrifying plummet.

Kkeeerrr ... rash!

Down I went, shaking the rink, legs in the air and arms akimbo.

'Yaaaahhhhoooo!' someone yipped, then a fearful ssshhh-iiissshhh and twin blades screamed to a halt inches from my head. Strong hands hooked under my arms and suddenly I was standing upright.

'You O.K.?'

Clutching the barrier fiercely I turned, encountering a young chap in a bright red sweater and ski-cap. 'Yes, fine ... thanks very much.'

'First time up?'

I pulled a wry grin. 'Don't it show?'

'Aw, you'll soon get the hang of it. Everybody's got to start sometime.'

'So they keep telling me.'

'Need any more help?'

'No, thanks. I'll just stagger around by myself. Thanks for the lift.'

'You're welcome.'

'He was off, generating that bewildering speed from nowhere, reaching four hundred miles an hour before he hit mid-rink.

I rubbed my bottom, massaged an elbow, and attacked it again, this time not so smart-assed, and by the time I'd reached the end of the second side was feeling pretty perky again.

A pause to rest, more from nervous tension than physical exertion, and another look at the crowd, feeling relaxed enough by now to concentrate more on the ladies.

They were indeed a splendid bunch of fillies. I mean, is there anything more delightful than the vision of a beautiful girl in skating outfit? The tiny skirt, short enough to show her lovely legs and cute little knicks, the bodice top that hugs the waist and emphasizes the breasts. It really is a very sexy get-up.

There were dozens of 'em out there – all gorgeous creatures with terrific figures and bags of style. Any one of them would have done just dandy. But strange as it may seem, not one of them appeared at all impressed by my prowess on the ice. They were either too busy showing off their own or were coupled with big handsome lads and highly unlikely to shoot me a glance even if I suddenly fell through the ice and drowned.

Ah well ... never mind. I'd got enough on my plate just trying to stay vertical. So ... with a deep breath ... and a girding of the loins ... off I went again.

I was half-way along the third side when I noticed Buzz was no longer doing a solo. He was cutting a fine figure-of-eight with a cute little dark-haired bundle in a jade-green outfit trimmed in white fur – not holding her but skating close, talking and laughing, as relaxed as though he was strolling in Hyde Park. Makes you sick.

Well, the sight of them stirred my determination. If I didn't at least get away from the barrier and out into the middle, I'd still be doing a solo when summer arrived. So – as I approached the next corner I took an even deeper breath, gritted my teeth and instead of running into the corner I cut across it to the fourth side.

Whhooooossshh! Oh, the exhilaration of free, untrammelled flight! Now I knew the bliss of birds (feathered variety) as they took to the air and soared aloft on spiralling thermals. O.K. – so it was only ten feet, but by golly I was upright all the way.

Crash! I hit the barrier, thrilled to the core. Nothing could hold me now. Off down the fourth side I streaked ... well, you know what I mean ... left ... right ... left ... right ... sssszzzzz! Now I was really getting the hang of it. The next ten yards I covered without once touching the barrier ... the following ten I actually moved *away* from it, maybe, oh, six or seven inches ... and then ... something started to go wrong.

Whether my right skate was longer than the left or it had a curve in it, I don't know, but on the next free-flight run I suddenly started to turn – inwards – towards the middle! Like a learner-swimmer suddenly out of his depth the ice-cold hand of panic gripped me. On I went, helplessly, arms outstretched like Frankenstein's monster, fingers clawing the air ... on and on ...

Ffzzzz ... sshhiisshh ... wwhhoosshh ... sswwiisshh ... skaters shot past me on both sides, one of the gayer blades performing a mid-air turn in front of me and grinning as he disappeared backwards.

Then suddenly it all started to go. My centre of gravity shifted to a spot two feet behind me and once again it was the windmill arms and batter-beater boots bit. Heeeelllppp! Jeezus, I was going ...! Oh, this was going to be a lulu ...!

But no! At a position roughly horizontal to the ice, my backwards plunge was suddenly and startlingly arrested. Two strong hands grabbed my right arm ... two others gripped my left, and in that ridiculous and ignominious posture I was steered towards the barrier.

'There yuh go, baby!' laughed Buzz. 'Man, now I call that

courage, risking the middle by yourself.'

Thud! I hit the barrier and doubled over it – and would've gone clean over the top if Buzz hadn't grabbed my coat.

'Hey, don't leave just yet!' he laughed. 'I want you to meet Beth Delewana.'

I turned to greet my other guiding hand. It was the scrumptious little dolly in the jade-green outfit.

'Hello,' she smiled, her teeth showing very white against her dark complexion.

'Well caught, ma'am,' I grinned sheepishly. 'Talk about saved in the nick of time Another second and I reckon the rink would've split from end to end.'

'Come on,' said Buzz, 'we're going to take you round, you can't hug the barrier all afternoon.'

'Hug the b ... I'll have you know, Malone, I've been gliding solo for the last ten minutes.'

'Good for you. Beth, grab his arm, we'll take him through the sound barrier.'

'Now, Buzz ...' I protested. But they had me. Out we went, my feet zooming all over the place. God, I felt ridiculous.

'Just relax ...' Beth said comfortably, 'we'll do the rest.'

'O.K.,' I nodded. 'I'm relaxed.'

'Tobin ...' said Buzz, 'your arms are stiff as railway lines. Come on, loosen up ... left ... and right ... and left ... that's it, now you're going ... and *push* ... and *push* ... *push* ...'

'Buzz, we're going too fast ...'

'No, we're not, you're all right ...'

'Buzz, I ...'

'Shut up and concentrate. We're coming to the end ... look up – don't look down at your skates ... just go with the curve, we'll guide you round ... that's Russ, look *up* ... head *up* ...!'

But I couldn't look up. The sight of my own feet fascinated me, hypnotized me, and suddenly I was dizzy, dazzled by the rushing ice, and as we turned into the bend it got worse. I weaved, staggered, teetered, tottered, then got my feet into the most goddawful tangle and slid sideways, right in front of Buzz's skates. Over he went, dragged sideways by my plummetting weight. Down I went ... the lovely Beth crashed down on top of me. Then in quick succession, amid copious cries of dismay, thud! ... biff! boof! ... three ... four more skaters piled into the heap and came crashing down on top of us.

Men cursed and women screamed. Flat on my face against

the ice with my leg bent under Buzz and his skate rammed hard into my side, I tried to push myself up an inch or two and turn my head . . . managed it . . . and found myself looking straight between Beth's widespread thighs in spectacular close-up.

'Owwww!' someone yelped.

'Aaagghh!'

'Ooooh!'

'Jeezuschrist!'

'Hell, will you guys get off the top, we're suffocating down here!'

Then, for some reason, the girls started giggling, not bothering to get up, but quite happy to lie there in a big warm heap and giggle.

'Hey, will you people please get the hell *off* up there!' I don't know who he was, I couldn't see him.

Gradually, one by one, laughing like daft things, the girls were pulled to their feet and the great load lightened. Beth became aware of my unavoidable eyeline and closed her legs in a hurry, struggled to her knees and finally got up, leaving just Buzz and me lying there.

'Cute step, that,' he acknowledged. 'Sort of sideways shimmy. Like to learn that, Tobin.'

'Buzz . . . do you think you could possibly remove your skate from my left lung. Hate to bother you, but it hurts when I laugh.'

'Sorry, mate . . . oh, blimey . . .'

He was on his feet in a flash, hauling me to mine, gaping with acute consternation at the six-inch tear in my day-old parka. 'Oh, my God . . . Russ . . .' He gingerly fingered the gaping hole, then looked at his fingers, gaping even harder. 'Russ, man . . . you're bleeding!'

'Hm . . .?'

'I've cut you! You're bleeding like a stuck pig! Jeezus, come on, let's get you inside . . .'

'Let me see,' insisted the lovely Beth, taking a butcher's, probing the hole with gentle fingers and bringing me out in goosebumps. 'No, I don't think it's too bad . . . thirty or forty stitches ought to do it.' She grinned at me. 'Better get it seen to, though.'

Funny how the fickle finger of fate chooses to change the course of our lives so unexpectedly. One minute I was the lonely barrier-hanger, feeling out of it because I couldn't skate, and now I was the centre of concerned attention. Between there and the barrier at least a dozen people shished up to ask how I was ... ten of them women.

'Oh, I'm fine, thanks very much,' I assured them, managing a brave smile and hanging on to Buzz and Beth as though in danger of imminent collapse. 'It's only a scratch.'

'Tobin,' muttered Buzz as we hit the coconut matting, 'I get the distinct feeling you're milking this.'

'Of course,' I grinned. 'Nothing like a wound to bring the little darlings round. If I can't impress them with my skating, I'll bowl 'em over with my blood.'

We reached the house and new heights of concern, this time from the top brass. Greg Douglas, spotting me through the window, came rushing up. 'Russ ... you're hurt!'

'Just a fractured rib, Greg. Buzz got jealous of my triple-leaps and put the boot in.'

He laughed. 'Seriously – is it bad?'

I shook my head. 'No, I don't think so. The parka hurts more than the wound, I only bought it yesterday.'

To Buzz he said, 'Get his skates off and show him through to the bedroom.' He gave me a comfortable grin. 'I'll get one of the girls to patch you up.'

'Oh, we can manage,' said Buzz.

I blistered him with a glare. 'Shut up, Malone, you've done enough damage.'

My boots were removed and the joy of once more standing on my own flat feet was almost too much to bear. Then we joined Greg in the party room and he took me through into the house proper, opened a door and waved me through, saying, 'Gee, I'm sorry about this, Russ ... we should've taken better care of you.'

'Heck, it was own daft fault, Greg. Buzz kept telling me to keep my head up. I guess I got the bends on the bend.'

'Well, go into the bathroom and take a look at it. You'll find antiseptic and stuff in the cabinet. I'll send someone in to give you a hand ...'

I grinned. 'No, really, I can manage.'

He cocked a humorous eye at me. 'You'd rather?'

'No,' I laughed. 'I thought you were joking.'

'Not at all. There's a harem out there. I reckon I can find one who'd like to give you a hand.'

I shrugged. 'Well . . .'

With a laugh he shut the door, leaving me impressed with his organizing ability.

I crossed the sumptuous bedroom, done out in blue, and entered the equally sumptuous bathroom. I stripped off my parka, gasping a bit at the extensive patch of blood surrounding the rip in my shirt; and with some apprehension took that off. At the wash-basin I inspected the gash in the mirror and was relieved to find it was only one of those daft superficial cuts that hardly severs the skin but bleeds copiously, this one having done it so much that I had to take my trousers off for a proper clean-up.

Well, I filled the bowl with warm water and was standing there with my Y-fronts pulled down an inch or two, sluicing away, when suddenly a voice immediately behind me said with a smile, 'Hi, how're you doing?' and frightened the life out of me.

I spun round, heart a-clamour, forgetting for the instant that I was practically indecent, and stood rooted, stunned by the vision leaning languidly in the doorway and blatantly inspecting me with a very amused smile.

Thud! The sight of her socked me in the ribs, doing more damage than Buzz's skate. She was wonderful, a slim, blonde-haired lynx, a graceful, green-eyed pussy-cat, exquisitely dressed in a black-and-white blouse and superbly-cut black trousers.

It is said that woman does not reach her sexual pinnacle until she's thirty. Well, if looks were anything to go by, this luscious lady had reached that plateau two years before her time, and was still climbing. She looked like a woman who had seen, experienced and enjoyed everything and, having decided she liked it, was making it a hobby. It was there in her lazy, familiar smile, in the light of her languid green eyes, in the carefree tumble of her mid-blonde hair and in the languor of her pose.

Her clothes, her style and the rings on her fingers told me she was a woman not entirely suffering the deprivations of absolute poverty, and as the immediate shock of her presence began to subside, I began to wonder why a bird like her should be standing in *my* bathroom.

'Hi . . .' I gulped.

Her eyes were travelling over me, unhurriedly, and as they

reached my nether regions, only partly covered by my very brief briefs, a tiny smile touched her full, perfectly-formed lips.

'I ...' I croaked, sneaking my thumbs into the elastic waistband and hoisting them a touch. 'I'm doing fine, thank you.'

'How's the wound? Greg asked me to look in, he's concerned about you.'

'Oh, it's ...' I glanced down, regretting there wasn't more to show, 'it's nothing – just a scratch. It bled quite a lot, but it's not deep.'

'Mind if I take a look?'

'Well ... no ...'

She eased away from the doorway and lynxed towards me, everything moving on well-oiled bearings. She came up very close, emanating shock-waves of heavenly perfume that caught hold of me and shook me senseless, captivated me, devastated me. Jeezus, she was overwhelming. The urge to touch her, enfold her was suddenly a very real and terrible thing. Her slender body was a powerful magnet, demanding to be caught, crushed, fondled and made outrageous love to, and how I resisted the urge to touch her I shall never know.

What I do know is that she reached out and touched me ... with long, delicate fingers, bringing huge goosebumps up all over my body and causing the hair on my scalp to rise like elephant grass.

The goose-pimples evoked a chuckle from her. 'Are my hands cold?' she asked, sweeping her eyes up to meet mine, then lowering them again to inspect the scratch.

'No,' I croaked, throat choked and heart a-thunder. 'No, they're wonderf ... very warm. It was just ... the way you touched me.'

She gave a laugh. 'I only touched you.'

'That's what I mean.'

She smiled to herself and asked, 'Does it hurt?'

'Not now.'

'Have you bathed it?'

'Well, I was sort of ...'

'Greg said there's some antiseptic in the cabinet. I think we ought to give it a shot to be on the safe side. That skate might have been rusty.'

'Yes ... I ...'

I didn't know what I was saying, I was just making noises.

She crossed to a wall cabinet, leaving me standing in a bemused trance, unable to believe what was happening.

'Ah, here we are ...'

She took out a bottle of blue stuff and a wadge of cotton wool, trickled her fingers in the water in the basin, tipped in some antiseptic, then dowsed the cotton wool.

'O.K., here we go ...' She turned to me with a grin. 'Need a bullet to bite on?'

I laughed, noting the edge of hysteria in the sound. I was quickly cracking up. 'I think I can stand it.'

Then ... she touched me again, her left hand coming to rest for support on my stomach and her right one dabbing at the wound.

I glanced down, noting two things simultaneously – the frantic pulsing of my diaphragm and the close proximity of her left hand to Herc, who, although lying dormant with shock, was still nevertheless patently obvious as a bulging curve beneath the skin-thin silk of my briefs.

Only three inches, four at the most, and the sudden thought of her touching him, holding him, brought on a surge of stifling excitement I had to fight by concentrating on a bar of soap if I wasn't to disgrace myself.

Now, in this position, being a tall bird, she had to stoop quite a bit to bathe the scratch, and the next thing she did to stop my breath was to go down on one knee, at my side, to get into a more comfortable position, but in doing so she altered the angle of her hold on my stomach and now her arm was touching my left thigh barely an inch from Herc! The lump in my throat doubled in size, the thump-rate of my heart trebled, because now I was sure she knew *exactly* what she was doing and to the nearest millimetre where she was touching and I just *knew* I was being methodically and very expertly seduced!

'Am I hurting you?' she murmured, raising her eyes and smiling that lazy, what-are-we-doing-out-of-bed smile.

'N ... no, not at all,' I croaked tremulously. 'You're very gentle.'

'Your name's Russ, isn't it? Russ Tobin?'

'Yes. Did Greg tell you?'

She nodded. 'Hm hm. I hear you're working for him – with Hire-A-Guy.'

'Yes, that's right. Just doing a few odd jobs for a couple

of weeks.'

She released her hold on my stomach, turned to the basin, rinsed out the pad, then came back, resuming, if anything, an even closer position to Herc than before. I was concentrating so hard on the soap I was sweating with the effort, but I knew I was fighting a losing battle. Any second now, I thought, Herc is going to become completely uncontrollable. He will rise up like Nessie, the Loch Ness monster and either split my briefs or shoot out of the top and break her wrist.

Was there a chance that she really *didn't* know what she was doing? Could she be a trained nurse or something – so used to handling bodies that she honestly didn't know she was drivng me potty?

Supposing she was – and I suddenly got a gigantic erection? Maybe she'd run screaming from the room yelling rape and then I'd be in real trouble – not only chucked out of the party but maybe out of Hire-A-Guy too. Down, boy, down! God, will you stop it, woman? What a position to take up – down on her knees with not only her hand tantalizing Herc but her lovely mouth, too. Surely she knew she was driving me bananas?!

'What sort of jobs have you being doing?' she asked, still dabbing away at the scratch with an application more befitting an appendectomy.

'Well,' I grinned, 'I've only done one so far – I was Santa Claus at Simpsons yesterday.'

She looked up, frowning humorously. 'Doesn't seem too much like you. You've hardly got the stomach for it. You're very slim and hard here.' She gave it a pat to prove it.

'It was an emergency – the regular Santa was ill. I was well padded up.'

'What . . . sort of jobs do you anticipate doing for Greg?' she asked, once more rinsing out the pad then once more resuming her position.

'I really don't know. I've heard his "guys" do all sorts of jobs – gardening, cleaning, decorating. I'll just have to see what comes along.'

'You sound pretty confident you can tackle almost anything. Are you handy around the house?'

'Not bad.'

She stopped dabbing and sat back on her heels, looking up at me, her head on one side, studying me, frowning a little.

'You know, you don't look or sound like an odd-job man. You're English, aren't you?'

'Yes.'

'What are you doing in Canada?'

I smiled. 'It's a long story'

'An interesting one?'

I shrugged. 'Possibly.'

'Would you like to tell it to me – over a drink?'

Oh, boy . . .

'Well, sure, I'd love to.'

She came to her feet. 'Let's have a look at that shirt.' She took it from the hook on the door and inspected it. 'Well, now, you can't wear this like this. I'll rinse it out and hang it on the rad, it'll be dry in a few minutes.'

'Oh, now, look . . . it's very kind of you, but I'll do it.'

'You won't,' she said firmly. 'Greg asked me to look after you and look after you I will. Besides – washing shirts is no job for a man. Tell you what you can do – go into the bedroom and dial 6 – it's the bar – and order some champagne for us. Tell whoever answers you're in bedroom ten, O.K.?'

'Right . . . but . . . I think I'd better put my trousers on, don't you – otherwise the barman might get some funny ideas.'

She didn't answer – just smiled – and turned to empty the basin.

I slipped my pants on, feeling more comfortable with pride-and-joy hidden, and went to the phone. By the time I'd finished ordering she'd rinsed the shirt and was bringing it into the bedroom. She hung it over the hot-air radiator then returned to the bathroom to have a go at the parka and was finishing cleaning that up when there was a knock at the door.

'Shall I answer it?' I asked, indicating my naked torso.

'Sure,' she smiled. 'I reckon he's seen a chest before.'

I opened the door. A white-jacketed waiter handed me an ice-bucket and two glasses, nodded and disappeared, superbly trained. The joys of money.

'Open it!' she called from the bathroom. 'I'll be right in.'

Plop! Fzzzzz! I poured two glasses. She entered, hung my coat on a rad and turned to take a glass.

'Happy Christmas,' she smiled. 'I hope it is being happy for you, seeing you're so far from home.'

'It's being fantastic,' I grinned, taking a gulp. 'Certainly one of the most . . . different . . . I've ever had.' I shook my head.

'You know, the most incredible things happen to me.'

'What sort of things?' She looked around, then headed for the bed and sat on it, swung her legs up and sat against the headboard. 'Hey, you've got some cigarettes. I took them out of your pocket. Mind if I have one?'

'Not at all.'

I went into the bathroom and got them, gave her one and lit it, then had a glance around, wondering where I should sit. I decided on an armchair, brought it close to the bed and sat facing her, setting my drink on the dressing-table stool.

As I lit a cigarette I looked up at her, catching her looking at me, and suddenly I felt embarrassed under the directness of her gaze. This really was the damnedest situation – a full-blooded party going on out there and here I was, stripped to the waist, sitting in a bedroom with a gorgeous, glamorous piece of crumpet I reckoned wouldn't have spared me a glance in the normal course of events, but who now at least *seemed* to be quite content to be here.

'You know,' I said, smiling at her, 'you've been looking after me for a quarter of an hour and I don't even know your name.'

She smiled very nicely. 'It's Dominique ... Dominique De Neve.'

'How very beautiful. Is it French?'

'French-Canadian.'

I couldn't resist a glance at her wedding finger. 'Is it Madam De Neve ...?'

She also glanced down. 'Was – up to a year ago. I still have the name but not the man.'

'Oh, I'm sorry.'

She laughed. 'How sweet – but you've no cause to be. It was a mutually congenial parting. We both got what we wanted.'

'I see. Well, I'm very glad ... and I'm also grateful – for your help. It was very kind.'

'My pleasure,' she said, sipping her champagne. 'You were going to tell me about the incredible things that happen to you and why you're in Canada.'

I gave a sigh. 'Dominique ... I can't help feeling you'd much rather be out there in the party than sitting in here listening to my life story. I really don't know what Greg thinks he owes me just because I fell down on his ice-rink, but I really consider your being here, keeping me company, compensation way above and beyond the call of necessity and I honestly would prefer it if you'd go back to the fun and ...'

She was smiling at me and shaking her head. 'Russ, you could not be more wrong. I'm very happy to be here keeping you company ... and if it helps any, Greg did not ask me to do it – I volunteered.'

The surge came again ... and with it the shakes. 'You did?'

'Huh huh,' she nodded.

'Well, that's awfully nice, but ... I can't think why ...'

'You mean because of all those rich, handsome men out there?'

'Well, sure ...'

'Dear man ...' she said softly, 'I *know* all those rich, handsome men out there. I've known them for five years ... party after party after party – that's the penalty for belonging to a rich, handsome "in" set. You have no idea what a ... pleasure ... it is to meet a new face ... especially such a nice face – and one that is not going to talk money and business and great new deals and killings on the stock market ...'

'Oh, I see.'

'I'm glad you do. Just as all this ...' she indicated the room, the house, 'may be new and exciting to you, so you are new and ... interesting to me. And if you'd like to pour us some more champagne, I'd really like to hear about these incredible things that have been happening to you.' She grinned and held up her hand. 'Honest injun.'

'All right,' I laughed, reaching for the bottle. 'Well, you're asking for it.'

'Yes,' she replied, holding out her glass, and the look she gave me over the rim damn near made me drop the bottle.

CHAPTER SIX

I knew, of course, that I was being used, toyed with, played with, but it didn't matter a bit. It was a classic case of poor little rich girl bored with her own wealthy clique and looking for sparks at the foot of Nob Hill and I was delighted. She was beautiful, fun and *very* exciting, and so, I thought, let battle commence. Whatever ensued just *had* to be chock-full of interest and would undoubtedly constitute, in retrospect, one of the most colourful moments in my investigation of life.

Ha! I didn't know the half of it.

All the time I was talking, and it was a good half hour, I knew she was only half-listening, but then why *should* my grubbing around in Liverpool, selling sewing machines and collecting debts interest a bird like her? Should the details of a courier's job either in Majorca or even in Africa set her aristocratic blood racing? And even the account of my experiences in Nassau and our later adventure (horrifying enough for Buzz and me at the time) in New York and the subsequent chase across the Canadian border could hardly be expected to evoke more than mild interest from a woman who had been everywhere and done everything herself – particularly as she had but one interest uppermost in her mind all the time – an interest so uppermost that she couldn't wait for me to finish prattling before she broached it.

Then broach it she did.

Watching me closely and smiling in that amused, secret way women like her do smile in these circumstances, she said, 'I admire your thirst for experience. Would you say you've learned a lot about life since you left Liverpool!'

I grinned. 'A little – though I realize there's an awful lot I don't know about it yet?'

'About women, maybe?'

'Yes,' I laughed, 'especially about them.'

'But you have learned *something* about them on your travels?'

'Oh, yes,' I laughed again, louder this time.

'Now, that ...' she said, sitting more erect as though taking fresh interest in the proceedings, 'was a laugh that smacks of experiences you haven't told me about.'

'Well ...'

'And are not *about* to tell me about – obviously.'

I shrugged. 'Well ...'

'Mmm ...' she went, then, with a smile, 'Were they fun?'

'Terrific,' I grinned.

'How many ... ten ... twenty ...?'

'No comment.'

'Thirty ... forty ...?'

'Still no comment.'

'How much does sex interest you?'

'Enormously.' It was out before I could stop it.

'Yes, I could tell,' she smiled.

'Oh? How?'

She shrugged. 'Who knows? It's just there.' Unexpectedly she looked at her watch. 'Heavens, it's half past two – you must be starved.'

'Strangely, I haven't given a thought to food.'

'There's turkey out there ... and all kinds of things being barbecued. Doesn't it appeal?'

'Only if it does to you.'

She shook her head. 'I never eat.'

'And it shows.'

'Thank you,' she smiled. 'Look ...'

'Yes?'

'I don't know how you feel, but if you weren't desperate to stay for the sleigh-ride ...'

'Hm? What sleigh-ride?'

'The ... well, if you don't know about it, you can't be desperate to stay for it, can you?'

'Hardly. Go on, what were you going to say?'

'Just that, if you *weren't* desperate, I wonder if you ...'

'Yes, I would.'

Her eyes, hooded and warm, met mine and a small, knowing smile lifted the corner of her mouth. 'Thank God you don't need everything spelling out. Get dressed, hm? I'll tell Greg we're leaving. I'll be back in two minutes.'

She moved quickly then, galvanized by her own secret plans, whatever, God help me, *they* were!

In a state of jangling excitement I pulled on my shirt, all sorts of wild imaginings tumbling through my mind. I recall an old chap once saying to me, Russ, you can't guarantee any good things happening to you out there in the big wide world, but you *can* guarantee they *won't* happen to you if you sit on your ass at home and just dream about 'em!

By heck, I'd had cause to remember his words often enough since leaving Liverpool, and here it came again, one more time.

I put my parka on and sat down, lit a nervous fag, drained my glass and was emptying the bottle of its last inch when she came back in, looking quite stupendous in a black mink jacket and matching hat.

'Wow!' I gasped, coming to my feet.

She gave a laugh. 'Ready? I've told Greg we're leaving.'

'Er, how about my pal, Buzz Malone? I think I ought to let him know.'

'Greg's going to do that.'

I grinned at her. 'You think of everything.'

'We'll go out the back way and avoid questions, hm?'

'Lead on.'

She found a rear door that led out into a rear courtyard bounded on one side by a line of garages. There were maybe thirty cars parked in the yard and not a common proletariat model among them. There were Lincolns, Buicks, Cadillacs, Jaguars, Aston Martins and a sprinkling of small, fast European jobs. But the one that dominated the scene was the one Dominique was heading for – a fabulous sage-green Rolls-Royce Corniche convertible with a pale-cream top.

'Oh, no,' I gasped. 'Don't tell me.'

'Don't tell you what?' she laughed.

'That I am about to realize one of the most fervent ambitions of my life.'

'What – to drive a Corniche?'

'*Drive* one? Heck, no – just *ride* in one.'

She held up tinkling keys. 'So why not drive it?'

'Wha ... oh, no, Dominique, it's not insured for me ... no, I wouldn't take the chance.'

'Come on – it's only round the corner, there'll be no traffic. Really, it's only about half a mile.'

'Well ...' I hesitated.

'Oh, come on,' she laughed, thrusting the keys into my hand. 'It's only a car.'

Only a car. A sentiment a bit difficult to accept when you've been brought up to regard the bicycle as the height of luxury transport.

Well, *one* thing I knew about Dominique De Neve for certain – if she regarded this as only a car, she was *loaded.*

I opened the front passenger door and bowed her in, making her laugh, then I skipped round the other side and nervously slid in behind the wheel, luxuriating in the sensuous comfort of the deep leather seat.

It was, I was relieved to note, automatic drive. I'd have died if I'd grated the gears.

I started the engine ... then sat listening. 'Is it going?' I whispered.

'Yes,' she laughed.

'Oh, boy ...'

I backed out of the rank of cars, slid it into forward gear and whiffled away down the drive, chuckling to myself at the thought of Buzz's face if he could see me now. Oh, the sheer, obscene luxury of it. So many times since a lad I'd longed for pots and pots of money, but never more so than at that moment. By gum, I'd have a Rolls Corniche before I died if it was the last thing I did.

'You like nice things, don't you?' she asked, obviously getting a great kick out of my enjoyment.

'Yes, I do. Oh, I'd like to be rich, Dominique ... I'm sure I could handle it.'

'What would you do if you had lots of money?'

'Oh ... travel ...'

'But you're travelling now.'

'Yes ... but not always in the way I want to. In New York, for instance, Buzz and I were stuck in a hotel that overlooked some rotting backyards and a multi-storey car-park. Imagine – all the views New York has to offer and we got that one.'

'One can tire of luxury as easily as anything else, though.'

I grinned at her. 'So they tell me. I'd certainly like to try it for a while, though.' A pause, then ... 'Mind if I ask you a question, Dominique? It's a bit personal.'

'No – shoot.'

'Were you ever poor?'

She smiled and shook her head. 'Nope. I was born into money and married more. I've always lived in big houses, gone to private schools, had ponies, cars, long, lavish holidays.'

'And you're glad?'

She laughed and nodded vigorously. 'Delighted! I see no joy in poverty ... turn left at the next junction.'

'Not even the joy of appreciation when something luxurious *does* come along?'

'Nope. I can appreciate just fine – all the time.'

'Good for you. I can't stand people who're ashamed of their rich beginnings. Oh, I tell you I am enjoying this car so much ...'

'It's nice to see. It serves to remind me of how beautiful it is.'

'Do you have any other cars?'

'Four.'

I laughed aloud. 'Four! And what are they?'

'Erm ... a Cadillac ... a souped-up Mini ... a station-wagon and a general run-around.'

'Wow.' I looked at her. 'Mind if I ask how many houses you've got?'

'No,' she smiled. 'I've got four of those, too. This one ... a summer place up-country ... a beach house in Florida and a flat in Paris.'

'Good God,' I gasped. 'And you never feel cornered by your possessions?'

'If there's ever a tendency I fight it fanatically,' she smiled. 'Next turning on your right, then sharp left through the first gates.'

I made the turns, swirled in through high wrought-iron gates and entered the grounds of a magnificent Georgian-style mansion. Man, oh, man, this was certainly the day for being impressed.

I gave her a comical look and she responded with a shrug. 'Not much – but it's home. Park it by the front door.'

I expected a butler to open the door as we stopped, but Dominique surprised me by using a key. We entered a fabulous hall, rich in antique furniture, with a black-and-white marble floor and a graceful white staircase sweeping up to a galleried landing.

I stood rooted. 'Dominique ... this is wonderful.'

'Come on up, I want to change.'

We climbed the stairs, went along the landing for some distance then entered a bedroom of vast proportions and breathtakingly beautiful furnishings, its huge bed a plateau of pale pink silk set in a veritable sea of multi-hued Chinese carpet.

Along two walls ran a series of white-and-gilt floor-to-ceiling cupboards, and over on the right, beneath the windows, was a line of matching drawers containing her dressing table and mirrors.

Oh, *how* the other half lives.

With the casual ease, not to say disdain, of the very rich she slung the mink jacket on to the bed and made for the line of wardrobe cupboards to our left, flung four of the doors wide open then stood back, finger at her lips.

'Mmm ... what do you fancy?'

'Mm?' I came up behind her to be floored by the array of men's clothing hanging there. In one compartment alone there must have been thirty suits. In another – trousers. In a third – shirts, dressing gowns, smoking jackets ...

'My ex's,' she explained. 'He hasn't been back for them.'

'Oh. But that was a year ago.'

'Hm hm,' she nodded. 'He left in kind of a hurry – with his secretary.'

'Good Lord. What did she have that you haven't?'

'Her face. He has since left her's for someone else's, he's that kind of guy. A year is a long, long time for Pierre. Ah! this should do it.'

She took out a short gown in cream silk edged in brown and held it in front of me. 'Yes, very you.'

She then closed those cupboard doors and opened others, revealing endless racks of her own clothes. Selecting a similar style of gown in yellow silk, she closed the doors and turned to me, smiling diabolically, advanced upon me, her manner completely changed, taunting, playful, devilish, came right up to me and kissed me on the nose, murmuring softly, 'Do you realize ... that you ... and I are the only two people left in the whole wide world?'

'We are?'

'Hm hm,' she nodded, throwing the gown on to the bed and reaching for the buttons on my parka. 'There's no one in the house ... and no one outside. There's just you ... and me ... what do you think of that?'

'Wonderful,' I croaked, my face stiff with excitement.

Ping ... ping ... ping ... the buttons parted. Her hands slid inside and eased the coat from my shoulders and dropped it to the floor. I was trembling. Something stupendous was about to take place, something ... fantastic, wicked, awesome, wonderful ... something so exciting I felt quite sick with it.

Now she began on my shirt buttons, every movement purposely slow, as though she was determined to extract the full sensual potential from each moment.

'You ... work for Hire-A-Guy ... right?' she whispered, still working on the buttons.

'Yes ...' I nodded.

'How would you like to work for me?'

'I'd ... love to. When?'

'Today.'

'Today?'

'Right now.'

'F ... fine ...'

'O.K., you're hired.'

'What do I have to do?' I smiled, a nervous tick fluttering in my cheek.

'Everything you're told,' she said, her tone theatrically ominous. Releasing the last of the buttons she eased the shirt out of my trousers, continuing, 'You are mine to command for the rest of the day. You are my butler ... handyman ... my general ... my slave – and all for a dollar a day.'

'A dollar, hm? That much. For a dollar I'd do just about anything.'

Her smile deepened. 'You may *have* to.' And the way she said it left *no* doubt as to what she had in mind.

The shirt parted company with my shoulders and dropped to the floor. For a moment she just stood there, her warm gentle fingers resting lightly against my chest, as though reading emanations from my flesh ... and then they dropped.

Snick! My belt was undone. Zziipp! went the zipper and the trousers dropped to my feet. Again a momentary pause, slowing progress in the interests of art, then her fingers slid into the waistband of my briefs.

This of course was all far more than Herc could stand and with a sudden rush he ballooned against the silk. Slowly she lowered the briefs, smiling to herself as they snagged on Herc, then gradually slid over him and released him with a twang. Up he shot, quivering like a spear stuck in a tree trunk, questing the horizon and ready for anything.

For a long, wordless moment she studied him, then, so unexpectedly, she spun away, ordering me over her shoulder, 'Get undressed and into that robe! Then fill my bath, I'll be back in a moment!'

The devil! So this was the game she wanted to play. With a loud hysterical laugh, so up-tight it had to come out somewhere, I kicked the clothes aside and slipped into the cool silk gown, then tidied up the clothes and went through the door she'd indicated.

It was the bathroom.

Perhaps you saw Elizabeth Taylor, as Cleopatra, taking a bath in the film *Anthony and Cleopatra*? Well, for all the plush splendour of her tub, this one would've had Cleo gnashing her Egyptian teeth with envy. The circular bath, in pale turquoise and gold tiles, was about ten feet wide and three feet deep, and set in a raised floor at the far end of the room. Climbing three steps to it, I stood gawping at it, and at all the other incredible turquoise and gold fittings in the room for a couple of minutes, then finally turned my attention to the job at hand – filling the bath.

Problem one – there were no taps.

I searched around and eventually found two gold buttons set in the rear wall, one marked 'In', the other 'Out'. Seeing nothing else that even vaguely resembled a tap, I pressed the 'In' button, expecting a thunder of water and great billows of rising steam.

I got nothing.

With a shrug I began searching again, moving around the room, inspecting the fittings, prodding this, pulling that, moving nothing. And then, so help me, I turned back towards the bath, intending to head across to the far side of the room, and got the shock of me life. The damn thing was filled!

I went to the edge, knelt down, felt the water. Perfect! Just nicely hot. A silent, swift, perfect fill – all automated. Whatever happened to gurgling, trickling taps?

'Tobin!' Her voice rang imperiously from the bedroom.

With a grin I went through, found her placing an ice-bucketed bottle of champagne on a bedside table.

'Is my bath ready?'

'Yes, ma'm.'

She turned and regarded me approvingly. 'You got it filled?'

'Yes, ma'm.'

'Good! I like enterprise. Pour the champagne.'

'Yes, ma'm.'

I popped the cork, poured two glasses, handed her one. She took a sip, eyeing me over the rim. 'Enjoying yourself?'

'I'm having a ball.'

'You ... like playing games?'

'Yes.'

'You think it's right to give free rein to one's fantasies?'

I shrugged. 'Why not? Fun is not all that easy to come by ... and we're not hurting anyone.'

'That's right. I'm ... very glad I wasn't wrong about you ... it could have been embarrassing.'

'I'm very glad you took the chance.'

'Everyone has fantasies, hm?'

'Sure ... but I'll bet very few get the opportunity to bring them to life.'

She sat on the bed and patted it. 'Sit down.'

I sat.

'Do you remember your very first fantasy?' she asked.

'Oh,' I frowned, 'no, I can't say I do. I suppose I must have been very young ... probably pictured myself as a cowboy or something.'

'How about ... sexual fantasies?'

I grinned. 'Oh, I can remember a couple of very strong ones – the first when I was about nine.'

'Nine! That was pretty young. Who was she?'

I laughed. 'A woman of, oh, twenty-five, I suppose. She worked in the boarding-house in Blackpool where we stayed on holiday. I was head over heels in love with her – a terrific crush. Nothing came of it, alas.'

She laughed and held out her glass for a refill. 'And the second lady?'

'Oh, I was about fourteen ... fifteen. She was a teacher – a real good-looking sexpot. She used to tease the lads unmercifully, then send them down to the head for the cane when they got randy. It's a wonder we didn't gang together and rape her, she certainly asked for it.'

'How?'

'Oh ... a lot of ways. Her desk was built up on a plinth at the front of the class and she used to sit with her legs half open so we could see her panties.'

'Oh, no,' she laughed.

'It's true. And she'd furtively watch us through her long blonde hair, enjoying every minute of it,' I laughed. 'The clatter of pencils on the floor was quite deafening. We used to drop them to get a better look.'

'Men,' she smiled.

'Also women,' I reminded her. 'She was enjoying it too.'

'And what fantasy did you have about her?'

'Well ... she had a small house near the school playing fields, some distance from the school, and she was always teasing us about inviting some of us for tea sometime, after a game of soccer. She never did – at least not to my knowledge – but I used to have fantasies about it happening to me.'

'And imagine what happening?'

I grinned. 'I used to make it last a long, long time – usually just before I went to sleep at night. I'd start with me walking up to her front door after the game, then I'd go back a bit in time to the game finishing, then to it starting. It takes a lot of concentration to produce a clear-cut fantasy when you're young.'

'Didn't you ever get into the house?'

'Oh, yes! Yes, I'd finally knock on the door and she'd open it, dressed in her school clothes – usually a blouse and skirt. She'd invite me in and there'd be a lot of small talk – about the game and the school – but all the time she'd be smiling at her own secret thoughts, and undressing me with her eyes.

'Then, after a cup of tea, she'd excuse herself and leave the room and I would secretly follow her. I'd see her go into her bedroom and take off her blouse and skirt, then admire herself in the mirror, dressed in just her bra and panties and silk stockings. After a bit she'd undo her bra and take it off ... then pull down her panties and I'd see a big bush of blonde hair framed by the silk stockings ... and at that moment I'd step into the room and let her see me.'

'And ... how did she react?'

'Oh, she'd pretend to be angry, but she'd never make any attempt to cover herself. She really wanted me to see her.'

'And then ...?' she smiled.

'And then ...' I shrugged, 'I'd make love to her.'

'How?'

'Oh ... just the ordinary way. I was only fifteen remember.'

'And ... how would you do it now?'

'I ...' My heart was hammering. 'Different ways.'

'How many different ways do you know?'

'A ...' I cleared my throat. 'A few.'

She looked at me for a moment longer, then slowly set down her glass, saying, 'Tobin ...'

'Yes, ma'm?'

'Undress me.'

CHAPTER SEVEN

I began with the buttons on her blouse. She stood inertly before me, her arms relaxed by her sides, her attitude that of complete acquiescence. Play with me, she was saying. Enjoy yourself.

Five ... six buttons were released and the blouse fell open, revealing full, firm breasts with large bright pink nipples, hard as plum stones.

'Do they please you?' she asked softly.

'You are very beautiful, Dominique.'

'Continue.'

I dropped the blouse on to the bed. A quick snick and the fastener at her trouser waist was open. With thumping heart I worked the trousers over the gentle mound of her hips and slid them down her thighs, encountering tiny green pants embroidered with little yellow flowers.

Now I dropped to my knees, took the trousers to her feet, and still staring expressionlessly ahead, she stepped out of them.

The trousers abandoned, I hooked my fingers in the elastic waist of her little panties, paused to gulp a breath, then slowly eased them down, experiencing a fresh surge of excitement as my fingers lanced in her hair. Then ... there they were – a heavenly cluster of light brown curls, shaped precisely like the continent of Africa.

Left leg ... right leg ... the panties were gone. And there she stood, gloriously naked.

'Does *every*thing please you?' she asked, very softly.

'Everything delights me, Dominique. How could it not? Everything is perfect.'

'Thank you.' She looked down at me, her expression serene. 'Well, then ... now that we know what the other looks like ... and each is delighted with what he sees ... shall we let the games begin?'

'Yes, ma'm.'

'Good. First – my robe.'

I got to my feet, tingling with excitement at the way she

was doing this. It was obviously going to be a marathon session, both in duration and in content. Her manner was suspect; she had something up her sneaky sleeve all right – and that, as much as the naked sight of her, told me I was in for an afternoon I woudn't forget in a hurry.

I held out her robe, regretting the loss of her nakedness as she slipped it on.

'Thank you. Kindly bring the champagne.'

Following her into the bathroom I found her standing at the bath's side, tipping a lotion into the water from a golden urn and turning the water a milky blue.

'Put it down at the side,' she commanded, corking the urn.

I put the bucket down, poured two more glasses, then stood, finding her waiting, arms outstretched.

'Disrobe me.'

I did so.

'Thank you. Now you may bathe me. Take that thing off.'

As she entered the water I dropped the robe and slipped in after her. The water was fantastic, waist-high, warm and incredibly soft. She handed me a sponge and a cake of soap and turned her back to me. I worked up a good rich lather and began on her shoulders, deriving great pleasure from such intimate contact with her flawless, golden skin and the perfect curves of her body.

'That's wonderful,' she murmured softly. 'You have a very gentle touch.'

'Women must be treated gently – until they demand otherwise.'

She smiled. 'You've learned a lot on your travels. And I'm sure you've been amply rewarded for your application.'

She turned, saying with quiet decisiveness. 'Now do my front ...' she removed the sponge from my hand and dropped it in the water, '... with your hands.'

Oh, boy ...

I worked up a good handful of lather and again began on her shoulders ... over their points and down her arms, moving inevitably to her breasts. At first contact with them her eyes closed and a soft groan escaped from her partly-opened lips. Tenderly I covered them, my hands sliding easily with the soap, her rock-hard nipples tickling my palms as I traversed them, back and forth ... back and forth ... and then, sneakily, I took them both between thumb and forefinger and gently squeezed.

The sensation buckled her knees. Her face contorted into a mask of sweet agony and she rolled her head. 'Ohh ...' she gasped. 'If you do that ... I shall come.' She made a move towards me, dropped her right hand and jolted me as she caught hold of Herc.

'If you do that, so shall I!'

'Do you want to?'

'No, not yet. Do you?'

She nodded, breathlessly. 'Yes.'

She caught my right hand and drew it down between her legs, then threw her arms around my waist and hugged me very tightly, moving against me in a flurry of jerks and in a matter of moments she was there, crying out as she plunged into her climax, thrusting hard again and again, gasping plaintively 'Ohh ... ohhh ... ohhh ...' until she was done. Then with a final long-drawn sigh she went limp against me and I held her tight, soothed her with a slow caress until she eased away and looked at me, smiling a contented, smouldering smile and sighing a grateful sigh.

'I needed that,' she laughed. 'It was very ... very nice.'

'I'm very glad.'

'And now ... you may dry me.'

We got out of the bath and in silence I rubbed her dry with a warm, fluffy towel, making no attempt to arouse her, though I could tell she was deriving great pleasure from the act.

When I had finished, she held out her hand for the towel and started on me, covering every inch of my body though making no sexual play whatsoever – until she was kneeling before me, drying my thighs. Then, in a spirit of devilry, she suddenly and unexpectedly caught hold of Herc and buried him in her molten mouth.

Before I had time to react she was up and away with a taunting laugh, throwing the towel in my face and snatching up her robe. 'Hide and seek, Tobin! Find me if you can! If you find me ... you can *have* me! The game is on!'

Flinging the towel aside, I grabbed my robe and was after her, though not *too* fast, giving her a sporting start. I ran into the bedroom, paused for a quick look in the wardrobes and under the bed, then out on to the landing, seeing her damp footprints going off to the right, fading quickly on the pale green carpet.

At the end of the landing I found a second flight of stairs and down I went, pausing at the bottom to listen. The silence was absolute ... and eerie. I was in a corridor of closed doors, all strangely forbidding.

On my toes I crept to the first and popped my head inside. It was a study, ponderous with books and dark leather, but with no place to hide. I closed the door and went on.

Well, there was only one thing for it – try every room in the house. I opened the next door, discovering what looked like a maid's room – a uniform hanging on the wardrobe door. I tiptoed across and tried the door, but it was locked. A quick peep behind the sofa and on again.

Three doors later I found a scullery and a utility room and finally the kitchen – and in it a hastily scribbled note propped against a coffee pot. 'You're cold, Tobin! Hurry! Don't forget the reward!'

Highly likely.

I left the kitchen and entered another corridor, pausing now and again to listen for creaking floors or closing doors, and it was during one of these pauses that I suddenly heard the sound of voices coming from a room on my left! I crept towards it, bewildered, now hearing the voices more plainly. They were men's voices ... arguing heatedly! Good God, there were people in the house! What was going on here!

Checked in mid-stride and wobbling like a high-wire walker, I hung suspended, wanting to hear more yet poised for flight in case the door suddenly opened and someone came out. What *was* going on?

And then, on the verge of running for my life, a single word broke through my fright-blanked mind and with a relieved laugh I put my ear to the door and heard:

'An' I'm a-tellin' *you*, sheriff, if them sheep-men don't git offa mah land, mah boys are gonna clear 'em orf – dead or alive!'

'Now, see here, Dave Crowley – you take the law inta yor own hands an' you're likely ta find yorself dancin' on the end of a rope!'

I opened the door and peered in. The bitch had switched on the telly. A quick glance round the room then back into the corridor.

It was four rooms later that I heard her calling me – from

the study I'd started at. 'Russ-ell To-bin ...! Russ-ell ... To-bin ...!' Very softly and seductively. 'Russ-ell To-bin ... Russ-ell To-bin ...!'

Ha ha! I thought, hand on the doorknob, the game's going on too long for her, she wants to get caught! Slowly and silently I twisted the knob, chuckling to myself at the fright she'd get when I bounded in with a roar.

'Russ-ell To-bin ... Russell To-bin ...!'

Crash! In I went with a yell. 'Gotcha!'

'Russ-ell To-bin ... Russ-ell To-bin ...!'

Tape recorders, I can report, are not easily frightened.

'Russ-ell To ...'

I punched the key and shut it up.

So ... madam was not eager to give up so quickly.

I quit the study and ran silently up the stairs, paused again to listen, then doubled back along the landing towards her bedroom, thinking that maybe the minx had been in there most of the time! Then another thought struck me – maybe she wasn't even in the house! Well, in her mood I wouldn't have put it past her to nip out and leave me to make an idiot of myself. These rich birds are a law unto themselves and boredom can induce weird inventiveness. I could imagine her sitting with a girlfriend next door, sipping a sherry and killing herself laughing at the thought of me scouring the house in my kimono, saying, 'I'll let him sweat for an hour then call him on the phone.'

Half-heartedly now, getting a bit fed up with this particular game and wanting to see her again, I went back along the landing, desultorily opening bedroom doors and peering in ... and it was as I put my hand on the knob of the fourth room that I froze, hearing faint sounds from within.

I put my ear to the door, mystified by the sound, unable to analyse the quiet mechanical rasp, then, slowly, I opened the door and peered inside, amazed to find the room in flickering semi-darkness.

It was a movie projector, set at the foot of a double bed on the right side of the room and casting a dull beam on to a screen, positioned at right angles to me, over on the left, its beam so modest that all I could make out in the otherwise ink-black room, was the lower half of the bed.

I stood there nonplussed for a moment or two, wondering whether to go into the eerie room or turn tail, but as the seconds ticked by my inquisitiveness as to what was being projected on the screen overcame my natural cowardice, and I took a couple of faltering steps inside. Then, as I still couldn't see the angled screen, I took a couple more steps, peering not only for the screen but around the room, expecting to find Dominique lurking there – but finding no one. And in four more steps I'd reached the foot of the bed.

It was pretty scary, I can tell you – the projector running all by itself and high cupboards looming all around, and so, keeping a wary eye on these, now expecting Dominique to leap out any second and scare the hell out of me, I backed up along the bed and finally, when I reached the head, managed a glance at the screen.

Instantly all thoughts of cupboards and a leaping Dominique vanished from my mind. With a thumping heart I lowered myself on to the bed and gaped entranced at the image on the screen, taking a moment or two to sort out the bewildering tangle of arms and legs, then finally realizing that what I was witnessing was a whizz-bang, flat out, thorough-going orgy!

Held hypnotized by this vision of unbridled fornication I slowly swung my legs up on to the bed and leaned back against the headboard, my mind blurred by the unexpectedness of the discovery. Dominique had obviously set the projector going, but why wasn't she here watching the film? What sort of game was *this* she was playing.

Well, no doubt she'd let me know in due course, but since I was obviously intended to look at the film, I reckoned in the meantime I'd do just that. It'd been a long time since I'd had a good laugh at a bluey. So, settling down, I began to concentrate on the proceedings and at that very moment, stap me, the film ended!

Well, stun me ... just getting nicely in the mood for a good chuckle and the curtain comes down. But no ...! Now the leader frames of another film were rattling through the gate and a moment later the title came up ... *The Milkman Cometh.* Yes, very *cinema verité.*

I glanced at the projector. It was loaded with a big reel which was about one-third empty, there being, I calculated, a good half hour to run. By gum, she'd timed this remarkably well.

I returned my attention to the screen.

The opening shot was a suburban street that looked English, there being no houses in the world like the British semi. Then into the frame trundled a horse-drawn milk float, stopping at number twenty-six.

Close-up of a big, handsome, broad-shouldered milkman, cap set jauntily on the back of his dark, curly head. He consults his delivery book, glanced towards the house, nods knowingly and grins with unabashed lechery. Then, in looser shot, he nips out of the van, slings two pints into a little crate and heads up the pathway.

Close-up of him at the front door, whistling happily. He prods the bell. The door opens – just a crack. A sleepy-eyed blonde pushes a curtain of crumpled hair from her face and gives a start of horror as she realizes who is at the door.

The milkman waves his account book at her and mouths something, obviously demanding payment. She shakes her head sadly, like she's flat broke. He holds up the two pints and shakes his head. No more milk, missus, until the account is settled. He turned to go.

Oh, *please*, she implores him – what about my old man's rice pudding!

No lettuce, no milk, he insists – unless ... an expression of unadulterated filth contorts his features. Well, now, perhaps there *is* some arrangement we could come to?

Horror strikes her. You ... you beast! ... you dirty, suggestive swine! How *dare* you!

He dares because in the meantime she has unknowingly (ha!) allowed the door to swing open and he is now ogling her stupendously boobed goodies semi-visible through her shorty nylon nightie.

And what a pair! Big as melons and twice as juicy. He covers her from toe to head, very slowly, and at last meets her offended eyes. Well, he asks again, holding up the bottles – what's it going to be – ten minutes with me or ten rounds with the old man when he shouts for his rice pudding?

By gum, the poor bird's in a terrible dilemma. What *is* she going to do? Finally, to everybody's great relief she slumps ... and nods ... then walks dejectedly back into the house, followed at a fast trot by Horny Harold.

A quick cut to her bedroom (one thing about blue movies they don't waste your time). Wifey walks dejectedly into frame, followed by Harold. For a couple of lascivious seconds he ogles her up and down, then advances on her, slides his hands into the neck of her nightie and with a masterful wrench, rips the thing asunder, right down the middle. By gum, she really is built – thighs like a couple of tree trunks, complete with a spectacular clump of high-summer foliage.

Now Harold starts ripping at his own clothes, hurls them aside in a frenzy of impatience, and as the last article is removed, his jockeys naturally, wifey throws up her hands in horror – and no blinking wonder.

Harold is built like his bleeding horse!

I mean, really – I have seen some preposterous sights on blue movies, but this lad takes the biscuit. The thing is positively inhuman. I reckon it's at least a foot long and as thick as an all-in wrestler's wrist! A stupendous great effort.

But is he at all abashed, in any way contrite? Is he buggery. The fella's brimming with pride – and also determination ... to stick it somewhere. Like in wifey's mouth for openers.

Down on your knees! he demands.

No ... no! anything but that.

Down, I say! Think of your husband's rice pudding!

Ah, that gets her every time. What a diabolical thing to hold over a woman's head. In fear and trembling she drops to her knees, her head averted, unable to face the great throbbing monstrosity.

But Harold advances upon her.

Now a change of camera angle and in it comes from right of screen, gigantic, awesome and in glorious, mind-boggling close-up, filling the screen. A pull-back on zoom to bring in wifey's face, horror-stricken in the extreme, a great little actress.

A couple of askance glances, then – tentative surrender to the inevitable. In comes her hand, tiny as a baby's by comparison, and grasps the pulsing phallus, covering a mere third of its diabolical length. This is now joined by her other hand and *still* a goodly yard and a half protrudes. This lad deserves to be in cinemascope.

Then her profile moves into frame. She begins to yawn ... wide ... wider ... widest. Good God, her lips will split! And at full stretch she lowers it over the life-size fireman's helmet and swallows it until her lips are touching her hands.

At this point the 'acting' is quickly abandoned – either that or wifey is stricken with an inexplicably swift change of heart, because she is now tucking in with gusto like she hasn't eaten for weeks. And while this is going on, Harold is having a good feel at anything he can lay his hands on and working wifey up a treat.

Two or three minutes of this and she's aching for something different, so as the camera pulls back Harold pulls out, yanks her to her feet and throws her on the bed. Fortuitously, she lands on her back with her thighs eight miles apart, and before you can say snuff, Harold is between them and ramming that terrible thing in to the hilt.

And is she distressed by this rapacious invasion of her person? Don't be ridiculous. She is having the time of her boring, penniless, depressing suburban life. She is smothering him with kisses and leaping up and down like there were tacks on the bed. By golly, she really does go – and Harold is no slouch at it either. I reckon before he became a milkman he must have been a stoker. Bang ... bang ... bang ... and bump ... bump ... bump. Anyone for shoveha'penny?

Suddenly she stops, smiles up at him with naughty, glowing eyes, says something to him. He grins, nods, then pulls out of her. Quick as a wink she's on her knees, head down into the pillow, and in goes Harold like a Bengal Lancer ... in ... and in ... and in ... good heavens, is there no *end* to it? Surely to God he'll puncture a lung!

Well, they're going at it like they've only got half an hour to live and I'm sitting there having a good chuckle when suddenly a ghostly apparition appears at the side of the screen and frightens the living wits out of me. My heart gives a sickening lurch, my hair rushes aloft like it was starched, and an ice-cold wave of terror engulfs me.

Now the pale wraith, swathed in drifting white, glided silently towards me and if a face hadn't appeared at that precise moment I reckon I'd have been off that bed and diving through the window in the next!

'Boo!' she laughed, leaping on to the bed.

'God!' I gasped. 'Dominique ... you frightened the life out of me! Where did you came from?'

From behind the curtain. I was watching you. You looked as though you were enjoying yourself.'

She moved up the bed and sat beside me, snuggled close. 'What do you think of the film?'

I laughed. 'Well, I just do not *believe* that milkman. My

God, he's built like a stallion!'

'Isn't he just. And to think I have to collect *my* milk from a supermarket.'

I turned to her, grinning, expecting to find her smiling, too. But she wasn't. She was looking at me very intently, her eyes half-lidded, lips parted.

'I have a new game for us to play,' she murmured huskily.

'Oh?' I croaked. 'What is it?'

She leaned towards me and very gently placed her soft, compliant mouth on mine. 'The milkman ... and the housewife,' she whispered.

I gulped. 'Oh.'

She gave a low, hungry chuckle and speared my mouth with her tongue. 'Your uniform is in *that* cupboard.'

We played the game for two full hours, our performance faithful to the very last frame of the film, and as 'The End' came up in a grand, shattering explosion, we collapsed in a tangle of limbs upon her bed.

'Ohhhh!' she gasped, flinging an arm across my chest, limp as a rope. 'Well ... if that poor housewife had to take what *I've* just taken ... that bastard got more than his money's worth.'

We fell into silence, too fatigued to talk, and drifted into private thought.

Christmas Day, I pondered. Ha! Incredible where life leads you. The permutations of movement that bring two strangers together have always fascinated me. If I'd missed that New York train in Miami instead of catching it by the skin of my teeth I wouldn't have met Buzz ... wouldn't have had that package thrown at me by mistake ... wouldn't have been chased over the border into Canada. I'd still be in New York doing ... what? I smiled to myself, very glad indeed I wasn't down there doing what.

I slid my arm around Dominique and brought her closer, and with a little happy mew she curled against me, obviously very content. A moment more and she was asleep, her lovely body rising and falling against me steadily and her heart throb beat for beat with mine.

Christmas Day, I thought ... and that was all I thought, for in two neighs of a milkman's horse I, too, was fast asleep.

CHAPTER EIGHT

We woke at nine o'clock, some three hours later, famished and fully restored. She sat up, bright and alive and obviously looking for trouble.

'I'm starved, how about you?'

'I daresay I could eat a peck or two.'

'Right – you fill the bath, I'll see what there is.'

She slid off the bed, pulled on her robe, then turned to me. 'I'm assuming rather a lot, aren't I . . .?'

'Mm . . .?'

'That you're free to stay, for instance. Had you planned to go somewhere tonight – with your friend Buzz, maybe?'

'No,' I smiled. 'No, we hadn't planned anything. But how about you? I'm surprised you're not fully booked Christmas night.'

She gave a light shrug. 'I could be.'

'I'm sure.'

She smiled mistily. 'But I kinda like it here . . . doing just what I want to do. How about you?'

I grinned at her. 'I'm having a terrific time.'

'Positive?'

'Absolutely. There's nothing I want out there.'

She smiled, mischievously this time. 'I'm very glad,' and turned towards the door.

I went into the bathroom, punched the 'In' button and by the time she returned I was wallowing in three feet of soft, warm water.

She came in carrying a big silver tray. 'Cold chicken . . . fresh rolls . . . and hot coffee – how does that hit you?'

'Right in the taste buds . . . wonderful.'

I did a fast crawl to the side, but she said, 'Don't come out, I'm coming in. I feel exceedingly decadent.'

'Splendid.'

Dropping the robe, she slipped into the water, immersed her shoulders and shot up with a rush, flicking water at me. 'Whhhoooo! . . . that's beautiful. Pour the coffee, slave.'

'Yes, ma'm.'

I set the plates and things out along the side and poured the coffee. 'Dinner is served, madam.'

'Rightee-ho, Jeeves.'

She came up close, took a chicken leg, removed a bite from it, then fell backwards and floated across the pool, waving it in the air. 'Don't you agree one *really* honest-to-God decadent day every now and then does you the world of good?'

'Indubitably,' I concurred. 'Clears the blood a treat.'

'Do you ever feel *really* wicked, Tobin?'

'All the time,' I grinned.

'No, seriously.'

'Of course I do – just now and then. Everyone does.'

'You reckon?'

'Sure – we're all built the same. I think the only difference between us is our readiness to *admit* we occasionally feel wicked. I don't believe there's a housewife, no matter how outwardly staid, who hasn't had the occasional urge to do something outrageous – like opening the door to the vicar stark naked or letting the window-cleaner catch her in the bath. I reckon people need a little sin without responsibility now and again to make the dull routine of life bearable. It kind of hones the need for another spell of respectability.'

I sipped the coffee, enjoying its warmth, and took a bite of chicken, then, grinning at her, said, 'You're feeling wicked today, hm?'

'Huh huh,' she laughed. 'You brought it on.'

'I did?'

'Certainly.'

'Why me?'

She gave a shrug. 'Chemistry. The moment I saw you everything clicked into place. I knew you were a man I could be happily wicked with.'

'And I felt the same way about you. You know, of course, that you're a *very* sexy-looking woman.'

'Mmm . . .' she nodded.

'You sizzle with it. The moment I saw you I wanted to make love to you . . . I guess every man that sees you does.'

'I wouldn't know,' she grinned.

'Like heck. Tell me . . . just *how* do you want to be wicked?'

She waded towards me, the closeness of her wet, erect breasts and glistening body reawakening my temporarily abated passion. A new, vigorous surge swept through me and once more the game was afoot. Sensing it and sharing it, she came right up to me and covered my lips with a slow, wet kiss.

'No specific way. I just want to feel I can do anything I like now that I've got you here to do it with.'

'But ... you could do this any time you liked. You're your own boss ... wealthy, beautiful, free ...'

She shook her head. 'I'm not free. I have a thumping great conscience about indolence. You can get awfully sick of too much ice-cream. Then again you can have a bellyful of meat, too, and yearn for dessert. You happen to have hit me after a surfeit of monotonous meat. I am *bored* with doing good works. I serve on every conceivable kind of do-good charity and my teeth were aching for an orgy.'

'I'm awfully glad I was around.'

She smiled. 'So am I. Tell me ... will you stay the night? *Can* you stay the night?'

'I can ... and, of course, I will.'

She smiled, seemingly relieved. 'Tomorrow I think I'll take off for Miami. I need the sun, this cold shrivels me. You'll be staying here with Hire-A-Guy?'

'Yes ... for a couple of weeks.'

She looked at me, thoughtfully, smiling strangely. 'I ... know someone that needs some jobs doing. Should I mention your name?'

'Well, sure – if you think I can do them.'

Her smile deepened, naughtily. 'Oh, you'll be able to do them all right.'

'Who is it?'

'A friend of mine.'

She slipped her arms around my neck, then slowly pressed her body against me, bringing old Herc up with a hell of a rush.

'Mmmm ...' she murmured softly, pecking my mouth. 'That sleep did you both the world of good.'

'Yes,' I croaked.

'Are you ... ready for another game?'

'Hm hm ...'

'I have another film.'

'You have?'

'Hm hm. This one is called ... *Rape at Little Big Horn.*'

'Sounds ... terrific.'

'Come ... let's go to the movies.'

As the titles faded, up came a clip from an ancient Western – a wagon train crawling across the vast plain far below.

A quick cut to a big close-up of Chief Big Horn – a big, muscular guy about as Redskin-looking as Audrey Hepburn.

'Charge!' he yells, then comes another clip from another ancient Western – a band of mounted Injuns roaring down a hillside and galloping off across the plain.

Crash! Bang! Wallop! Thud! Bullets and arrows are flying thicker than flies in May. Now a close-up of a delicious blonde, hair awry and tits bursting from her torn blouse. Her hand flies to her mouth in horror as Big Horn himself bursts into her wagon.

A quick grapple, a masterful sock on the jaw and she's out like a light, then an easy heave-ho over his shoulder and, by God, she's all his.

Fade out.

Fade in – to the interior of his teepee.

Dominique wriggles closer and slides her hand on to my thigh. She gives me an outrageous grin, pecks me on the cheek and returns to the film.

The teepee flap is thrown aside and in staggers Big Horn with Blondie over his shoulder. Poor fellow looks all in. Thump! Unceremoniously he deposits her on a pile of buffalo furs and glowers down at her with blazing, rapacious eyes, mouthing the Apache equivalent of 'At last I have you in me power!'

Blondie stirs, her eyes flutter open, then fly wide, seeing him standing over her. 'Jeezuschrist!' she cries, hand to her mouth again, overdoing it a bit, really.

Cut to Big Horn, pointing down at her clothes. 'Gerrum off!' he commands.

'Get stuffed,' she replies valiantly. 'You will have to rape me – I will never surrender!'

Right, he says, have it your way, love.

Casting aside his bow and arrow, he whips out his bread-knife and goes in for the slice. Whhoosshh! Away goes her blouse, severed asunder, and out pop two of the juiciest grape-fruit he's clapped eyes on all summer.

Whey-hey, he shouts, quite carried away, then kneels down and sinks his gums into the left one, sucking hard like he's trying to get the whole thing in his mouth.

Blondie, meanwhile, is going quietly barmy, beating him

on the shoulder with all the power of a limp lettuce leaf. Now tiring of grapefruit, Big Horn makes a grab for her skirt, inserts the knife-blade into the waistband and rriipp! away it goes, revealing a pair of milk-white thighs that he suddenly fancies more than his Palamino – which for him is saying something.

Now, clad only in a flimsy pair of see-through knicks (a blatant anachronism) and a pair of black leather thighboots, she falls back against the buffalo furs, aghast, her hand once more to her mouth and her legs unaccountably wide apart, a sight to set even the most placid Injun aflame with rampant desire.

Abandoning the knife, he comes in fast for a bit of hand-to-knicker combat, gets his huge paws under her comely bum and down they came, Blondie thrashing her legs about as though in defiance, but in reality helping him more than a bit.

Whhoosshh! ... away they come, leaving her spread-eagled in despair and benumbed with mortified anticipation.

Dominique moved close, whispered in my ear. 'Enjoying it?'

'What do you think?'

'I think you're enjoying it.'

'What about you – are you enjoying it?'

'I'm enjoying it. Ssshhh!'

Back to the film.

Close-up of Big Horn, eyes flaring with lechery and tongue flicking hungrily. He lowers his eyes and slowly the camera panned down ... over his manly chest ... across his flat, corrugated stomach ... and we see his loincloth standing out like Billy Smart's big top.

Cut to Blondie, staring with horror, her hand, would you believe, at her mouth.

Back to the loincloth ... and the Chief's hands untying the string. The cloth drops ... and into view springs a tool that made the milkman's thing look like a shrivelled pinkie! It is a *monstrous* great dick, reminiscent of a navvy's forearm clutching a bowling ball.

'Good God!' I gasped.

Dominique laughed, excited as hell.

'I do not believe it!' I laughed. '*That* is faked!'

And by the look on Blondie's face, she thinks so too. 'No ... no!' she mouths, eyes bulging, and this time *both* hands at her mouth. 'For Godsake, not *that*!'

'This!' insists Big Horn (how *aptly* named), taking it in both hands and giving it a shake. Then he takes a couple of steps forward and stands above her.

Reverse shot – on Blondie's eyeline. Oh, my God, from down here it is unbelievable.

Back to a looser shot. Blondie shakes her head, appalled. She will *not* take the beastly thing!

Big Horn drops to his knees, tries to open her thighs, belts her across the mouth, but she's curled into a ball and sticking like glue. He can't get to first base. So what does he do? He does what any brave, ruthless, self-respecting rapist would do – he calls for help.

Into the teepee run three war-painted braves, Freeman, Hardy and Willis. They come to an astounded halt, then grin with glee at the sight and plight of the buxom Blondie and pitch right in to help the boss.

Producing four wooden pegs, four lengths of rawhide and a mallet from a handy box that ought to have been marked 'Do-It-Yourself Rape Kit', they proceeded to bind her wrists and ankles and peg her to the ground like a starfish.

'Aha!' cried Big Horn, standing above her and giving it a shake. 'Your hour has come, me beauty ...!' then down he drops and in he goes ... and as he sank it home so Dominique moved, pulled me down and gasped into my ear, 'I want you ... now!'

Film abandoned.

She took me hungrily, thrusting into me with a wild flurry of jerks, fingers driving into my back.

'Oh ... God, that is marvellous!' she cried.

'Fantastic!'

'I'm not going to last!'

'Me, neither!'

'Russ ... I'm commmiinngg ... oh, God, I'm commiinngg ...!' With a wild cry she exploded, yelled and bucked and hammered my back ... on ... and on ... and on ... not descending from her climax but holding up there, travelling on a continuous peak of ecstasy, yelling, 'OHHH ...! OHHHH ...! OHHHH ...!' as though she was hurtling down some wondrous, unbelievable, torturous tunnel.

'Come ...! Come ...!' she cried, insisting, pleading, commanding ... and then I went, drawing an explosive gasp, 'Oh ... *God!*' from her as we clung fast together like a couple of frenzied limpets, stunned by the titanic impact of our joy.

Into the ensuing silence crept the click ... click ... click of the film as its tail slipped through the spool. She uttered a long-drawn groan and straightened her legs beneath me, as I wrapped my arms around her and gently kissed her cheek.

'Happy Christmas, ma'am,' I said ... and she answered with a smile.

'It was ... it was ... it was ... it was. One of the happiest ... I've ever ... had.'

CHAPTER NINE

She dropped me at the hotel at ten the next morning. Coming to a halt a few yards down the block, she cut the engine and turned to me with a loving smile, looking all cuddly and bed-warm in a short fox jacket, her blonde hair tumbling around the collar.

'I'd ... like to give you something, but I'm afraid you'd be insulted.'

'What is it?'

'Money.'

I smiled and shook my head. 'I wouldn't be insulted, but I wouldn't take it. Thanks all the same.'

'I don't like the thought of you having to work for it. You should be free to enjoy yourself for a couple of weeks. You won't see much of Canada if you have to work for it.'

'Well ... maybe not, but I prefer it this way.'

'You're very stubborn,' she smiled. 'Pride goeth before a fall, you know.'

'So that's what keeps causing it, I wondered what it was. Have a wonderful time in Miami, Dominique. I'll be thinking of you.'

She put out her hand and squeezed mine. 'Thank you for a lovely day.'

'And I thank you.'

'If you're ever in Toronto again – look me up.'

'That, ma'm, is a fervent promise.'

I leaned across and kissed her then opened the door and got out. 'Goodbye, lovely lady.'

'Goodbye, Tobin,' she smiled. 'Watch out for Injuns.'

And then she was gone.

I stood there watching the Rolls out of sight, then turned towards the hotel, coming to a shocked halt as I spied Buzz standing in the hotel doorway, fixing me with a very old-fashioned eye.

'My ... *God*, Tobin, it is said that some guys get all the luck, but even among *them* you take the flamin' biscuit! How in hell did you manage to pull a bird like her!'

I shrugged. 'Wit, charm, beauty, intelligence ...'

'I'll bloody bet!' he laughed, clapping me on the shoulder. 'Come on up, I've got to pack yet.'

'You're, erm, just coming in, I presume – from Greg's party?'

He yawned extravagantly. 'Well ... yes. I did kind of ... "go on" somewhere afterwards, you understand.'

'Perfectly. To Beth Delwana's, I presume.'

He just grinned.

We took the lift up to the room, ordered coffee and drank it while Buzz was packing.

'So ... a gay old time was apparently had by all,' he said, smothering another stupendous yawn. 'You seeing her later on today?'

'Nope. She's flying down to Miami for a rest, said she needs at least a month to recuperate. Funny, that, come to think of it ...'

'What is?'

'How my women keep taking off the day after I meet them. Lily Longlegs nips off to London and now Dominique to Miami. Buzz ... I haven't a personal problem even my best friends won't tell me about, have I?'

'Yes,' he nodded. 'You're a randy sod, that's your problem.'

'Jazus, look who's talking – Six Gun Malone, the Fastest Nob in the West.'

'"Was",' he grimaced. 'I think it's dropped off. I heard an ominous thud in the shower this morning. It *might* have been the soap, but I've got a nasty feelin' ...'

'No doubt you'll find out for sure during the flight to Victoria.'

'With a bit of luck,' he grinned. 'Well, I think you're a nutter. If you'd played your cards right I reckon you could've been on your way to Miami with that lovely creature right now instead of bumming around here for a fortnight.'

'I thought about it – and I think the offer was there – but . . .' I gave a shrug. 'Ah, I'm out of her class, Buzz. Hell, I'd have had to borrow a quarter from her every time I felt like an ice-cream.'

'You know, of course, that she's a multi-millionairess?'

'I gathered as much. You should see the house.'

'I should be so lucky.'

'How did you know she was a multi-millionairess?'

'Greg told me.'

'Oh, yes, how did he take my leaving like – without saying goodbye?'

He shrugged. 'He was furious.'

'Oh, hell. What did he say?'

'He said how come a penniless bum like Tobin can pull a bird like Dominique De Neve when I've been trying for a year and can't get past her doormat.'

'Did he really?'

He laughed. 'Did he hell.'

'Well, it *is* an apt question. I suppose the answer is that in poverty lies anonymity.'

'What you mean is – she fancied a bit of rough, Tobin.'

'Something like that,' I grinned. 'Seriously, though, did he say anything?'

'Yes – he said he'd give you a call here tomorrow if he has a job for you. So – what are you going to do this afternoon?'

I shrugged. 'I don't know – probably take a bus round town. Just get on one and see where it takes me.'

'I sure wish I wasn't flying off until you'd got your bearings, I feel responsible for you.'

'Buzz,' I laughed, 'I've just travelled solo half-way round the world. I'll be all right.'

'Well, look – at least let me leave you fifty bucks in case of emergencies. You don't have to spend it, just keep it as a stand-by.'

'Well, that's very good of you. All right.'

He signed a traveller's cheque and gave it to me, then closed his case and checked his watch. It was time to go. We caught a cab outside and within half an hour were at the airport.

'Well, so long, son . . .' he said, shaking my hand. '*Try* and keep out of trouble, there's a good chap. I don't want to have to bail you out of nick or identify your corpse when I get back. And keep away from women, for Godsake.'

'Guide's honour,' I swore, sticking up two fingers, then reversing them. 'Nary a bird shall pass my portals until you return.'

'They don't get a chance to pass, you bugger – you whip 'em inside too fast.'

'Best of luck in the tournament, Buzz. Come back with a cup or something – better still, money. And watch out for those pigeons at 30,000 feet. Get one of those sucked into your engine and ... Buzz, you are not listening to a word your father is saying ...'

'I am ... I am ...' he mumbled, staring across the concourse at two very dolly airstews who were heading our way. 'Man, oh, man, I do believe they could be on my flight ...' He flashed me a lascivious grin. 'Tarra, son, I'll drop you a line, let you know how I get on. I imagine it'll be something like this ...' With a skip he was off, cocking one leg in the air as though trying to mount a walking horse, following the birds through the barrier, then, as they disappeared into the Departure Lounge, he turned and gave me a victory fist and followed them out of sight.

Chuckling to myself, I sauntered back across the concourse and made my way out to the taxi rank, wondering what indeed the next two weeks held for me. Two weeks in a strange town. Sounded exciting, full of potential. Well, for a start I'd go back to the hotel, have a bite to eat, then maybe take that bus ride until dark. After that ... an early dinner and bed. I reckoned I needed at least ten hours solid to put me back in working order, ready to face the rigours of my Hire-A-Guy duties, whatever they were.

Yes ... that was what I'd do.

But it didn't quite work out that way. I got back to the hotel all right, that part went according to plan, but as I was crossing the foyer the porter called me from his cubicle.

'Er, Mister Tobin ...!'

I went to him. He turned from the letter slots, an envelope in his hand. 'Letter for you, sir ... came in by hand.'

'Oh ...?'

Puzzled, I took it, felt the hard bulge inside it.

'Who delivered it?'

'A guy from the hotel garage.'

'Garage?' I frowned at the envelope, unable to identify the hand that had written 'R. Tobin Esq.'. 'Well, thank you ...'

'You're welcome.'

'Er ... *when* was it delivered?'

'Just a coupla minutes ago, sir.'

'Thank you.'

'You're welcome.'

I turned away, slit the envelope, took out the key and the note. It said 'Dear Proud Man ... At least use this – how can I possibly drive five at once? She's gassed up *and* insured – ready to go. Don't worry about refilling it, the hotel's got full instructions. *Please* use it – I'll be hurt if you don't. Besides – it needs the exercise. Thanks again for a wonderful Christmas. I'll be thinking of you, too. D.'

Well, I'll be ... well, what do you know about that. The lovely bird had lent me a car!

With a flurry of excitement, quite touched by the thought, I turned back to the porter. 'Where do I find the garage?'

He told me. Five minutes later I was entering it and a young guy in uniform was coming out of his little office to me. 'Yes, sir?'

'My name is Tobin. I believe somebody left a car here for me?'

'Yes, sir, that's right.' He wheeled away, heading across to a line of cars.

'Probably an English Mini,' I added.

He checked in mid-stride and turned, frowning at me. 'A *Mini*, sir?' His frown became a mocking grin. 'This baby ain't no Mini, sir ... not by about sixty-five feet.'

'Oh? Well, which ...?'

He pointed across the garage – to a breathtaking metallic-blue, cream-topped Cadillac convertible! He gave a chuckle. 'That your idea of an English Mini, sir?'

'No,' I gulped.

'Mine, neither. Anyway – she's all yours.'

'Are you ... positive? I mean ...'

'If your name is Tobin and you've got a key to fit this, I'm positive. Got instructions from the lady – keep her gassed up and see to any running repairs. Use it as much as you like and leave it here for pick-up when you're finished with it. O.K.?'

I nodded, numbly. 'Yes ... wonderful.'

'Well, she's all yours. Are you taking it out now, sir?'

'Er ... well, yes, sure. It'll give me a chance to get used to it in light traffic.'

He laughed. 'You'll need all of ten minutes with this baby – she drives herself.'

He opened the door and bowed me in with a grin, getting quite a kick out of all this. I slid into the lush, cream-leather upholstery, thrilling to the smell and the opulence of a very expensive car, and glanced at the dials. It had everything – including automatic transmission and stereo tapes.

I inserted the key and turned on the ignition, pressed a switch, and the passenger window went down ... pressed another, and the aerial rose ... yet another, and the seat began reclining.

'Got the feel of it?' he asked.

I nodded. 'Think so. Well, here we go ... if I'm not back in two weeks, call the cops.'

With a roar the mighty power unit exploded into life, dropping instantly to the faintest flutter as I eased off the gas. Into drive ... handbrake off ... and away we went.

'Keep her down to two-hundred in the city!' he laughed, waving me off.

Out of the garage and into the street, concentrating fiercely on driving on the right side of the road. Within a few blocks I was beginning to feel more confident and was able to risk a glance at the occasional girl. Oh, *boy*, it felt good. I only wished Buzz had been with me – this sort of thing is five times more pleasurable when you've got someone to share it. Buzz ... or Dominique. I'd have given anything to be driving her around right then. Well, never mind, I was mighty grateful for the car. What a lovely thought.

Now ... where to? North, south, east or west? I knew Lake Ontario lay to the south and fancied a look at that, so I turned at Bathurst and cruised down to Lakeshore Boulevard, now seeing the vast expanse of water ahead of me.

On to the boulevard, a turn to the west, then out along the lake shore at a leisurely lollop. Time now to think about music. The stereo slot was already loaded ... a touch of a button and the car filled with the romantic beat of a gentle bossa nova. Da ... di ... da da ... da da ... di ... da da ... Ah, this was the life ... money ... money ... money. Maybe it *wasn't* everything, but at least you could be miserable in style.

Tobin, I thought, it's about time you got yourself rich, about time you started applying this mind of yours to accumulating some real lettuce instead of staggering from pound to pound, dollar to dollar, peseta to peseta. Just think of the life you could have with a million in the bank – a car like this, a girl like Dominique, fourteen holidays a year and a hamburger just when you felt like it – like right now for instance.

I wheeled the Caddy into the parking lot of the drive-in restaurant and came to a halt, then drove right round the deserted lot and out on to the boulevard again. The flaming place was closed.

See what I mean?

With a million in the bank I'd be down in Miami with Dominique now, down in the sunshine where the drive-in restaurants are always open.

Da ... di ... da da ... da da ... di ... da da ...

I drove for two hours, covering the city and finishing back at the hotel as it was getting dark. Well, that had been lovely but not as good as it might have been. The glamour of the car and the romantic music had got me yearning for female company, and so it was in a mood of some disgruntlement that I entered the hotel and went up to the room.

Strange how different a room can seem when you're suddenly alone. You actually notice the wallpaper. Bad, that.

Well, I thought, no good sitting around feeling sorry for yourself, Tobin. You know the world's out there, but it sure as heck doesn't know you're in here – so make up your mind what you want to do – go out or stay in.

But it wasn't that easy. I guess weariness had something to do with it, but I just couldn't make up my mind. I considered a movie, but abandoned that, I wasn't in movie mood. I sat on the bed and lit a fag, took three drags and stubbed it out. I wasn't in the mood for that either. Hell, come on, Tobin, what's the matter with you?

The matter was, of course, that the past few weeks had been crammed with excitement and activity – the hairy old time with Stud Ryder in Nassau, the four days in sunny Miami and their riotous climax with the gorgeous Evie Shoemaker, the incredible train journey with Buzz to New York, the wild chase into Canada and all that had happened since ... and now everything had suddenly come to a screaming halt. I simply wasn't used to the silence!

Well, there was only one way to fix that – get out and stir something up!

Right – a quick shower, a change of clothes – then a drink in the nearest bar. Things always happened in bars.

Well – almost always. The first one I entered, just after six, was the exception. There was only the barman in the place.

'Yeah, what'll it be?'

I felt he might have been glad to see me, but he reacted like I was disturbing his meditation.

'Er ...' I didn't even feel like drinking! 'Vodka tonic, please.'

He was a middle-aged guy, balding, portly, dead miserable. He placed the glass and bottle of tonic down without a word and sauntered back down the bar to read his paper.

'Very quiet tonight,' I remarked.

'It don't come much quieter.'

'Any reason for it?'

'Probably because the place is empty.'

Oh, wry ... very wry.

'You have a good Christmas?' I persisted.

'Lousy – the cat got run over.'

'Oh, I'm sorry.'

'Don't be – I hated the goddam thing.'

'Oh.'

'But the wife was bananas about it – she spent the whole goddam day at the cemetery and burned the turkey. Some Christmas.'

'Maybe New Year will be better.'

'I doubt it. She's gettin' another goddam cat.'

'Oh.'

I swallowed the drink, threw some money on the bar and left.

By eight o'clock I'd had four drinks in four different bars and hadn't talked to a soul. So I nipped into a hamburger joint, ordered one without onions and got one smothered in them. It just wasn't my night.

Ah, well, there was only one thing for it – bed. I strolled back to the hotel feeling better now that I'd made the decision. You just can't fight a night like this. Much better to call the whole thing off and succumb to the inevitable.

I entered the room, threw off my clothes, cleaned my teeth, then hit the mattress. Wonderful. Maybe there was nothing wrong with the world after all; maybe it was just me. Good-night world, see you in the morning. Who needs you?

I put out the light, emptied my mind (not difficult when you start with nothing), closed my eyes and slept like a babe for ... oh, all of twenty minutes. The telephone shattered me awake.

With pounding heart I fumbled in the dark for the receiver, not knowing what time it was, but feeling I hadn't been asleep all that long.

'H ... hello,' I croaked, feeling for the lamp switch,

A pause ... then a husky, low-pitched hell of a voice, so three-dimensionally sensuous she could have been smashed, murmured, 'Mister Tobin?'

Oh, boy. 'Er ... yes?'

'Hi.'

*He*llo, I thought. Now here was a way to wake up.

'Hi,' I laughed, wondering who the wonderful creature could be and *where* she could be and just how much of that blatant sexual innuendo she'd back up with action. 'Who is this?'

'Oh, you don't know me,' she smiled, dropping the voice another octave. 'But you do know a very close friend of mine – Dominique De Neve.'

Oh, brother. Oh, my sainted aunt, here we go again.

'Oh, yes ...' I quavered, heart erupting. 'Yes ... I ...'

'She telephoned me this afternoon ... told me all about you.'

'She did?'

'Mmm ... said you were just the man I needed ...'

'Oh?'

'... to do some ... odd-jobs around the house.'

'Oh!'

'You are working for Greg Douglas's Hire-A-Guy, aren't you?'

'Oh, yes, certainly.'

'Dominique told me you'd done ... one or two little jobs for her and that she was very satisfied with your work.'

'Well, that was ... nice of her ...'

'And she suggested I give you a call. I hope you don't mind.'

'No, no ... not at all.'

'My name is Lucille Koeller-Jurling. I have one or ...'

'Er, sorry, could I have that again? Lucille ... ?'

'Koeller-Jurling,' she laughed. 'It's Swedish – from way back.'

'Ah.' Ah! 'Er, is that "Mrs." Koeller-Jurling ... or ...'

'Yes – Mrs. As I said, I have one or two odd jobs you could do for me if you'd like. Dominique said you needed the money.'

'Well, yes. I'm kind of stranded here for a couple of weeks ...'

'She explained your circumstances.'

'Oh. Er, what ... sort of jobs have you got for me, Mrs. Koeller-Jur ...'

'Oh, nothing *too* difficult. A little decorating ... an attic I want cleared out.' The sexy smile came again. 'I don't think they're beyond your particular talents.'

You know, I believe she was smashed – not falling down motherless, by any means, but she had a nice little tipsy slur going. Hell, she had to be – no woman could get that degree of uninhibited sexual innuendo into her voice, talking to a stranger, stone cold sober. Could they? I don't know, maybe *she* could. Maybe she was that kind of bird. Then again, maybe Dominique had pre-sold me so well that Lucille felt she could dispense with formalities and get right down to basics straight away. You never can tell over the phone; they can be very deceiving.

Well, whichever it was, one thing was certain – she sounded a *very* exciting bird and the prospect of meeting her had me stammering and breathless.

'F ... fine,' I said. 'Well, I'd be delighted to come round and ... when did you have in mind?'

'Tomorrow?' she suggested.

My heart sank. I felt sure she was going to say 'right now'.

'Yes, all right ... about what time?'

'Say ... eight o'clock? How does that suit you?'

'Eight!' I gave a laugh. 'Yes, all right, I can be there at eight.'

'You sound surprised. Is eight an unusual time?'

'Well, no, I supose not. I know you Canadians start work early ... it's just that you personally don't sound a "crack of dawn" lady. I'd have thought ten was more your mark.'

'Crack of dawn?' she repeated, then poured a throaty chuckle in my ear. 'Hey, you thought I meant eight in the *morning*!'

'Well, yes ...'

'Oh, no, honey. You're right – I am *not* that kind of lady.

No, I meant eight tomorrow *night*.'

'Oh . . .!'

Oh!

'A kind of preliminary meeting was what I had in mind. I thought you'd like to look the jobs over before committing yourself – then if you don't want to take them on you haven't wasted a working day. And if you *do* want to take them on, you could start the next day.'

'Ah, I see! Well, that's very thoughtful of you, Mrs. Koe . . .'

'Besides, I'm going to be out all day tomorrow.'

'Right.'

'So – how about it – is eight all right?'

'Perfect. You'd better give me your address.'

'You'll be driving . . . yes, of course you'll be driving,' she chuckled. 'Dominique told me she'd lent you her buggy. You must have impressed her, Mister Tobin.'

'Well, I . . .'

'You have a pen?'

'Er, two ticks . . .'

I skipped out of bed, got my pen and address book from my jacket, fumbled for a page. 'Right, I'm ready.'

'Good,' she smiled, and gave me an address in Rosedale that sounded so inviting I was tempted to suggest I nip out there right then.

'Fine,' I said. 'Well, see you at eight.'

'Wonderful,' she breathed, and rang off.

That, of course, did it as far as sleep was concerned. I was now wide awake, full of bounce, impatient to get there. I lit a fag and strolled the room, trying to imagine what she looked like, how old she was – and what Dominique had told her about me.

In my mind's eye I came up with a girl very like Dominique – in her late twenties, tall, blonde, willowy, with a wide Swedish mouth and a curtain of tumbling hair. Then I realized that of course *she* wasn't necessarily Swedish – perhaps she'd just married a Swede. She certainly didn't sound Scandinavian; that rich, throaty burr was pure Canadian.

And as to what Dominique had told her about me . . . well, that was anybody's guess. What *do* birds like these two tell each other?

What, I wondered, were Lucille's circumstances. She'd implied she was married, but was she, like Dominique, divorced – and also like Dominique, rich, footloose . . . and bored?

Speculation on all these matters ran riot for the duration of another cigarette, then, realizing that no good could come of it, I put her out of my mind. No good building up my hopes too much. To find one bird like Dominique was miraculous enough; to expect another was just plain greedy. She probably *did* have a couple of genuine odd-jobs for me to do. Why shouldn't she? Anyway, to avoid disappointment, I made up my mind that's all there was to it. Anything else would be a pleasant surprise.

So thinking, I cleansed my teeth again and got back into bed, wondering how I was going to fill the next day till eight o'clock, finally deciding I'd just follow the Cadillac's nose to wherever it took me.

But, ah, the plans of mice and odd-job men. Mine was shattered just after nine the next morning – by Greg Douglas's secretary.

'Hello, Mister Tobin . . .?'

'Yes, speaking.'

'Good morning, this is Hire-A-Guy. Mister Douglas wondered whether you'd like a job this afternoon? Something just came in.'

'Yes, sure . . . what is it?'

'A private wedding reception needs a waiter – a man to hand round sandwiches and drinks and empty ashtrays, you know the sort of thing. Nothing difficult. It's in a house on Charles Street – very local. We can pay twenty dollars.'

'Yes, fine. What are the hours?'

'Start at two, finish at seven.'

'Great, that works in all right.'

She gave me the address.

'What about uniform?' I asked.

'None needed. It's very informal – just a house party.'

'Right, I'll be there.'

I thanked her and put down the phone. Well, there was a break. I could still do a spot of sight-seeing until two, twenty dollars coming in the afternoon, then Lucy Koeller-Jurling to look forward to in the evening. What a lovely day it was turning out to be. All very interesting.

Ha!

I didn't know the half of it.

Perhaps she didn't know, but what she'd omitted to tell me was that this was no ordinary wedding.

This one was between a couple of fellas!

CHAPTER TEN

All unsuspecting, I rolled up to the house at a quarter to two and parked the Caddy eight hundred yards down the street. I had to. There wasn't room to park a bike near the house. Big do, I thought – I'd be kept busy so that time would pass quickly.

The house was a down-at-heel three-storey job in an endless row of similar edifices, all totally uninviting. My spirits wavered as I mounted the six crumbling stone steps, banged on the knocker and stood listening to the din from within – deafening party music and the raucous babble of voices.

It took five hard wallops on the knocker before anyone answered, and as the door opened I knew there was something quaint going on. I mean, the bloke standing there was clue enough – a very strange lad, skinny as a ball-point pen and dressed in green velvet trousers, an open, frilly yellow shirt, his long crinkly red hair draping his narrow shoulders and 'I Love Yours' tattooed on his sunken chest.

He gave me a surprised, then disturbingly approving search from toe to head and shot his orange eyebrows up about a foot.

'Well, hel . . . lo! Come in . . . come in!'

Aye aye, I thought, wrong house.

'Er . . . Mister Daniels?' I enquired, without much hope.

'Not personally, angel – he's inside.'

'Oh! Er, this is the wedding reception, then?'

'With a vengeance, love, but, er, do we know you?'

'I'm . . . the waiter . . . Hire-A-Guy,' I said, regretting it instantly. I should have said I was a neighbour complaining about the noise – then scarpered.

'Ohhh!' his mouth dropped open. 'Ohhh! come in . . . come in! Oh, splendid! I thought I hadn't seen you before. I'd certainly have remembered.'

I'll bet.

I stepped over the threshold – into a wall of strangely perfumed incense – or maybe it was perfume! – now certain that something was not quite jake around here.

'Who's getting married?' I asked casually.

'Dicky and Frances,' he replied cosily, closing the door. 'And what's your name?'

'Tobin. Russ Tobin.'

'Wonderful. This way ...'

He moved off down the hallway, and with some misgivings I followed, peering around, a wave of disenchantment engulfing me at the dinginess and odd-ball decor of the place. Each stair of the carpetless staircase was painted a different, garish colour, as were the bars in the bannister, and the wall behind was a vast disturbing mural, a panorama of naked fellas gambolling through a nightmarish Dali landscape of finger-sprouting trees and three-eyed boulders. All very jolly.

'By the way ...' he said, pausing at an open door through which the tumultuous noise was blasting, 'my name's Sandy ... Sandy Sillitoe. I'm the sort of organizer of it. Anything you want just come to Sandy, but I'm sure you'll manage just fine. Come in and get acquainted.'

I followed him in, into a huge two-roomed room crowded with men who all looked like Sandy Sillitoe, the spectacle of noise and colour quite stunning me.

'Everybody ... *every*body ...!' yelled Sandy, attracting a sea of faces which immediately transferred to me and held, embarrassing the hell out of me. I felt like a bug on a pin.

'Everybody ... this is Russ Tobin from Hire-A-Guy who's helping out with the drinkies and the eats. Anything you want – just ask him, I'm sure he'll be only too pleased to give it to you ...'

'Oooh, lovely ...! Me first!' said a smart-assed character in pink and everyone roared with laughter.

'Now, now,' said Sandy, wagging his finger, 'you leave our waiter alone, Benjy Doyle, he's got work to do.' He turned to me, his eyes shining with some inner glee, and slipped me a nauseating wink. 'Never mind him, he's just kidding. We're all so excited today. Come on, I'll show you the bar.'

At the far end of the room trestle tables had been erected almost wall-to-wall. In the centre of them stood a huge glass punchbowl filled almost to the brim with blood. Well, it looked like blood. To one side of the bowl was a great stack of glass cups, maybe a hundred of them, and on the other side reposed a veritable mountain of food – plates of sandwiches, sausages, meat pies, chicken legs ... and a dozen or so bowls of jelly and trifle.

Sandy led the way through the narrow gap between table and wall and I followed.

'Right, then, here we are,' he said, rubbing his hands together, 'more than enough for everybody. All you've got to do is give them what they want ... fill the punch cups and dish out the plates – oh, *and* keep the music going ...'

He turned and pointed to a pile of records and a turntable on the floor. 'Doesn't matter which you put on, they're all nice and lively.'

'Where are the happy couple getting married?' I asked. 'A local church?'

He gave me an odd sort of look and laughed. 'Good heavens, no – right here. Upstairs.' He glanced at his diamante watch. 'In ... thirty-two minutes precisely.'

'Oh.'

'Then we'll have a *super* party until seven ... then we all go over to their house for a little celebratory send-off. You'll be finished at seven though.'

'Where are they going for their honeymoon?'

He laughed. 'Niagara Falls, where else? Well, now, any problems?'

'No ... yes – one. What happens when the bowl's empty?'

He gave a shrug. 'Make some more – here, there's stacks of booze under here.' He pointed under the table.

'Fine – but how? What is it?' I gave the bowl a sniff and winced. 'Wow! Smells potent.'

He laughed tinklingly. 'It's my own concoction. I call it "Wedding Night" – exhilarating, intoxicating and mysterious.'

I'd have called it Bloody Mess. It looked terrible.

'What's in it?' I enquired.

'One bottle of gin, one bottle of vodka, half bottle of brandy, one bottle Cinzano Bianco, one bottle Campari, a tin of tomato juice and a dash of bitters. It's fantastic.'

'You better write that down, I'll never remember all that.'

'Of course you will. Gin, vodka, brandy, Cinzano, Campari, tomato juice and bitters. Think of a sentence to remember it by ... er ... gay virgin bashfully comes creeping to bed, how about that?'

'It'll do,' I grinned. 'Gay virgin bashfully comes creeping to bed. I'll remember that.'

'Splendid. All right, then ... well, I'd better pop upstairs and see how things are coming along. The preacher should be here by now. Now, remember – no one gets a drink until after the ceremony. No doubt they'll try the moment I disappear, but be firm.'

'Firm,' I nodded.

'This stuff is so potent they'll all be legless before the "I do's." '

'Roger. By the way, where are the happy couple now?'

He jabbed a finger at the ceiling. 'Upstairs.'

'Nervous, I suppose?'

'Shaking like jellies, poor lambs.' He glanced again at his watch. 'Whoops! Almost two-fifteen, I must go. See you later.'

He passed back through the gap, tucked his bum in as he squeezed between two chatting chaps and disappeared into the crowd.

Well, now ...

Feeling suddenly spare, I picked up a tea-cloth and began polishing the glass cups for something to do, surreptitiously having a butcher's at the assembled company. What a motley lot they were – all colours, shapes and sizes, all talking nineteen to the dozen and waving their hands around as though trying to catch flies. A *very* strange wedding reception, I concluded. I mean, if the bridegroom *was* an artist – fine. That would explain this crowd of gaudy layabouts. But what about the bride? Didn't she have any girlfriends? There wasn't a blooming bird in the room. Sad state of affairs.

'Penny for them,' cooed a voice on my left.

I shot round. He was five foot two, but all woman – a real Queen of the May, clad in a floral shirt, gold dingle-dangle round his neck, a dyed silver streak standing out like a brooch in his dark, luxuriant hair and I swear he was wearing false eyelashes.

'Pardon?'

He smiled cutely. 'I said "penny for them". You looked very deep in thought.'

'Yes, I was.'

'Alvin Woodthorn,' he announced, proffering a slender,

bejewelled hand.

'Russ Tobin,' I answered, making it an unmistakably butch connection.

'Yes, I know. How very nice of you to come and help us out.'

I shrugged. 'I'm grateful for the work.'

'Ah, Dame Fortune not smiling too brightly upon you at the moment?'

'Not at all – just a . . . temporary inconvenience.'

'I see.' He sounded quite disappointed. 'If . . . you *are* in difficulties, I'm sure I could help.'

I'm sure you could – and in return for what, I thought. 'Well, that's very kind, but I'm really all right.'

'You're English, aren't you?'

'Yes.'

'A long way from home.'

I laughed, not un-nervously, grateful the bar was between us. 'Home is wherever I happen to be. I don't get lonely.'

'Fancy,' he mocked, smilingly. 'A rugged individualist. I like that.'

And who gives a stuff, I thought, disliking the way the conversation was going and knowing what was coming.

'You . . . live alone?' he enquired with transparent nonchalance, picking an immaculate polished nail.

'Always.'

'Terribly independent, aren't you?'

'Terribly. I can't stand other people's underwear in the sink.'

He rolled his eyes in horror. 'God for*bid*! I couldn't stand that myself. How long are you staying in Toronto?'

'A couple of weeks.'

'And where are you staying?'

'The Y.M.C.A.,' I lied.

'Oh, God, not really.'

'Needs must.'

'Poor lamb, you really are hitting bottom.'

Maybe – but not yours, love.

'And you mean to say you never get lonesome in that dreary place?'

'Never have time,' I said, picking up another cup and rubbing it busily. 'Far too busy – day *and* night.'

'Oh, come *on* . . .' he chaffed. 'You mean to say you never take a night off ... never go to a party or a movie?'

I shook my head. 'Never.'

'Now, don't tell me you're putting a kid brother through college, sugar.'

'No ... I won't tell you that.'

'What then? I mean, no one in his right mind works all those hours voluntarily.'

'I'm ... paying off a fine.'

'A *fine*?' he frowned. 'You mean traffic or something?'

'No – assault and battery.'

'Uh?' he gaped, backing off a step.

'I hit a guy in a pub. I'm paying him compensation for a broken nose.'

'Oh,' he gasped. 'What ... I mean, why ...?'

I shrugged. 'He was trying to pick me up. I hate that sort of thing, don't you?'

'Er ... yes ...'

'I told him to leave me alone, very nicely – twice, in fact, but he persisted. Very silly.'

'Yes ... funny – you don't look the violent type.'

'Well, you never can tell, can you? It's always the quiet ones you've got to watch.'

'Yes, well ...' he glanced quickly across the room. 'Ah! there's ... would you excuse me?'

'Certainly. Nice talking to you.'

'Yes ...'

He went.

I had a quiet chuckle to myself and polished a few more glasses, and suddenly there was another one there, a handsome young lad with dark curly hair and dimpled cheeks, smartly attired in black slacks and a red shirt.

'Hi,' he smiled, flashing his teeth.

'Hi.'

'How about a drink?'

'Sorry – Sandy's orders, nothing until after the wedding.'

'Oh, come on, just one, I'm parched.'

'Sorry. If I gave you one I'd start a stampede.'

'I could nip round there and duck down behind the bar. No one would see me.'

'You want me fired?'

'No, of course not.'

'Have a sausage, it'll take your mind off it.'

'Aw, don't be mean – just one.'

'Nope – sorry . . .'

'Tobin, isn't it?'

I looked at him, disturbed that he'd remembered. 'Yes, Tobin.'

'First name Russ?'

'Russ.'

'Short for Russell?'

No, George, you berk.

I nodded. 'Short for Russell.'

'Mine's Rodney.'

That figured.

'How d'you do.' I nodded.

'Not just a *teensy* drink?' he insisted, bathing me in charm, giving me the teeth, dimples and a cute, raised eyebrow.

'Not even an itsy-bitsy one,' I grinned, giving it all back to him.

From the corner of my eye I noticed the emergence from the crowd of an odd-looking character in aubergine floral slacks and a purple shirt, his hair dyed so blond it was almost white, giving him a weird albino appearance. As he squeezed into the small clearing in front of the bar he shot me a look of such unadulterated malice it quite stunned me for a second and before you could say 'just good friends' I had a right old barny on my hands.

'And *what* . . . d'you think *you're* doing!' it demanded, coming to a fraught halt, hands on hips, everything jiggling and wiggling.

'Mmm?' I gaped.

'I *said* . . . what do you think you're *doing*?'

'I'm . . . polishing this cup.'

'*Don't* get funny with me – you were chatting up Rodney, bold as brass!'

I shot a look at Rodney, who had a curious little smirk going, obviously enjoying the moment and obviously not about to leap to my rescue.

'I . . .' I started to say.

'Just keep your lecherous eyes off him, I warn you!' continued Flock Slacks, pointing his finger threateningly. 'He's spoken for – so keep your nose out!'

'I . . .' I gave a helpless laugh, overwhelmed by the unexpected vehemence of the attack. 'Look . . . you've got it all wrong!' I turned to Rodney. 'Well, tell him ...!'

Rodney half-shrugged, his expression vague and enigmatic, leaving ample room for doubt. 'My dear Boofy, you're getting your panties in a twist over nothing at all – as usual. Russ and I were merely discussing the booze situation. You really will have to curb this irritating jealousy. I can't speak to anyone without you barging in with your teeth bared.'

'You're a lying bitch!' Boofy snorted. 'I was watching you! You were *not* talking about the booze situation, you were *drooling* at each other! Well ...' he huffed, 'if you prefer a bloody bar bum to me, take him and welcome – he's just about your class.'

'Hey, you ...!' I gasped, blood rising, 'watch your mouth. You're wrong about everything, sunshine – and especially about me. I'm not interested in Rodney or anyone else in this room – I'm with the other lot. So I'll accept your apology and you both push off and leave me alone.'

'Ha!' he scoffed. 'That'll be the day when I apologize to a bar bum.'

I threw down the drying cloth and squared up to him, aware that we had the full and fascinated attention of the entire room – and from their multiple expressions it was disturbingly obvious whose side they were all on. Understandably, since I was the square peg in so many round holes, if you'll forgive the expression.

Faced by this encroaching wall of antipathy, to say nothing of animosity, I suddenly felt trapped – and scared, and I wanted out of there very badly, but there was nowhere to go.

Now, secure in the support of the room, Boofy's attitude became openly insulting, infuriatingly insolent.

'You were about to say something, *bar bum*?' he sneered.

'Boofy ...' Rodney half-heartedly interjected, no doubt realizing that the thing was about to get out of hand.

'Shut up!' snapped Boofy. 'Go on, you.'

I shot a glance at the sea of faces, finding vindictive amusement and not a friendly eye in the house. The buggers were enjoying this, and I knew that a word from Boofy and they'd be on me like a pack of hyenas.

I made a lightning evaluation of the situation, realizing it was fast becoming a very dangerous one, and decided my best way out was a direct appeal to the gallery.

Heaving a sigh of bewilderment, I said to Boofy, 'Look ...

I was standing here polishing these glasses and Rodney came up and asked me for a drink. I told him that Sandy's orders were not to serve anything until after the ceremony. He tried to persuade me ... I insisted no – and suddenly I'm being accused of trying to seduce him ...'

'You're a liar!' rapped Boofy.

'Then ask him your bloody self!' I bellowed.

'*He's* a liar!' he yelled.

'And you're a bloody nutter!' I bawled, up to here with Boofy and Rodney and the whole cockamamie outfit by now. 'Look, if you don't want me here, I'll get out right now!'

I made an angry move towards the gap between table and wall, but Boofy was there before me.

'Oh, no, you don't!'

'Eh?' I gaped.

'You don't get away that easily ...'

'I ... get out of my flaming way, you ...!'

I reckon in the next split second, mob or no mob, I'd have landed him one because I was beginning to hate the sight of him, but at that instant Sandy's perplexed and very welcome voice shouted from the door, 'My God, what's going *on* here ...! Let me through ... good *God*, don't tell me someone's fighting ...!'

He burst from the crowd, wide-eyed and mortified. 'Wh ... what on earth's going *on* here?'

'It's him!' sniffed Boofy. 'He's a trouble-maker. Tried to pick up Rodney.'

'God *Almighty*!' I gasped. 'Look, Sandy, it's a bloody lie and I want out of here – right now! Rodney was only asking me for a drink, but this guy is so rotten with jealousy he won't believe me. Now he's got the whole room hating me and there's no point in my staying any longer. Forget the money – just let me get out of here.'

Sandy turned on Rodney and speared him with a fierce glare. 'Is it true? *Were* you just asking him for a drink?'

Rodney shrugged, answered nonchalantly. 'Of course. You know Boofy. If I asked someone the time he'd insist I was being raped.'

'I *saw* the look you were giving him!' insisted Boofy.

'For God*sake* ...' sighed Sandy, 'will you stop it – all of you! There's Dicky and Frances upstairs about to be married and you're down here fighting like cat and dog. Now, come on – everybody, get upstairs. The vicar's *waiting* ... come on, *please*!'

I made a move to leave the room, but Sandy caught me by the arm. 'Russ, *please* ... I'm sorry about all this, I really am. I know what Boofy's like, he's *terribly* jealous of Rodney – and Rodney teases him unmercifully. Please stay, we need you. There won't be any more trouble, I promise.'

'Well ...'

'Oh, you are kind. Look, I've got to fly, the preacher's waiting to begin. See you in twenty minutes. Have a drink and cheer yourself up. It'll be a super party, you see. Be down soon.'

Suddenly I was alone.

Ah, what the heck – a few more hours and it would be all over and I'd be twenty dollars happier. And there was Lucy Koeller-Jurling to look forward to.

The thought of her dissipated the unpleasantness like snow in an oven, and in more cheerful mood I went back to the bar and inspected the punch.

What a weird concoction. I gave it a stir, sniffed it again, ladled some into a cup and sipped it. By gum, it wasn't too bad. I took another sip, sat down, lit a fag and settled down to wait.

Ten minutes passed. I finished that cup and filled it again. I was really quite enjoying myself, thinking about Buzz and how he'd be getting on in Victoria. Bet he was serving more than aces, the randy devil. I wished he could have been there at the wedding with me, we'd have had a few chuckles. Never mind, he'd be back in a couple of weeks, then we'd have some fun before he flew off to Australia.

Another ten minutes passed and I realized I was getting nicely shickered. The room had taken on a rosy glow and all my cares were vanishing in a delightful alcoholic haze. 'Blimey,' I laughed aloud, 'you'd better watch this stuff, son, it's potent!' Always a reliable indication when you start talking to yourself.

Still no sign of the crowd and I was overjoyed. Every minute that passed was a minute nearer Lucy Koeller-Jurling, and I much preferred sitting in quiet contemplation of her than serving scrumpy to this bunch of idiots.

I was deep in reverie about that lady and half-way through my third glass of splodge when a voice, distant and ethereal, called out, 'Hi!' from the direction of the door.

I peered down the room, locating a French beret, long, lank, dark hair and a huge pair of sunglasses, leaning in, disembodied, round the door.

'Upstairs?' he enquired.

'Er ...' I had to think. 'Oh, yes! Yes, they're doing it now.'

He gave an annoyed tut and moved into the room, a dapper little fellow in bell-bottom hipsters, a blue-and-white striped T-shirt and fur-lined flying jacket. He approached the bar, drawing on a fag stuck in a foot-long ivory holder, his demeanour quite distraught, countenance pale.

'I just *knew* I'd be late, *knew* it!'

'You look as though you could use a drink.'

'How right you are ...' he peered into the punchbowl and made an expression like he was going to be sick. 'My *God*, what's that?'

'Punch.'

'Looks more like bleeding Judy.'

'It tastes all right. I've had three.'

'Well, if you say so ...'

I filled a cup and gave it to him. He took a tentative sip, relaxed his pained expression, nodded approval and drained it.

'You're right – not bad at all.' He held out the cup for a recharge and, in passing, I topped my own up. 'Cheers,' he said, swallowing half of it. 'Oh, that's much better. What a lovely fellow you are, you saved my life. The name's Bobby D'Angelo.'

'Russ Tobin – temporary barman. How come you're late?'

'Oh,' he tossed his head, 'domestic quarrel just as I was leaving. *Terribly* distressing. How many are here?'

'Hundreds ... well, about sixty.'

He gave another tut. 'And I wanted *so* much to be on time. He did it purposely, you know – because he wasn't invited. I just *knew* he'd pull something like this at the last moment. Dicky and Frances can't stand him ... and after this I'm not sure I can.'

'The course of true love,' I observed sagely, having difficulty getting the words out and really not knowing what I was talking about. 'Never mind, you're here now, so you may as well enjoy yourself. They should be down soon, they've been up there nearly half an hour.'

He groaned a groan and drained the second half absently. 'Oh ... and I *did* so want to see them do it.'

'Another belt?'

'Mm ...? Oh, yes, lovely ...'

I slopped in another ladleful. 'What sort of party do you reckon it's going to be?'

'Mm ...?'

He didn't get a chance to answer. Sandy Sillitoe burst into the room. 'They're coming ... they're coming ...! Bobby, love, where on *earth* were you? Oh, you missed a *beautiful* ceremony ...'

'Oh, God ...' wailed Bobby.

'But beautiful! Everyone cried. Russ, quickly, get the top record on – the one on the top of the stack – they'll be down any second. Everything ready ...? Yes, wonderful ...' He hared back to the door and peered out. Now I could hear the sounds of shouts and laughter from the stairs and the thunder of feet as the gang poured down them. A moment later and they were flooding into the room, hysterical with joy, some of them still crying into their hankies.

'Two lines ... two lines ...!' shouted Sandy, pushing and shoving them into position. 'Come on, form an aisle ...!' He turned to me. 'Right ... start the music!'

I dropped to my knees, reached for the record on the top of the pile, knocked the pile for a purler, fumbled for the right record, slapped it on the turntable, dropped the stylus down, there was a moment's pause, then out blasted Elvis Presley in 'Jail House Rock'.

To a roar of laughter from the crowd, up stormed Sandy, beside himself with fury. 'No ... no ... no ... ! For Godsake – the Wedding March!'

'Well ... you did say the top record ...'

'Get that off! Get it off! Someone's been messing with the records. Oh, Jesus, quick, find the bloody Wedding March ...!'

'What colour label?' I asked, so squiffed I couldn't read the titles.

'Yellow! No – orange! Christ, I don't know ... who's been messing with the bloody things? I had them all sorted out – Wedding March on top!'

'Ah! Here it is ...!' I pulled out one with a blue label,

slipped it on, swung the arm across ... and out roared The Wedding Samba!

'Tobin ...!' he wailed, racing round the table and falling on his knees. 'Have you been at that *punch*?'

'Me!'

He dived into the pile of records, scattered them left and right, yanked out one with a pale brown label and thrust it at me.

'Get it on!'

With considerable difficulty I located the hole, dropped the arm, and as the stirring opening chords of The Wedding March filled the room, Sandy shot to his feet and raced for the door.

'They're here ...! They're here ...!'

Now I was up on my toes, craning over the crowd for a glimpse of Dicky and his blushing bride, then lost my balance and fell against the table, slopping the punch over the cloth.

Quickly I mopped it up with a tea-towel, missing all the action out on the floor, and the next time I looked up I saw two grinning, bashful lads, holding hands, coming down the aisle towards me, resplendent in Sunday-best jeans and sweaters.

I only had time for one good gape and then the hordes were upon me, demanding booze. For the next few minutes I was working flat out and when everyone had been served ... a sudden hush.

'A toast ...' declared Sandy, raising his cup. 'Long life and infinite happiness to our two dear friends ... Dicky ... and Frances!'

'Dicky and Frances!' the crowd responded.

Well, it takes all sorts, I thought, raising my own glass.

'Russ ... the music!'

I bashed on the first thing that came to hand, a lively jiggy number, and the party was away in fine style, everyone dancing and having a great time. A few more drinks were served and the bowl was empty. In went another batch of booze – gay ... virgin ... bashfully ... comes ... creeping ... to ... bed. A quick stir and we were back in business.

'Coping all right?' called Sandy as he swept past doing a quickstep with Alvin Woodthorn, obviously restored to good humour.

'Fine! I've made another batch!'

'Good fellow! Give 'em all they want!'

I did – and by four o'clock there wasn't a soul present feeling any pain whatever.

'Hello, there . . .' It was that bloody Rodney again, fluttering his eyelashes so hard I could feel the draught.

'Oh, not you,' I said, peering round the room for his nutty soul-mate. 'You'd better clear off before Boofy sees you.'

'He's gone upstairs for a pee. Would you like to dance?'

'Are you kidding!'

'Just one.'

'Rodney, I may look daft – and also a bit squiffed – but I'm on to your little game, so push off. Go and make Boofy jealous with somebody else and let *him* take the lumps.'

'It's . . . not a game,' he said earnestly, giving me the dimples. 'I really do fancy you.'

'Tough titty. I happen to like dancing with the other sex – you know, the ones with those funny bulges up here.'

'You're prejudiced.'

'True.'

'You're anti-gay, aren't you?'

'Not at all. Live and let live is my fervent belief. Two of my best buddies are gay, lovely blokes. I've also got mates who are Jewish, Catholic, Baptist and Hindu, but I don't go to church with them. Now, toddle along, there's a good chap before Boofy returns and murders me.'

Well, he went, though reluctantly – and with an expression that somehow told me he'd be back. I didn't trust that sod and, as events later proved, I was right. Rodders was out to make trouble and make it he did.

I *knew* I should have left after that dust-up with Boofy.

CHAPTER ELEVEN

Well, time went on and by six o'clock I'd settled into the routine very nicely, making up fresh dollops of punch when needed and dispensing it with the aplomb of somebody who didn't have to pay for it, handing out plates of food and bringing in fresh supplies from the kitchen, keeping the records going without a break, emptying the ashtrays and generally keeping the place tidy, yet all the time with an eye on the time and wishing it would hurry up and be seven o'clock.

The party, as Sandy had predicted, was going well, everyone enjoying themselves madly, giggling uproariously, playing daft games like Postman's Knock and Queenie, Queenie, Who's Got My Balls, all of them tight as ticks and some a sight tighter.

Of Rodney and Boofy, that well-known firm of psychopaths, I had seen, thankfully, little, since they were upstairs most of the time, presumably patching up their quarrel, bless them. And with those two out of the way, and therefore all source of unpleasantness removed, I was moving freely about the room, stopping here and there to swap a crack and generally feeling very relaxed, little realizing, poor fool, that behind the scenes a plan of diabolical mischief – in which I was to suffer the leading role – was being hatched at that very moment, a plan that in just one hour would, to my shock and horror, be revealed to me.

Six-thirty – and all was still well.

Only half an hour to go, I muttered to myself, sick to death of Sandy's punch by now and pouring myself a straight vodka.

Then up strolled the lad himself, squiffed, though by no means falling down.

'You did a wonderful job, Russ ... just great.'

'Glad it went all right, Sandy.'

'Look, I've got to go over to the other house now, get things organized over there. Everyone will be leaving at seven so you can start clearing up pretty soon. Here ...' he took an envelope from his pocket. 'Twenty, wasn't it?'

'That's right ... thank you.'

'I may not see you before you leave, so I'll say cheerio now ... and thank you for doing so well.'

'What do I do about all the dirty dishes and things?'

'Just stack them in the kitchen, I've got someone coming in later to do them. Then give the place a bit of a tidy and you can go.'

'Right.'

He departed, taking a dozen or so guys with him. The party was beginning to break up.

Time – six-forty. I decided to make a start.

Loading a tray with used plates and cups I took them out to

the deserted kitchen and piled them on the already crowded work-top. When I returned for a second load even more people had left. The place was emptying fast. Two more trips to the kitchen and there was no one left in the party-room, though I could hear laughter from upstairs.

Well, that was it – my first gay wedding. Not a bit different from a straight one – well, almost. I raised my glass, made a silent toast to the happiness of the bride and groom and emptied it, then loaded the remnants of the food – a few curly sandwiches, half a bowl of trifle and a sausage or two – stripped off the stained cloth, tidied the records and picked up the tray. A final glance round to see everything was ship-shape, then I returned to the kitchen for the last time.

I'd just finished emptying the tray when I felt, rather than heard, a presence behind me, at the door. I turned, finding Boofy, Rodney and Benjy Doyle filling the doorway with two others behind them. Trouble, I could tell from their faces, was in the offing.

For several long, tense moments I held Boofy's gaze – his expression languidly insolent, mine a tight-lipped glower, then I turned away and finished unloading the tray, my heart banging with the sure knowledge that I was in for it.

Individually I wouldn't have been worried about any one of them; they were hardly Charles Atlases. But five-to-one were very dicky odds and I did not relish a physical confrontation with them one little bit. My mind was now racing, trying to formulate some kind of tactic, plan, get-out if they started something, but all that emerged was a blind, panicky confusion. I'd just have to wait and see what happened, there was nothing else I could do.

Boofy, naturally, opened the bidding, his tone sneeringly insolent. 'Finished your housework, dearie? Shame – he's still got all those dirty dishes to do. Don't you think that's a shame, Rodney? He's going to be *very* late home tonight.'

'Shame,' agreed that swine Rodney, all, presumably, because I wouldn't dance with him.

Inwardly trembling, I outwardly ignored them and continued stacking the dishes, wondering how I was going to get past them to the front door. I looked at my watch. It had just gone seven. I now had a perfect right to leave.

I decided to play it boldly – just walk right through them, collect my coat in the hall and march to the front door.

Drawing a steadying breath, I turned, took half a dozen steps at Boofy and murmured, 'Excuse me.'

He didn't move. 'Tobin ...' he leered, 'you have been a very rude boy. You came to this house as a hired bar bum and you misbehaved yourself. You tried to seduce poor Rodney here. Now, we don't think that such behaviour can go unpunished. You've got to *pay* for taking advantage of your situation, hasn't he, fellas?'

They chorused agreement. It was all, of course, pre-planned. The whole thing had been cooked up upstairs as a drunken amusement – the sort that frequently ends in disaster.

Well, I didn't intend to let it reach that stage because I had no intention of letting it start.

Levelling a stern eye at Boofy, the obvious ring-leader, I growled in a low, angry voice, trying like hell to hide the flutter. 'I'll just say this once ... I was hired to do a job and I've done it – to the satisfaction of the man who hired me. The job is now finished and my time is up. I now wish to leave ... so I'd be obliged if you'd get out of my way and let me through. I have another job to go to at eight ...'

'Well, lucky old you,' sneered Boofy. 'But we disagree that you've finished your job. Look behind you ... at all those dirty dishes. You can't possibly go until you've washed all those.'

'Correction ... I can and will go without washing all those. I was hired as a waiter, not a dishwasher. There's someone else coming in to do them.'

'But we prefer *you* to do them, sonny boy. We've taken a vote on it ... and decided we like your company so much, we want you to stay a bit longer – say ... till ten o'clock.'

'Now, look ...!'

'Tobin, you'd better make up your mind – you do *not* leave this house until you've washed all those dishes ... I mean every single one.'

'You're bloody mad ... you can't keep me here ...'

'Who says we can't? There *are* five of us, Tobin ... we can make you do anything we like.'

'Like hell you can,' I growled, now livid with this sneering idiot. 'Come on, out of my way ...'

He shook his head slowly, murmured threateningly, 'No way,' and came away from the doorpost in an attitude of readiness, the other four bunching around him protectively.

'I wouldn't advise you to try anything, Tobin. There's a general misconception about us – that we don't resort to physical violence. You try and make a break for it and we'll beat you to a pulp, I promise you. Now ...' he took a step towards me and the others came with him. I took a step back, panicking, my heart thundering. This was going to be the real thing ... five-star punch-up. They kept coming and I kept going – backwards, until I ran into the sink, then they still kept coming until they hemmed me in in a tight half-circle.

'... do you do the dishes ... or do we beat you up?' drawled Boofy, making a sudden dart behind me for a bowl-half-filled with liquifying trifle then inspecting it meaningfully, swirling the juice around the bowl with a wry, pursed smile, intention obvious.

Well, what was I going to do? – stand there and take all this – the threats, the insults *and* no doubt the remains of the trifle? Or was I going to burst through them and run like hell for the front door?

God, how many times I'd promised myself when in a fix like this that I'd take up judo and karate and kung fu the moment I got out of it. Five half-drunk punks would be easy meat after a few kung-fu lessons. Wham! Thock! Biff! Chop! A quick kick in the Brussels sprouts and I'd be stepping off their groaning, writhing bodies to freedom. I really *must* do something about it after this.

'Well, bar bum ...?' leered Boofy, raising the bowl above my head. 'What's it to be? Do you like trifle, Tobin?'

The other four were grinning like imbeciles, their eyes glued expectantly on the bowl, which I knew was tilting. Well, this was it – the moment of truth. In another second that sticky mess would come slithering out of the bowl and land with a plop on my nut. Was I going to let it happen?

Was I buggery.

In a wave of anger I shot my hands aloft, grabbed the bowl, wrenched it out of Boofy's hands and slammed it down on his immaculate blond head. Splut! Trifle cascaded down his hair and into his eyes, blinding him. Taken completely by surprise, the other four stepped back, horrified, giving me a sliver of room and a momentary advantage.

Biff! I bashed Rodney in the chest, driving him back across the kitchen, caught Benjy Doyle a back-handed clip on the ear, bulled through the other two and raced for the door.

'Get him! Get him!' bellowed Boofy.

With bursting heart I hared down the hallway, grabbed my coat off the wall and ran on, knowing by the time I'd reached the stairs that I'd never get the the door opened in time. They were on me! A lightning change of plan. In mid-stride I grabbed the bannister rail, swung myself round the newel post and clattered up the stairs, three at a time.

'Get him! Get him!' screeched Boofy, quite demented with rage. 'Kill him!'

Feet thundered up the stairs behind me. I reached the top, swirled around that post and raced along the landing, passing two ... three ... four doors, all closed. I needed time – just a second or two – to get inside one of the rooms and lock the door.

At the end of the landing another flight of stairs led off to the left – and at the bottom of them stood a pedestal with a potted plant on top. I ran up two or three stairs, turned, leaned over the rail and tipped the pedestal sideways, on to the stairs, blocking them, then up I went like a flaming rocket, straight through the first door I encountered, felt inside for the key, slammed the door and locked it.

I collapsed against the wall, gasping for breath, wondering just how much a human heart can take, then felt for the light-switch and snapped it on.

Thump! Thump! Thump!

'Open this door, Tobin!' It was Boofy, quite hysterical.

'Get stuffed, you nutter!'

'Open ...' Thump! '... this ...' Thump! Thump! '... door!' Thump! Thump! Thump!

'You're a bleeding head-case, mate! You think I'm going to stand there and let you tip trifle over my head?'

'I'm going to get you for this, Tobin!' he raged, giving the door a hell of a kick. 'You've got to come out sometime! And, by God, when you do ...!'

'You'll do *what*?'

'You're going to be sorry you ever came to this house!'

'You're too late, mate – I've been sorry ever since I clapped eyes on you!'

'Open this DOOR, DAMN YOU!!'

Crash!

Another terrific kick then a yell of anguish. 'Jesuschrist!'

I let out a bellow of laughter. He'd crippled himself.

'Right, Tobin ... that's something *else* you're going to pay for!'

'Oh, get knotted. Go and play with your marbles – or Rodney's!'

'You'll have to come out sometime ...!'

'Look, who the hell d'you think you are, Boofy? You can't keep me locked in here!'

'Then come on out – and see what happens to you!'

'Well, whatever happens to me, *you'll* never walk the same, you crumb ... because if it's the only thing I get a chance to do, I'll kick your nuts off! If you've got any.'

'Let's break down the door!' I heard Benjy whisper.

'No ... Sandy would be furious. He'll have to come out sometime ... and when he does ...'

'What shall we do to him?' asked that louse Rodney. 'Tar and feather him?'

There was a thoughtful pause, as though Boofy was earnestly considering the suggestion, then Boofy answered, 'Not a bad idea, Rodney – except we haven't got any tar ... but we *do* have some black gloss paint!'

'Yes!' gasped somebody.

'Let's strip him and paint his balls!' hissed someone else.

'Why stop at his balls?' leered Boofy. 'Why not paint him all over?'

'Yes!' they chorused.

'Are you listening, Tobin?' laughed Boofy. 'We're going to paint you all over with black gloss ... every stupid inch of you!'

'You're raving lunatics, the bunch of you!' I shouted, scared witless because I knew they were drunk enough, and mad enough to do it. 'You lay a finger on me and I'll have the cops around here so fast ...'

They dissolved into jeering laughter and gave the door a contemptuous bash. 'Come on out, Tobin ...!' wheedled Boofy. 'Come and get pain ... ted! Don't be long now ... we'll be waiting for you at the bottom of the stairs!'

Laughing uproariously they clattered down the stairs. With my ear pressed to the door I heard them reach the bottom and then ... silence. For a full minute I stayed there, straining to hear their feet on the lower staircase but hearing nothing and not really knowing if they'd gone down or not.

I slumped against the wall, trembling with fright and anger

and in danger of collapse. What a stupid, rotten turn-up! What a bloody unbelievable thing to happen! What a crazy, cock-eyed world it really was. You come to a house to do an honest, helpful job and wind up locked in a bleeding attic about to be painted black by a bunch of half-drunk fruit-and-nut cases! I mean, really ...!

I tell you something, I don't blame people for becoming recluses, you know ... I don't blame them one bit for shutting themselves away behind high walls and turning guard dogs loose in the garden. There are those among us who think Howard Hughes is a mite quaint, the way he shuts himself away from the world, but at times like this I don't blame him at all. Trouble, they say, only enters your life when people enter it, and the more I knock around this lunatic globe the more I'm inclined to agree. I mean, who could have guessed when I walked into this house that five hours later I'd be locking myself in this flaming room to escape being painted?

Painted!

Oh, my God, just look at the time! Seven thirty. Aw, this was ridiculous. I had to be in Rosedale at eight! How could I be here when I was supposed to be there! I *had* to be at Lucille Koeller-Jurling's at eight o'clock! They couldn't keep me here against my will, it was ... criminal! I could charge them with intimidation ... violence ... abduction ... threats. Didn't they realize how *serious* it was!

Ohh ... bollocks. How could this be happening? I'd had the evening all planned out. There was an exciting, sexy woman not two miles away, waiting for me to arrive any minute. I couldn't stay here. I had to go!

Bewildered, confused, I looked around the room, really seeing it for the first time. There was not much in it – just four big wooden packing cases and a couple of travelling trunks. I crossed the bare wood floor to the window, an ancient sash type that hadn't been opened for fifty years. Without much hope of opening it I gave the lower part three or four good thumps, but it was locked solid. Then I peered through the grimy glass and realized it wouldn't do me much good if I did get it open. There was nothing out there except a thirty-foot drop to the yard.

Back to the door for another listen. Nothing. Silent as the grave. My spirits slumped. What in hell was I going to *do*!

Well, after a minute or so I yanked my slumped spirits to

their feet and had a little heart-to-heart talk with myself, moved by anger at the ridiculousness of the situation.

How *dare* those five kooks inflict this ... this indignity upon me ... deprive me of my freedom, threaten me with violence! Good God, they couldn't keep me here when I wanted to be elsewhere! It was preposterous!

Right! I would simply open the door and march out – straight down the stairs, chin up, shoulders back. I would defeat them with the aloofness of my bearing. And if they *did* physically try to stop me, get hold of me, touch me in any way, I would ... I would ...

I looked around the room, crossed to the packing cases, finding the weapon I needed in a sliver of wood, three inches wide and two feet long ... I would clobber the bastards!

Back! I would say, eyes blazing, shrivelling them with white-hot menace. One step nearer and somebody dies! Open-mouthed they would drop back, casting terrorized glances here and there for avenues of escape. That's better, my beauties, *back*, I say! By God, this is Tobin you're dealing with, not some spineless ninny! Back, you dogs ... back! And thus I would march right through them and out of the front door.

Right ... here I go!

I strode purposefully to the door, snapped the key in the lock, took a firm grip on my scimitar, pulled open the door ... and let out an unholy shriek! They were there – right outside the door!

'Got you!' Boofy's shout rang jubilantly out as he flung his shoulder against the door. Then my own shoulder was hard against it, a shoulder fortified by craven fear and maybe a bit more weight.

'Help, you guys ...!' he bellowed, giving it another thrust.

I shot back a few inches but countercharged immediately, all but closing the door ... another inch or two ... push, man, *push*!

Then into the gap slid Boofy's soft-suede boot.

'We've got him!' he cried ecstatically.

'Like fuck you have!' I replied and brought the chunk of wood down on his toe with one hell of a chop.

'Yooowwww!!' he yelled and fell back from the door. 'OH, you crummy bastard ...'

Slam! The door hit the frame and the lock went home.

'Jesus, Tobin ...!' he screamed, hopping around on one

foot. 'My *God*, you're going to pay for this! Right ... come on, you guys, I've got a way of getting him out of there! Now, I *want* him!'

Oh, my sainted aunt, what had I done now?

With thundering heart I listened to them clumping down the stairs and along the lower landing, out of ear-shot. And now I really *was* worried. I did not like the sound of Boofy's threat one little bit. It sounded extremely like he intended setting fire to the room and easily mad enough to do it!

Well, stuff me, what was I going to do now? What were *they* going to do?

I paced the room in a fuddle of worry, glanced at my watch and released a sickened groan. It was ten to eight! Even if I left this minute I'd be late! God*dam* the bloody, blasted, buggering, stupid arseholes ... ohhh ... buggerit!

With all my strength I flung the length of wood at the wall and, damn me, it shot back and hit me on the head.

Well, that did it. With a heartfelt groan of anger and frustration and disbelief I slumped against the wall by the door and slowly slid down until I was sitting on the floor, then dropped my head into my hands and heaved a big, tired sigh of complete capitulation.

And there I sat, waiting for the end ... and waited ... and waited ... and waited.

Something was wrong. They should have been back by now, the mood they were in. Then again maybe this suspense was all part of the torture. I just didn't know what to flaming well think. Maybe they'd crept back again, like they'd done before, and were right outside the door now, this time prepared for a concerted rush the moment I opened it.

What a terrible dilemma.

I was a bundle of jangling nerves, straining to hear the slightest sound, occasionally sniffing at the keyhole for signs of smoke, gas, any damn thing. That last boast of Boofy's really had me worried – 'I've got a way of getting him out of there!'. What *did* he have in mind!

I put myself in his position. What would I do to get *him* out of this room? Well, I ... that was the trouble – I couldn't think of anything, and it was having no idea what *he* was up to that had me so damned worried!

Another half an hour crept by, the house as still and silent as Anfield cemetery. I thought again about Lucy Koeller-

Jurling. What a diabolical shame – her sitting there and me sitting here. What was going through *her* mind? Disbelief that I hadn't turned up, probably. Well, I'd more than likely get a very cool reception when I did finally turn up – *if* I ever did.

I'd telephone her and explain what happened ... ha! A nice job I'd have convincing her I was telling the truth, too! Sorry, Lucy, but I had to lock myself in an attic to escape five gay fruitcakes who fancied painting me black! Didn't *quite* have the ring of truth about it, somehow.

Ten to nine and still not a sound. What in hell were they *doing*! Building a bleeding ladder?! Aw, this was now getting just plain silly ... and I was getting very fed up!

Right, I thought, I'd give them another fifteen minutes and then, come what may, I was going! I'd go through that door and down those stairs swinging the chunk of wood like a claymore – and God help anyone that got in the way!

You can push Tobin just so far, you know, and then, by golly, you've got a tiger on your hands. Biff! Thock! Wallop! They'd go down like ninepins, screaming agony and clutching bloody heads.

Roused thus to a fine fit of pique, I got to my feet and executed a flurry of vicious slashes with my weapon, getting the blood boiling nicely. O.K., Boofy, your hour has come ... THUCK! One to the side of the neck ... and ... POW! another in the guts. Now your turn, Rodders, you *nasty* little man ... TWACK! What ho, Benjy ...! CRUMP! And you other slobs ... SPLAT! ... KLUNK!

I was ready. Gripping Excalibur so hard my fingers hurt, I silently turned the key, took a deep, determined breath and flung back the door. Arm raised high I leaped out on to the landing, 'YAAAHHHH!!', instantly feeling a right double-dyed cunt because there wasn't a soul in sight.

Well, there might have been.

Somewhat deflated, I approached the stairs and with my heart driving straight lefts into my ribs, I began to descend, eyes peering into the gloom below and skin crawling with anticipation of momentary attack.

Half-way down I stopped and listened hard ... not a damn thing. Nary a voice, creak, tinkle or click. I went on, reached the lower landing, becoming increasingly suspicious as each stifling second passed that the house was completely and unbelievably deserted.

The bums ... the bastards ... the dirty, unmitigated swine. They'd gone! Hopped it! Scarpered!

Appalled by their gall, angered by their vindictiveness yet elated by the prospect of freedom, I now threw caution overboard, ran along the landing, clattered down the stairs and raced towards the front door. I was there! Free! I was at the door, turning the catch, pulling it open ... and staring face-to-face with Boofy.

'YAAAHHH!' I cried, sightless with shock, my arm jerking high to open his skull.

'YAAAHHH!' screamed Sandy Sillitoe, falling back, *his* arm jerking high to protect himself.

'Sandy!' I gasped, lowering the plank.

He peered at me wildly, arm still raised, then, seeing I wasn't going to decapitate him, slowly lowered it. 'Russ ...! Russ ... what ...?'

'I thought you were Boofy!'

'Boofy? But why ...?'

I slumped. 'Come in.'

Still boggle-eyed, he entered and I closed the door. 'Russ ... what's going on ... why are you still *here* ...?'

'There's been some trouble ... Boofy, Rodney, Benjy and two others ... I was clearing up at seven o'clock, just about to leave, and they ... got funny.'

'Funny?'

'Mean ... aggressive. Told me I couldn't leave until I'd done all the washing up. It was Boofy ... you know, the trouble we'd had earlier on about Rodney. They were all half-cut. I locked myself in a room upstairs. They threatened to strip me and paint me all over with black gloss ...'

'They ... *what*!'

'You know, I think they'd have done it, too.'

'But ...' he frowned, very perplexed, '... they've been at the other party for an hour or more. I've just left them. They ...'

I gave a wry laugh. 'Yes, I guessed as much. They knew I had another job to go to at eight o'clock. About an hour ago, upstairs, Boofy told the others he had a way of getting me out of the room and then they came down. I've been waiting up there in a state of mild terror ever since, expecting them to burn the door down or something. I suppose I should've guessed they'd left the house a long time ago, but ...'

'Oh, my God, how terrible! You've been locked in that

room, waiting for them to ... oh, Russ, how awful for you! I ... I don't know what to say ...!'

'Well, it's not your responsibility.'

'But I'm most certainly going to *make* it my responsibility. After all, I hired you. They're not going to get away with this ...'

I gave him a weary smile. 'Forget it. Put it down to liquor. I'm not hurt.'

'But your other job ...!'

I shrugged. 'It's too late to go now.'

'But ... how much was it worth?'

'I don't know. There were a couple of things to do ... a bit of decorating ... possibly fifty dollars, I really couldn't say.'

'Well, you won't be out of pocket over this, I promise you.'

'Oh, listen, Sandy ...'

'No!' He held up his hand. 'I think Boofy's behaviour was disgraceful and he's going to pay for it. He *and* the others. I will not have this sort of thing going on in my house. The very least they can do is compensate you for loss of earnings.'

I smiled. 'Well, you do what you think is best.' I checked my watch and winced. It was twenty to ten. 'I must go. Thanks again for the job. I'm glad at least the wedding went off all right. What time do the happy couple leave on their honeymoon?'

He smiled a bashful smile. 'They've just left. We gave them a lovely send-off.'

'Splendid. Well, I must be off ...'

I moved towards the door, but he leapt to open it, apologizing profusely as I went through it. 'Goodnight, Russ,' he called 'and don't worry, you'll be hearing from me. I'll be in touch through Hire-A-Guy!'

'O.K., Sandy ... goodnight.'

I turned on to the street, pulled my coat around me against the bitter cold and heaved a sigh of relief that I was out of the house. By gad, Tobin, you know more ways to find trouble than Soft Mick. You wouldn't be safe shackled to the wall of a padded cell in an abandoned nut-house on a deserted desert island!

Reaching the car I unlocked it, slid into the freezing leather seat, started the engine and sat there thinking about Lucille Koeller-Jurling. To call or not to call – that was the question. And if I did – what sweet bundle of unadulterated mayhem would be waiting for me there!

The question, as things turned out, was not entirely inappropriate.

Oh, boy.

CHAPTER TWELVE

I sat there for some minutes pondering the problem. What, I wondered, would her reaction be to my not turning up at eight o'clock? What would it be if I turned up now? Ten o'clock is a difficult sort of time to call on people, isn't it? – a bit too late yet *not* too late, if you see what I mean.

I certainly felt a strong compulsion to call because I was dying to see what she looked like, and yet I didn't want to ruin it completely by making her mad. Well, at least I could take a look at the house, see if the lights were still on. Maybe the house itself would give a clue as to what to do.

I got out my street map, located her road in Rosedale, no more than five minutes away by the looks of things, then drove along Charles Street into Mount Pleasant, entering the district of Rosedale almost immediately.

Aha, this was more like it – a very different pile of bricks to Charles Street. Ultra-modern, ranch-style, mock-Georgian, the houses lay well back from the streets, half-hidden behind trim hedges, exuding money and an aura of splendid, effortless superiority, haughtily forbidding to the casual intruder and a monumental warning to any would-be purchaser that the price of residency was very high indeed.

I found Lockwood near the end of a lovely cul-de-sac on the borders of Rosedale Park. It was, like Dominique's, a magnificent neo-Georgian in light-sand brick, a modest little ten-bedroomed job fronted by a graceful sweeping drive and seventy yards of landscaped, snow-covered garden.

There were lights in the downstairs rooms and none upstairs, so I guessed she hadn't gone to bed yet. Well, here I was – now what was I going to do?

I was going to tell her the truth, that's what I was going to do. I was going to knock on the door, apologize for being late, tell her the whole story and throw myself on her mercy, because the worst she could do was chuck me out and that would leave me no worse off than I was now!

So, with my heart breaking into a gentle canter, I swung the nose of the Caddy through the open wrought-iron gate and scrunched up the snowy drive to the porched front door, cut the engine and got out.

My pulse-rate slipping from canter to gallop, I rang a lighted button and got dulcet chimes, and seconds later, through the bullseye glass panels in the door I got the wavy outline of an approaching female figure, dressed in black.

The door opened, cautiously, on a chain, and a *very* lovely young face with huge grey eyes, and short light brown hair peered wonderingly at me through the gap.

'Yes?' she enquired.

'Er ... Mrs. Koeller-Jurling?'

'Zis is her residence, yes,' she answered cautiously with a delicious French accent. 'Who is calling, plis?'

'My name is Russ Tobin. I was supposed to be here at eight o'clock, but I got held up. Mrs. Koeller-Jurling asked me to be here at eight ... she has some jobs she wants doing ...'

'Ah!' Her transformation was quite startling. Her manner became bright, sparkling, her eyes grew twice the size and her lovely mouth popped open. 'Yes, of course! Would you wait one moment, plis?'

For you, love, I'd wait for ever. 'Sure,' I smiled.

'I'm so sorry, but I shall 'ave to close ze door.'

'That's all right – go ahead.'

'I won't keep you a morment.'

'Don't worry about it.'

With a sexy little smile and some excitement she closed the door and disappeared. A minute later she was back again, unlatched the door and opened it.

'Plis – come in. I'm sorry to keep you waiting. May I take your coat?'

I stepped into a hall large enough to land a helicopter in and sank up to my knees in the pile of an off-white patterned carpet that must have cost around a dollar a tuft.

As I slipped off my parka I had a good look round the palatial place, finally coming face-to-face with Fifi, a breath-taking little button with a belting figure and stupendous legs, who was patiently waiting for my coat and having a damn good look at me while she was doing it.

She released the cute, flirtatious smile and said, 'Madam is in the lounge, sir – you may go right in.'

'Is she ... mad at me for being late?' I whispered.

'Aw, terr*ib*ly mad,' she frowned, sending me up. 'You should nev*er* keep a lady waiting.'

'I try not to,' I grinned, getting on splendidly with this little buttercup and wishing she was Lucy Koeller-Jurling. 'Erm ... what is your name, may I ask?'

'My name is Brigitte. I am maid to Mrs. Koeller-Jurling.'

'Lovely. I must say you do it very well.'

'Sank you,' she laughed, dropping a curtsy.

'You work late, hm? How do you get home?'

Her eyes widened and she glanced up the stairs. 'But I am 'ome! I live 'ere.'

'Wonderful. Well, I'd better go in and face the music.'

'I will announce you.'

She nipped past me and with a cute little wiggle headed for the lounge door, really turning it on. I followed, silently whistling 'Sank 'eaven For Leetle Girls', half of my mind on Brigitte's gorgeous bottom and the other half on Lucy Koeller-Jurling, wondering what I was about to come upon.

'Meester Russ Tobin ...' Brigitte announced, making it sound like someone else's name entirely.

I entered, slipping Brigitte a wink before I cleared the door, then coming to an astounded halt as I rounded it.

No two ways about it – Mrs. Lucille Koeller-Jurling was a real heart-stopper. Opulently gowned in a sheath of white satin trimmed with ostrich feathers, she lay reclined along the entire length of a pale-pink velvet couch, one hand supporting her lovely head, the other holding a foot-long ivory cigarette-holder to her exquisite lips while she peered at me through a curtain of pale gold hair in the attitude of Mata Hari receiving Count Rudy Von Tickleknicker of the German General Staff into her boudoir.

For what seemed like a quarter of an hour time stood still while she inspected me from hoof to hairline, her fine, wide-eyed features expressing languid off-handedness as though she was trying to make up her mind whether I should be there or not, and I was on the verge of getting a bit fed up with this when a playful, sexy half-smile dissolved the tension and told me we were going to be good friends after all.

'Well, they *do* say better late than never,' she drawled

mockingly, the slur of her words suddenly explaining the sleepiness of her eye.

On a low green marble table in front of the couch stood, besides a silver cigarette box and table-lighter, a cut-glass goblet half filled with a colourless liquid. The lady was charmingly smashed.

'I'm ... very sorry, Mrs. Koeller-Jurling ...'

She was shaking her head. 'Lesson one in this sweet life, Mister Tobin – never apologize. Well, come and sit down and let me look at you.' She waved to an armchair near the couch. 'And of course you'll have a drink. What would you like?'

'Vodka tonic?'

'Good choice – no smell, no hangover. Brigitte, honey, get Mister Tobin a drink.'

I settled nervously into the armchair, heart banging, feeling Lucy's eyes on me, knowing I was in for a *very* interesting evening. I looked up, met her gaze, and my pulse erupted at the playful, amused intimacy in her eyes. God knows what was going through her mind, but it certainly wasn't attic clearing.

Although two-thirds of my mind was paralysed by the opulence of the house, the blatant sensuality of this lazy-eyed creature and by a devastating glimpse of Brigitte's thighs as she crouched at a low cupboard for a bottle of tonic, I had sufficient control over the remaining third to manage a little detailed analysis of Lucy herself.

She was, like her pal Dominique, in her late twenties, immensely attractive and sizzling with sexuality. It was there in the languor of her pose, in the intimacy of her manner, and in the seductive mode of her dress. That satin gown hid everything yet nothing, moulding to her long slender legs in a way that revealed more than if she'd been stark naked.

I risked no more than a fleeting glance at her body and yet she saw it and her smile deepened, knowing what effect she was having on me.

'Cigarette?' she asked, leaning forward to push the box towards me, the gown opening slightly to reveal a glimpse of completely sun-tanned breasts.

'Thank you.'

I took one and lit it with a silver lighter, glad of something to do.

Brigitte moved from the cupboard with my drink, catching

my eye and bathing me in a glowing, knowing smile that I found both exciting yet somehow uncomfortable, feeling that the two of them had cooked up some naughty plan together and were delighted that I was fitting into it perfectly.

'Zere you are, sir.'

'Thank you, Brigitte.'

She turned to Lucy. 'Madam?'

Lucy demurred with a shrug, 'Why not?' drained her goblet and handed it to Brigitte who returned to the cupboard, refilled it and placed it on the table.

'Will zat be all, madam?'

'For now, honey, thank you.'

'Sank you, madam.'

She bobbed a little curtsy and trotted from the room. I felt compelled to watch her go. As the door closed I turned back to Lucy, finding her smiling to herself.

'Cute, hm?'

I smiled. 'Very.'

'She's a treasure, I love her. Drink your drink, you look as though you need it.'

'I do.' I took a swallow and winced. It was nine-tenths vodka.

'Too strong?' she smiled.

'No ... beautiful.'

'A drinking man.'

'Now and then.'

'Are you ... in a hurry to get somewhere?'

I shook my head. 'No, I've nowhere to go but bed ... I mean, back to the hotel. But what about you? I really am very sorry I'm so late. Am I keeping you up?'

She released a laugh. 'No, you're not keeping me up. I'm very glad you came.'

'Thank you. I nearly didn't get here at all.'

'Oh?' She raised a quizzical brow. 'Change of heart?'

'No, not at all. Force of circumstances. I've been locked in an attic for the last couple of hours.'

She spluttered in her drink and gasped, 'You've what!'

'True. I had a job this afternoon ... as a waiter at a private house party down on Charles Street. I was supposed to finish at seven o'clock. It wasn't until I got there that I discovered it was a reception for a gay wedding.'

She gasped again, then laughed aloud. 'My *God*, you're

joking!'

'No, really ... two fellas got married. Nice couple.'

'But what a shock for you!'

'Mm ... so so. It wasn't that that worried me – there was a spot of bother. One of the guests got a bit naughty.'

Her eyes crinkled. 'Poor you.'

'Oh, not sexy naughty. He got insanely jealous because he thought I was trying to pick up his boyfriend.'

'And ... were you?'

I laughed. 'What do you think?'

'It would very much surprise me – after what Dominique said about you.'

Aye, aye ... now we were getting to it. With that old lump throttling me again, I said, 'Oh ...? What did she say?'

She smiled smokily. 'Oh ... this and that. But go on – what happened?'

'Well, I was getting ready to leave at seven when five of them got nasty and insisted I wash all the dirty dishes up before I left. They threatened to beat me up if I didn't.'

'Good God ... unusual for gay people, isn't it?'

'Very. They were all pretty high, though.'

'So you did the dishes?'

'Nope – I ran ... but I couldn't make the front door, so I bolted upstairs and locked myself in a storeroom.'

'My God, you didn't ...!'

'I couldn't get out. They were waiting outside – planning to strip me and paint me all over with black gloss paint!'

She let out a whoop and slapped the cushion. 'No! Oh, you poor thing! Well, how did you finally get out?'

'I got mad enough to take them all on and stormed out wielding a big stick – but they'd gone, left the house. I'd been sitting up there for an hour and a half unnecessarily.'

'Oh, what a mean trick. Well, under those circumstances you're forgiven.' She swallowed another throatful and put down the glass, fitted another fag in the holder and leaned towards me.

'Light, honey?'

As I held the lighter towards her she touched my hand to steady it and raised her eyes in a teasing smile.

'Nervous?'

I nodded. 'A little.'

'Why?'

I shrugged. 'Well . . .'

'Think I'm going to eat you?'

I gave a laugh. 'I don't know.'

She lay back against the cushions and studied me for a moment. 'Tell me . . . what's with this Hire-A-Guy thing?'

'Pardon?'

'You don't look the type – an odd-job man.'

'Didn't Dominique tell you?'

'A little. You're broke, hm?'

'Well, pretty bent – I've got some money in England, but I'm not allowed to transfer it here. I'm waiting for an Australian pal to come back from Victoria, he's a pro tennis-player. He knows Toronto well and we're going to do the town together. So for a couple of weeks I thought I'd take this on, meet a few people and earn some money.'

'And get into a little trouble, too, by the sound of things,' she grinned. 'You seem to have a knack for it.'

I shrugged. 'It does seem that way. I certainly don't go looking for it, but it seems to find me all right.'

'Dominique told me about the trouble you had on the New York train. It sounded serious.'

I laughed. 'It was.'

'Tell me about it.'

I knew what she was doing, she was getting me relaxed, making me talk – so I talked . . . and became more relaxed. Half an hour and another drink later it was like I'd known her all my life. She was that kind of woman.

'Boy,' she smiled, shaking her head, 'things really do happen to you, don't they?'

I shrugged. 'I reckon they happen to most people if they knock around the world.'

'True. Do you . . . enjoy things happening to you?'

I grinned. 'It's better than dying of boredom.'

'Yes . . . infinitely. Well, there are one or two little things you can do for me if you'd like.'

'Certainly I'd like – if you're sure I *can* do them.'

A smile as she tipped the glass to her lips and emptied it. 'I think you can. How'd you like to get me another drink for a start? And get one for yourself.'

'Thank you.'

I picked up the glasses and went to the cupboard, and while my back was turned she asked, 'Do you . . . play games, Russ?'

I damn near dropped the bottle. Aye aye, I thought – here we go again. I half-turned, finding her draped over the arm staring at me. 'What ... sort of games, Mrs. Koeller-Jurling?'

'Now, ain't that one hell of a mouthful?' she laughed. 'You'd better call me Lucille. I mean games – like football, tennis, squash ...'

'Oh ...' I shook my head. 'No.'

'You surprise me. You have an athletic build.'

'Thank you.'

I returned with the glasses, but before I could sit down she asked, 'Know anything about hi-fi sets?'

'Hi-fi ...? Not too much – a little.'

She nodded across the room to a magnificent piece of scrolled furniture.

'That thing refuses to work. Think you could take a look at it?'

'I'll certainly have a look.'

She swung her legs off the couch and stood up, shook back her long blonde hair and headed across the lounge, swaying gently. I'd been right about the figure, it was perfect, undulating in all the right places, the satin of her gown running smoothly and excitingly over the firm neat mound of her bottom.

'Do *you* play games, Lucille?' I called after her and she turned on the walk and threw me a devilish grin.

As I joined her, she went into a crouch at the side of the stereogram, the gown moulding tightly around her slender thighs and parting temptingly above the knee.

'What ... d'you think's the matter with it?' I asked, dragging my eyes from the gap and crouching beside her.

'I don't know. Last night it was playing fine, tonight it refuses.'

I slid the doors open and had a look inside, conscious of her closeness and her perfume. Not really knowing what I was doing and not caring while she was this close, I switched on the set, worked the auto mechanism, watched the arm descend on to the record and winced at the wretched scratching that ensued.

The fault was not difficult to find. There was no stylus in the head.

'Uh huh,' I murmured, sounding like a brain surgeon discovering the cause of a mystifying paralysis. I went inside, had a look around and found the little devil lurking in a corner. Seizing it between finger and thumb I withdrew and held it up to her. 'The culprit.'

'What is it?'

'Your stylus.'

She chuckled. 'You know I never knew I had one. How thrilling.'

'Everyone should have a stylus.'

'Do ... you have one?' she asked, mock-innocently.

'Certainly. How else can I make music?'

'True.'

I pulled off the head, slid the diamond in and replaced the head. A moment later dreamy late-night music came slithering out of the speakers.

'My hero,' she announced. 'Oh, I'm going to enjoy having you around the house.'

I shrugged modestly. 'It was nothing, really. I just happen to have a doctorate in stylus replacing.'

'Really,' she smiled, getting to her feet. 'And how about dancing – do you happen to have a doctorate in that, too?'

Her arms came up and in I slid, my insides erupting at the touch of her slender, satin-clad body, so warm and lithe.

'You're trembling,' she smiled, her cheek lightly against mine and the perfume of her hair making a terrible mess of my composure.

'Yes,' I gulped.

'Why?'

'You really don't know ...?'

She chuckled warmly in my ear. 'Tell me ... what went through your mind when I telephoned?'

'Well, I ...'

'Be honest, now.'

'Well, I ... took it at face value,' I lied. 'Dominique knew I was looking for work and I thought she was trying to help.'

She eased away and gave me an old-fashioned look. 'Come on, now ... you mean to say you didn't wonder what sort of a bird I was ... whether I was bored ... lonely ... frustrated? Can you honestly say you didn't weigh up the possibility of taking me to bed ...?'

'I ...' I was stunned by her forthrightness.

'Of course you did,' she laughed, settling back into position, seemingly satisfied now the air had been cleared. 'It's a situation every man dreams of, isn't it – the lonely, frustrated divorcee deprived of physical comfort?'

'Well, yes ...' I croaked. 'Erm ... *are* you divorced?'

'No.'

'Oh.'

She laughed gaily. 'Relax. Mister Koeller-Jurling is not going to walk through the door any moment – he's in South Africa ...'

'Oh.'

'And has been for six months.'

'Oh?'

'You're still not relaxed. Come on, loosen up.'

'It has nothing to do with your husband ... it's you. You've got me tied in knots.'

She broke away, laughing. 'You're very sweet. Dominique was right – you are fun. Come on, let's have another drink ... take your jacket and tie off.'

She slipped my coat off and threw it on to a chair, then resumed her pose on the couch while I got my tie off and sat again in the armchair.

'You liked Dominique?' she asked, reaching for a cigarette. I lit it for her, then one for myself, feeling the need.

'Very much,' I said, then added, 'very much.'

'Do you find us at all alike?'

'Very.'

'In what ways?'

'In many ways – style ... manner. You're both very forthright, I'll say that.'

She laughed. 'It saves a lot of time. You find it off-putting?'

'Not in the least. I find it very exciting.'

'Spoken like an enlightened lover. Well, so far we'll give Dominique ten out of ten. Tell me ... why do you really think I phoned you and invited you over?'

I shrugged, not too sure how to answer. 'Because you were intrigued ...?'

'And because I was lonely?'

'No. I'd be surprised if either you or Dominique ever get lonely. I'm sure there's a plethora of rich, handsome men only too ready to ... pop in and chat.'

She laughed brightly. 'Pop in and chat,' she repeated. 'So – if you don't believe we get lonely – how about bored?'

'Oh, yes, I can believe that. You're obviously both extremely wealthy ... you don't *have* to work for a living – so I imagine it's very easy for you to get bored ...'

'I'm enjoying you, you know that?'

The sudden earnestness of her manner stopped me cold.

'I ... well, thank you.'

'Shall I tell you *why* I'm enjoying you ...? Because you *are* fun ... and because you're nice ... and you're not on the make ... and also because you're the first man to set foot in this house for six ... long ... months.'

'I ... really?'

She nodded. 'Really. And you are also the first man I've been able to drink with ... laugh with ... relax with for six long months ...'

'Oh ...'

'And shall I tell you why?'

'Yes ... please ...'

'Because I am being watched, night and day, that is why. And if I am caught in the company of a man during the next three months – before my divorce comes through – well ... it could be *very* disastrous for me.'

'Oh.'

She released a slow, smouldering smile. 'How would you feel if you didn't talk to a girl for six long months?'

I laughed. 'I'd be climbing up the wall. Wow ... and is your husband doing this to you?'

She nodded emphatically. 'He's doing it. He is doing his damnedest to come up with one shred of evidence that he can use as a counter-claim. Fortunately I learned that he is having me watched, round the clock – in this house, when I go out, everywhere, and I have taken the utmost precautions not to be seen with another man since the day he walked out.' Her smile came again, 'Naturally it is taking its toll ...'

'Naturally.'

'... and when Dominique told me about you ...' she laughed, 'well, it was too good to be true! You have a perfect right to be in the house. You're employed by Hire-A-Guy, aren't you?'

'Certainly, I am,' I grinned.

'Certainly, you are. And for as long as you want to stay you will be doing odd jobs around the house for me, will you not?'

'Certainly, I will.'

'Right! And the first job I want you to do for me ... is dance with me. I haven't danced in a *very* long time.'

She held out her hand to me. I came to my feet, brought her to hers, and once more we were locked in zinging juxtaposition.

'Oh, that is ... lovely,' she sighed. 'How good is the feel of a real, live man ...'

'Real live girls aren't so bad, either.'

'You dance so well.'

'This is dancing?'

We hadn't moved an inch.

'The kind *I* prefer,' she said dreamily, snuggling in even closer. 'We match pretty well, hm?'

'All the way down. You ... feel awfully good.'

'I do?'

'And smell awfully good.'

'So do you – like a man.'

'I'm afraid that if we do this much longer ...'

'Mmm ...?' she murmured sleepily.

'I ... I'll have to kiss you.'

She raised her head from my shoulder, regarded me for a pensive moment with heavy-lidded eyes, then placed her lips very softly on mine. Next thing we were devouring each other.

For three or four minutes we kept up this hysterical bash then she finally broke away, gasping, staring wildly, her breasts heaving under the satin gown.

'My God, I feel faint ...'

'Would you like to sit down?'

'Sit! I'll have to lie down!' She laughed quickly and shook her head. 'Phew! I must be out of practice. *You're* obviously not. Do you have a doctorate in kissing, too?'

She came in close again, panting, murmuring, 'My God, what have you *got* down there?'

'I'm sorry ...'

'Don't you *dare* apologize. It's ... it's been longer than I realized. You really got to me, you know that? You really had me going just now.'

'I'm very glad. I don't have to tell you what you're doing to me.'

'No,' she chuckled, 'no, that's plainly obvious. Tell me ... have you ever had a Turkish bath?'

'Mm . . .? No, I never have.'

'Would you like one?'

'Where . . .? You mean *here*?'

She nodded. 'Hm hm . . . come on, bring the drinks.'

I followed her out of the room and up the staircase to a room off the main landing, a fabulous bedroom with a huge silk-draped four-poster bed. A door on the far side led into a bathroom, another Hollywood set not unlike Dominique's, but in white and gold and with the Olympic-size bath set in the floor, not on a raised dais.

Moving quickly, she crossed to another door that led into a dressing room, complete with massage bed, already prepared with snow-white towels. And from this room she entered yet a fourth door, releasing billows of steam as she opened it. She closed it again quickly and came back to me.

'It's all ready.'

'In there, hm?'

'In there.'

'What do I do?'

She laughed. 'Well, first off it's advisable to get undressed.'

'Er . . . yes . . .'

'So, while you're doing that, I will fill the bath. Just go right in and sit on the lowest tier, I'll join you.'

'Right.'

Laughing to herself, she went back into the bathroom and a moment later I heard water gushing into the bath.

Quickly I stripped, hung up my clothes, opened the door and slipped inside – straight into a scalding London pea-soup fog. My God, it must have been two thousand centigrade in there. Arms outstretched I stumbled across the duck-boards, located a wooden tier, picked up a bathtowel and sat down, wondering who in his right mind would sit here for pleasure.

Already I was cascading with sweat, fighting for my breath, half afraid to breathe in case I scalded my lungs. I tell you, I was near to panic in there, and if it hadn't been for the knowledge that people did this all the time for the betterment of their health (impossible to believe), I'd have been out of there before you could say dripping.

'You all right?' Her voice came from the direction of the door, ethereally, on drifts of red-hot mist.

'I think I'm shrinking!'

'Stay with it, the panic will pass. I'm coming in right now.'

'Don't be long – there's not much of me left!'

Her laughter echoed through the room. There was a few moments silence, the door opened, closed, then a shadowy figure, draped in a huge white towel, emerged through the steam.

'Is that you?' I asked.

She laughed. 'Who else? How's it going?'

'Rapidly. Now I know what a lump of lard in a hot pan feels like.'

'It's good for you – sweats out all the impurities.'

'That's what I'm afraid of. Take those away and there's nothing left.'

She bent down and kissed me on the nose then sat beside me. 'Fun, huh?'

'Great. Next time let's go the whole hog and sit in the central heating furnace. You ... wouldn't happen to have a cigarette on you, would you?'

'Oh, very droll. Look – over there!'

She pointed over to my right. I turned, peered through the steam, seeing nothing. I turned back to her. She'd gone!

'Hey ...!'

I looked all around, now heard a slight movement above and behind me.

'Up here!' she called, way up on the highest tier.

I turned to look and woomf! got her towel in the face.

'I'm lying down!' she said.

So she was – stark naked. I couldn't see much, just a drooping arm, the curve of her left thigh and the mound of her breast, but it was enough to start the hammers going again.

'Why don't you throw that old towel away and come on up?' she drawled. 'It's warmer up here.'

'It may get a damn sight warmer still if I do.'

'I love the heat.'

With a grin I discarded the towel, told Herc to behave himself, climbed on to the tier I'd been sitting on, then knelt on the tier above, which brought me face-to-face with a very naked body.

'Hi,' she smiled, turning her head.

I gulped.

'Go ahead – look if you want to.'

I did, breaking out into an even greater sweat that had nothing to do with the steam heat.

'You ... may also touch if you want to,' she murmured softly, looking at me very intently.

Tentatively I placed my hand on her leg then very delicately ran it up her thigh and over her firm, flat belly, smoothing the moisture from her skin. Round and round and round ... she flinched as my fingers entered the perimeter of her thick, dark pubic bush and her thighs contracted in a spasm of pleasure. Up now to her breasts which were rising and falling quickly, their bright pink nipples standing high and hard in readiness.

'Lucy,' I whispered, breathless with excitement, 'you are really something to see ... to touch ... to taste.' Then I lowered my head and took her left nipple gently between my teeth.

She released a pent-up gasp. 'Oh, Russ ...!' A tiny, plaintive whimper ... she rolled her head, arched her body, took my hand, murmuring breathlessly, 'Oh ... oh ... ohh!' as she twisted, writhed, thrust hard against my hand, then with an erupting cry flung herself against me, clung to me, jerking and quivering, until, with a long-drawn, satisfied sigh she relaxed, went limp against me and slowly uncoiled until once more she was lying on her back, smiling wistfully, shaking her head.

'Good?' I laughed.

'*Beauti*ful,' she murmured sleepily. 'Just beautiful ... that didn't take long, hm?'

'About twenty seconds.'

'My God, I needed that ... I've been storing that one up for a very long time.'

'Got any others?'

She nodded, still breathing hard. 'I reckon one or two. I never was a one-time gal – not if *I* could help it.'

'I'll do my best.'

She laughed. 'You know, I've got a feeling your best will do just fine.'

Recovering swiftly, she rolled on to her side and peered over the edge of the tier. 'Now ain't you in a mess!'

'Somewhat.'

She came into a sitting position, her legs over the side, parted around me. 'Stand up.'

I did.

'My God ...' she chuckled, taking me gently in both hands and caressing me with feathery fingers. 'Nice?'

'Fabulous,' I croaked.

'I'd almost forgotten what they looked like.'
'Almost,' I grinned.
'Oh! I don't believe it ...'
'What?'
'The brute's growing even bigger! Come on, you'd better cool down or you won't get through the door!'
She skipped down the tiers and out of the door. Feeling a trifle absurd in my condition I followed. As I reached the massage room I heard a splash as she entered the water and in two ticks I was standing poised on the edge, about to plunge.
'Oh, I wish I had a camera!' she hooted. 'One thing you'll never be short of is a place to hang your hat!'
'Very funny.'
Splash!
'YOOOOWWWW!' I howled. The water was freezing cold! 'OOOH! OOWWW! WOW! Geez, what a dirty trick!'
'Oh, did I forget to tell you!' she laughed.
'God, I'll get pneumonia!'
'Ha ha!' she pointed. 'How are the mighty fallen! That brought him down in a hurry.'
Splot! She slung a sponge at me, hitting me in the chest. I made a flying lunge at her, missed and went to the bottom, came up spluttering. She was already out and running dripping for the massage room.
'Come out of there, you'll catch pneumonia!'
Shivering and turning blue, I clambered out. Herc was nowhere in sight. What a disgrace. I ran into the parlour, finding her wrapped in a big warm towel.
'He he!' she chuckled. 'And who's a big boy now?'
'Just you wait,' I threatened, grabbing a towel to cover both my shame and a skinful of goosepimples. 'Aw, I'm freezing.'
'Do you the world of good. In a few minutes you'll be glowing.'
'I should live so long.'
'Come – dry my back.'
I hobbled over, let the towel drop and began on her.
'Feeling better?' she asked.
'That was an extremely dirty trick. I have a natural aversion to any temperature below eighty.'
'You'll be warm in no time – I have the remedy. You may massage me.'
'That'll get *me* warm?'

'You'll see.'

She turned to me, pecked me on the nose and nodded at a wall cupboard. 'You'll find some oil in there.'

By the time I'd collected it she was lying on the table on her tum – naked.

'You don't need much, just a touch. I don't want to be sliding out of bed all night.'

I poured a drop into the palm of my hand and moved close to her. Suddenly, perhaps because the hilarity was over, her nakedness once more stirred me, the feel of her velvet skin becoming a matter of conscious, sensual pleasure.

I began in the small of her back and moved outwards in gentle circles, spreading the oil thinly up over her shoulders and down again to her lovely bottom, then on again down each leg to her feet. Having covered her totally, I then returned to her waist and began working on her spine, massaging upwards and outwards in small, firm circles.

'Hey ...' she murmured sleepily, 'you're pretty good back there. Where did you learn to massage?'

'I once had a girlfriend who was a physiotherapist. She used to do me for hours for practice.'

'And vice versa, I'll bet,' she laughed.

'No comment. Where did you get your fabulous tan?'

'Miami.'

'No bikini stripes, I note.'

'Of course not. Dominique and I wouldn't be seen dead with them.'

'Of course not. Tell me, where do you sunbathe in the altogether down there?'

'At Dominique's place.'

'That must give the locals a thrill.'

'It does. We charge them a spectator fee – make enough to pay the rent.'

'You're very good friends, aren't you?'

'The best. We like the same things.'

I grinned. 'So I noticed.'

I continued working down her body, paying particular attention to her thighs which produced a complexity of shivers, jumps, sighs and groans depending on how close I got to what.

'Watch it,' she muttered.

'I am. Don't fall asleep on me, now.'

'You're kidding.'

A little light pummelling on her calves, half a minute of each foot and this side was done. I slapped her on the bottom. 'Right – turn over.'

She raised herself up on her elbows and peered at me through her hair. 'I don't trust you.'

'Who – me? Whatever gave you that impression?'

'That!' she nodded. 'Quite his old perky self again, isn't he?'

'Turn over,' I grinned. 'I promise to be good.'

'In that case what's the point?'

Smiling, she flipped over and started my motor running again. I poured a drop more oil into my hand and delicately applied it to her stomach, then once again began working in small, slow-drawn circles, upwards towards her breasts, not touching them but teasing her by touching everything else. Now a fleeting contact with her nipples, a soufflé touch with the palms of both hands that brought them up instantly, hard as football studs.

Her eyes shot open. 'You're wicked!'

'Evil.'

For a while longer I worked round them, avoiding them, then nipped in for a quick tweek that made her shudder and tightened all the muscles in her stomach.

'You ... devil!' she gasped. 'You don't know what that *does* to me!'

I grinned down at her. 'I think I do. And I know what this does to you ...'

I went in for keeps, capturing each between a finger and thumb and teasing them into full extent.

'Ohhh ...!' She brought up her knees, made fists of her hands, gasped, 'Don't ... don't!' but meant 'Do ... do!' Squirming deliciously, she shot her legs out straight, braced together, taut as mooring cables, then continued to writhe, roll, gasp, and moan as another big something boiled up within her and came rushing to the surface. Now, really not knowing what she was doing, she threw an arm around my waist and pulled me close, then abandoned my waist and dropped her hand, grabbed Herc and squeezed him unmercifully as she rushed towards her climax.

'Ohh ... Ohhh ... OHHHH!' She curled into a tight ball, her face pressed into my stomach, kissing and pecking furiously anything that caught her fancy, then she was once more over the hill and sliding down the other side.

As she reached the bottom she released me and rolled on to her back, staring up at me with bright, laughing eyes and a shake of the head, panting, 'You're one *heck* of a masseur, you know that? You're going to kill me!'

'You want me to stop?'

'You want a broken leg! *Oh*, boy ... I reckon it was worth waiting six months for this. Right – you now have a permanent job ... at a hundred thousand dollars a year. Come on ...' she sat up and slid to the floor, still panting, 'now I'm going to do you.'

I climbed on to the table, face down, finding it somewhat difficult with Herc in full bloom.

'Don't be ridiculous,' she said. 'Turn over.'

I did, feeling a trifle conspicuous.

She tipped some oil into her hand and slapped it on my belly, making me laugh, then quickly smeared my chest, slowing as she recrossed my stomach and continued heading south.

'Vive la difference,' she murmured, shaking her head at him, then caught him in both hands and sent me through the roof with an exquisite caress.

'Nice?' she whispered.

'Awful,' I croaked. 'I'll give you ... exactly four years to stop.'

Suddenly she did stop, her expression changed, earnest. 'Russ ...' she held out her hand and took mine, '... come.'

Almost dragging me off the table, she led me out of the door, across the bathroom and into the bedroom. There, hurling back the silk coverlet, she leapt on to the bed, turned on to her back and reached for me, drew me over her and took me instantly, omitting a mournful moan and erupting into a fury, a veritable *avalanche* of bucking thrusts that brought us both to wild, frenzied climax in no time at all.

'Ohh, God ... GOD!' she howled, gripping my back and driving up into me time and time again, and for a full minute more we bounced and lunged around the bed until, with a great, rushing gasp she collapsed beneath me, groaning and 'ohh!-ing' and rolling her head, and there we lay, her arms tight around me, everything slowly coming to an exhausted and supremely satisfied halt.

For a long, breathless time we lay there, the oil of our bodies mingling warmly and deliciously, letting exhaustion take us and wallowing in floaty nothingness.

'That ...' she murmured weakly, 'is as it should always be.'

'It certainly doesn't come any better.'

'I could sleep for a year.'

'Two.'

She laughed, a low, sexy chuckle. 'No wonder Dominique sounded happy on the phone. I'm just amazed she went to Miami ... *aw*fully glad she did, though.'

She rolled over me and kissed the end of my nose. 'How long did you say you were staying in Toronto?'

I shrugged. 'A couple of weeks.'

'Hmm.' She smiled, thoughtfully.

'Why?'

'Oh, I was just wondering ...'

'What?'

'How I'm going to find enough jobs around the house to keep you steadily employed for two weeks.'

I laughed and patted her bottom. 'I'm not a very quick worker, you know.'

'Ha! You're joking!'

'I reckon the attic would take at *least* three days to tidy.'

'You do, hm?'

'At least. And what other jobs did you have in mind?'

'Oh, I'll think of something. One thing, though ...'

'What's that?'

'I don't want you to be out of pocket on this. If you weren't coming here you'd be earning money somewhere else.'

'True. O.K., I'll take the money – but on one condition ...'

'What's that?'

'That I really do the work for you.'

She smiled and nodded. 'O.K., it's a deal.'

'I think it's time I went, don't you? If the house *is* being watched ...'

'Yes, you're right.'

'What time shall I be here tomorrow?'

'Oh ... say ten o'clock. Russ, I won't be here during the day.'

'You won't?'

'No, I'll go out. I want to make it appear as though you're really working here. I'll get back around four o'clock.'

'All right ...'

We got dressed and went down to the hall, Lucy turned to

me and said, 'Let's do the thing properly, I'll get Brigitte to see you out.'

She came close and kissed me lightly. 'See you tomorrow around four. Get plenty of sleep, hm?'

'You bet.'

She walked into the lounge, pressed a wall bell, slipped me a wink and closed the door.

A moment later a door on the opposite side of the hall opened and out came the delectable Brigitte, patting her hair into place.

'Ah, you are leaving, monsieur?'

I gave a cough. 'Er, yes, Brigitte, but I'll be back tomorrow morning at ten. I have some jobs to do.'

'Ah, that is nice,' she smiled, giving me the eyes. 'You are coming ... just tomorrow?'

'No ... for a few days, I think. Mrs. Koeller-Jurling has ... a number of things she wants done.'

'No doubt,' she giggled. 'There are so *many* things in a house that only a man can do, non?'

'Er, yes, I suppose you're right.'

'Per'aps madam would allow you to do a leetle somesink for me while you are 'ere. I 'ave a lamp in my room zat does not work. It is such a nuisance because wizout it I cannot read in bed. I sink per'aps I ask madam – provided, of course, zat you are willing to do it for Brigitte.'

I grinned at her. 'I'd love to do it for you.'

' 'Ow kind.'

'Not at all. Any time.'

She swung her hips to the door and opened it for me. 'Bon soir, monsieur. See you in ze morning.'

'You certainly will,' I said and exited, whistling.

CHAPTER THIRTEEN

I awoke at nine, a couple of minutes before my switchboard alarm call was due, and skipped out of bed feeling full of beans. I'd slept like a felled log for a solid eight hours and felt fitter than Superman.

Crossing to the window, I flung back the curtains. It was

snowing like fun, but I hardly saw it. My mind was on other matters.

A quick pause at the wardrobe mirror to inspect my general condition, then a leap across the room with balletic grace to answer the phone.

'Your call for nine,' drawled the female operator.

'Lovely. And how are you this bright and beautiful morning?'

There was a stunned pause. 'Have you seen out yet – it's blowin' a blizzard!'

'Nevertheless, it is still a bright and beautiful morning.'

'Anythin' you say, Room 486 ...'

'Tell me, how does one set about acquiring a pot of tea and some toast in this salubrious establishment?'

'Mostly by just askin' for it. I'll put you through to Room Service.'

'You are too kind. Have a nice day, now.'

'Oh, it's gonna be a lulu, I just know it.'

She clicked off and Room Service came on. I ordered tea and toast then plunged into the shower and was singing so heartily I didn't hear breakfast arrive. It was there when I emerged.

Ah, Buzz, I thought, sitting by the window, nibbling a slice of under-done brown and watching the traffic struggling through the snow, if you knew what you were missing back here you'd pack your racquet and hit the first plane back. What a situation to fall into – pleasuring a lovely piece of grumble like Lucy Koeller-Jurling *and* being respectably paid for it *and* having the pleasure of the daytime company of that cute little pot of French mustard, Brigitte who, if the truth were known, I would have the greatest difficulty refusing if she ever got around to asking me.

Lucy ... and Brigitte. The thought of them quite spoilt my appetite for toast, so I swallowed a cup of Rosy and checked my watch.

It was time to go.

Feeling three queens to a pair of twos, I collected the Caddy, rolled it out of the garage and headed for Rosedale, a Christmas candlelight in the virgin snow. Into Lucy's driveway I swirled, noting her exiting tyre tracks in the snow, the old ticker beginning to quicken as I approached the front door and gave the chimes a going over.

The familiar, shivery silhouette of Brigitte approached and opened the door, quite taking my breath away. By George, she really looked something this morning, almost dressed in a blue uniform, so short at the hem and plunging at the neck that I could see a good nine inches of leg and seven-tenths of a most delightful pair of knockers.

'Bon jour, monsieur!' she beamed. 'Pliz come in. What a dreadful day.'

'How can it be dreadful when it starts with such a vision of loveliness?' I said, pouring it on a bit.

'La, what nice things you say.'

I stepped in and took off my coat. 'Mrs. Koeller-Jurling has gone, hm?'

'Oui, she left just a few minutes ago. I 'ave a letter for you.'

'Letter?'

'A leetle note from madam. I go get it for you.'

I watched her go, grinning at her sexy little wiggle. She was back immediately, handing me an envelope.

'Here you are, monsieur. Would you like a cup of coffee before you start?'

'Start?'

'In ze bedroom,' she grinned. 'We start in ze bedroom.'

'Terrific ... er, yes, please, I'd love one.'

'Come zis way. We shall have it in ze kitchen.'

Kitchen ... bedroom ... anywhere you like, love – maybe both!

I followed her through into a superb modern kitchen, all stainless steel and gleaming Formica, and sat on a stool at the peninsula unit.

While Brigitte busied herself pouring the coffee, I slid out the note and read it. It said, 'Good morning. Trust you slept well? Gave more thought to our discussion and feel you ought to be *seen* to work here. Brigitte has the details. Please feel free to avail yourself of her help. I'm sure she'll be only too willing. I believe you've made a second conquest. Till four. L.P.S. Swallow this note.'

I laughed out loud, got out my lighter, set fire to the paper and threw it in the ashtray.

'It was funny?' asked Brigitte, placing a mug of steaming coffee in front of me and sliding on to a stool opposite, showing me another tenth of her very generous charlies in the process.

'Thank you, that's lovely. So you don't know what was in the note?'

She shook her head.

'It said that you know all about the jobs I have to do ... and that I can ask you to help me with them.'

'Ah, oui, bon!' she beamed. 'I would like zat. So – we start in ze front bedrooms – cleaning all ze windows!'

'Windows? Oh, now, that's a surprise, Lucy ... er, madam didn't say anything about windows. Still ...' I shrugged, 'it's quite all right. Then what?'

'Zen we fix a curtain rail – also in ze front bedroom.'

'What's the matter with it?'

She gave a secretive grin. 'Nossink – you just pretend to fix it.'

'Mm?'

She leaned closer, showing me yet another tenth of her beauties. There was only one-tenth to go and it was getting very hard to concentrate on what she was saying. 'Zere is a man watching ze 'ouse – you know?'

'Well, sort of. Madam did say last night she thought ...'

'Ah, so! Well, it is true. So she is being ver' careful. She is out when you arrive ... and you work in ze front of ze 'ouse to show him zat you are here to work and not for anysink else.'

She gave a little giggle and sipped her coffee, raising her eyes sexily at me over the rim.

'Erm,' I said, putting on the big dumb act, 'I don't quite follow, Brigitte ... what else *could* I be here for?'

'Haw,' she went, eyes a-twinkle, 'so innocent. You sink I don't know what you did to madam last night?'

'Eh ...?' I could feel myself blushing under her teasing grin. Dammit, the minx knew everything!

'I tell you – my room is next to madam's and I hear every-sink,' she laughed. 'And madam looked so 'appy when I took in her breakfast zis morning.'

'Did she now?' I said, finding it hard not to smile.

'Ah, oui, very 'appy.'

'And how come you just happened to *be* in your room at the time, Brigitte ... you were downstairs when I left.'

'Well, I ... I can be in my room anytime I like!'

'You were listening purposely,' I accused her. 'You're a

naughty girl.'

''Ow can I 'elp but hear – you make so much noise! I sink you must be a ver' good lover, non?'

'Drink your coffee,' I grinned.

'Shall I tell you what I was sinking while I was listening to you and madam making such big love . . .?'

Blimey, the little devil was getting me going!

'Now, Brigitte . . .' I tried to pick up my coffee, but my hand was shaking and I spilled it, making her laugh.

'I shall tell you what I was sinking, Monsieur Russ . . . I was sinking that maybe you could fix the reading lamp in my bedroom today, non?'

'Brigitte, you're a very naughty girl.'

'Ah, oui,' she agreed, 'when I get ze opportunity.'

I had to cough to clear my throat. 'I . . . think we'd better get on with those windows – I mean I'd better get on with those windows.'

Her eyes widened. 'You mean you don't want me to 'elp you? Madam did say . . .'

'I know what madam said.'

'Then you *must* let me 'elp you.'

'You . . . stay down here and get on with your work.'

'But I 'ave no work to do – it is all done!' Her eyes crinkled disarmingly. 'I work very 'ard before you come and finish it.'

I laughed and shook my head at her. 'By golly, you've got it all worked out, haven't you?'

'Ah, oui. I want to enjoy a nice, funny day wiz you.'

'It'll be funny all right.'

'You make madam laugh – so you make me laugh also. In fact . . . *every*sink you make madam do, you make me do, non?'

'Brigitte, you're not just naughty, you're downright wicked!'

'But you like me . . . just a *leetle* bit, hm?'

'You know darned well I do. Come on, let's get those windows done.'

'Ah, yes – madam says for you to wear white coveralls when you work in front of ze 'ouse – make you look more like a workman – O.K.?'

'Yes, all right.'

'I get zem for you.'

She spun off the stool and went to a long cupboard, took

out the coveralls. 'I will fill a bucket wiz water while you put zem on . . . zen we go upstairs.'

Dammit, she made even washing windows sound like a potential orgy.

I climbed into the coveralls, but my mind wasn't on it – not while she was stretching across the sink to fill the bucket, the hem of her mini-mini outfit riding up almost to her waist. She shut off the taps and turned quickly, catching me looking, then smiled, knowing exactly what she'd been showing me. 'You carry it upstairs for me?'

'Of course.'

I heaved the bucket out of the sink and followed her into the hall, stopping at the foot of the stairs. 'After you,' I suggested.

'Merci,' she smiled.

Up she went, her cute little bum swinging like a metronome. I gave her six stairs lead then followed. Oh, brother. It was all so delightful I slackened pace to an eight-stair lead and got so bewitched I tripped up a stair and slopped some water.

Breathless, and not from the climb, I reached the landing and followed her round to a lovely bright bedroom at the front of the house.

'Nice,' I said. 'Whose room is this?'

'No one's – it is a spare room. I wish it was mine. Don't you sink zat is ze most deliciously comfortable-looking bed?'

'Yes, I sink,' I said, averting my eyes and heading for the windows.

I soaked the leather, wrung it out and started, at the same time having a look outside for the guy who was supposed to be watching the house. There were a few snow-covered cars parked along the street, but I couldn't see anyone in them. Perhaps he was quite a way off, watching through binoculars. Then again maybe he'd taken off after Lucy when she left the house.

'How long have you worked for madam?' I asked Brigitte.

She came up close and leaned languidly against the wall, arms folded, emphasizing her cleavage. 'Three years.'

'That long, hm. You obviously know her very well?'

'Ah, oui, I do.'

'And her husband?'

'Yes,' she scoffed, 'I certainly knew him.'

'What's he like?'

'He is a peeg.'

'You didn't have to think twice about that one. Why is he a peeg?'

'Because he is rich and fat and rude and mean and sinks he is God.'

'Mm, that sounds enough to be going on with. So – madam is divorcing him for adultery?'

'She could divorce him a hundred times over for it.'

'Oh, bit of a lad, was he?'

'Ha! A *beeg* bit of a lad! No girl was safe when he was around.'

'Oh?' I grinned. 'He try it on with you?'

'Sheee!' she went. 'Everywhere! In ze kitchen ... ze dining room – even when I was serving at table! Oop! would go his hand.'

'Well,' I laughed, 'I can't say I altogether blame him. I'd be terribly tempted myself – especially if you were wearing that uniform.'

'So?' she smiled, her eyes softening again. 'Well, now, maybe I would not mind if *you* did.'

I cleared my throat and moved to the next window. 'So madam has really got to watch her step where men are concerned, hm?'

'Only for another two months and zen ze divorce will be through. But it 'as been ver' 'ard on her.'

'Oh? How so?'

'Because it has been going on for such a long time – for six long months. For all zat time she has not been able to go wiz another man – in case her 'usband also claims adultery.'

'Yes,' I agreed, 'six months is a very long time.'

She smiled. 'In madam's case it is an eternity. She is a ver' sexy woman, no?'

'And ... what would happen if madam *was* caught ... well ... entertaining a man?'

'She would stand to lose about two million dollars.'

I gaped at her. 'T ... two *million*? God Almighty ...'

'Monsieur is a ver' wealthy man,' she continued, somewhat unnecessarily.

'Two ... million ... dollars,' I muttered, absently wiping the last window. No wonder Lucy was taking pains to establish me as a workman.

'There,' I said, throwing the leather in the bucket. 'Do you think we've given whoever's out there a big enough eyeful of coveralls?'

'I sink so.'

'Right – on to the next room.'

Along we trotted and repeated the window washing, then I took down the curtain and pretended to fix the track.

'Two million dollars,' I said for the third time. 'Almost worth giving up sex altogether for, isn't it?'

'Almost,' she grinned. 'But not quite.'

'And how much would it take to induce *you* to give it up?'

'Monsieur ...' she cooed, 'zere is not so much money in ze whole world.'

'Hm hm,' I said, getting down from the chair. 'Well, if he hasn't seen me by now, he just ain't looking. You really think there's someone out there watching the house. I'd have thought he'd be following Madam?'

She shrugged. 'Maybe zere are *two* men watching – maybe *three*! Who knows? her 'usband would do anything to catch 'er.'

'Well, he's certainly got plenty of incentive,' I agreed. 'Right ... now what?'

'Now we can relax and do whatever we want – our duty is done.'

'And I hope it did madam some good. I'd rather die than be the cause of her losing two million dollars. Erm, what about this attic. Does it really need clearing out?'

She shrugged. 'Yes ... but it is a nasty, 'orrible job.'

'Shall we at least take a look at it?'

Again the shrug, very French. 'O.K.'

'Right – lead on.'

That was the place to keep, all right – right in front, especially while climbing the second flight of stairs. Up she went, reached a tiny landing, opened a small door and I followed her in, expecting a grim, musty, cobweb-strewn attic, but it wasn't that bad at all. It was a long, dormer-windowed room with a slanting ceiling and bare-wood floor, full of old junk.

I raised the lid of a big cardboard box, finding it full of carpet trimmings and odd lino tiles. 'The stuff people hoard,' I said. Another box contained ancient newspapers; yet another books. There were battered travelling trunks, a set of newer cases, golf clubs, a tailor's dummy, a big wicker laundry basket, an old wind-up gramophone and a stack of dusty 78s

... you name it, it was there.

'Does madam just want it cleaned up or cleared out, Brigitte?'

'Aw, just cleaned up, monsieur ... and all zis stuff stacked neatly by ze wall.'

'Well, that's not too difficult ... and, by the way, don't you think you'd better stop calling me "monsieur"? You know my name's Russ.'

She grinned. 'Russ ... O.K.'

I slapped my hands together. 'Right – where do we start?'

'Well ...' she had a little think about it, '... if you could move ze sings from zat end, I could wash ze floor ... zen you put ze sings back and stack everysink else around zem, non?'

'Sheer genius, yes. And what are we going to wash the floor with.'

'I shall get a scrubbing brush from downstairs. It needs a good scrub.'

'Right – you nip downstairs and I'll fill the bucket in the bathroom. It's too heavy for a delicate little thing like you.'

'Aw, you are too kind,' she smiled, creating a draught with her eyelashes again.

'It's a pleasure. It's really nice working with you.'

'And I wizz you, mon ... Russ.'

'Right, you pop off and get your brush – and, er, maybe you could make another coffee while you're at it, hm?'

'Mais, oui ... certainement. *Anysink* you want – all you have to do is ask.'

With a giggle she was off, singing happily all the way down to the hall, a girl of simple pleasures and lovely to be with.

I nipped down to the bathroom and refilled the bucket, then went back to the attic and began shifting the rubbish from one end to the centre of the floor, thinking how pleasurable the most mundane job can be when you're working with a cute little custard like Brigitte. Who notices the dust and debris when you've got legs and things like hers to think about?

I was struggling with a trunk of old clothes when she came in, carrying a tray with two coffees and a load of cleaning materials on it.

'Voilà! Deux cafés au lait!'

'Attagirl. I've cleared this end, you can start any time you like. But ... how are you going to scrub it? Haven't you got one of those long mop things?'

'A mop! Zat is no way to clean a floor. No, I shall scrub it wiz my 'ands.'

'What – down on your knees?' I frowned.

'Mais, certainement – what is wrong wiz zat?'

'Well ...' I shrugged, 'bit hard on the knees, love. Tell you what – I'll make a pad out of this old carpet.'

'Ah, you are so thoughtful.'

'Well, we can't have you ruining your lovely knees, can we?'

'You ... sink I have nice knees?' she asked demurely, inspecting them.

'I sink you've got fabulous knees – and fabulous everysink else, too. I've never seen a nicer pair of ... legs in my life.'

'What – never?' she chuckled.

'Not ever, no.'

'Mmm ...' she said thoughtfully, hoisting her skirt another six inches, 'per'aps zey are not so bad.'

'Er ... hey! how would you like some music while you work?'

'Music?'

I pointed to the old record-player. 'If it works.'

'Oh, zat old thing.'

'Well, we can give it a try ...'

I opened the lid, took out the handle, stuck it in the side, gave it a few turns and released the brake. 'Well, at least it goes round. Let's see what records there are.'

I sifted through them, blowing the dust off and squinting at the faded labels. 'Good lord ... Nat King Cole ... Benny Goodman ... Hoagy Carmichael ... Bing Crosby ... probably worth a fortune, these. Let's try Nat King Cole and "The Tunnel Of Love".'

I slid Nat on, fully wound the motor and lowered the forty-pound head on to the record ... and after a few scratchy revolutions out struggled the Nat's Trio, circa 1950.

'Ah, they don't make records like this any more,' I sighed.

'Sank 'eaven,' she laughed. 'It sounds as though they recorded it in a bathroom!'

'The tun-nel of lo-o-o-o-o-ve ...' I sort of sang along.

Brigitte winced, picked up the bucket, carried it to the far end of the room, threw down the pad and went down into kneeling position, her back to me. Then, giving the brush a good soak and soaping, she made a lunge for the corner, blowing my mind with an eye-boggling shot of just about everything she'd got.

'The tun-nel of lo-o-o-o-ve ...' warbled Nat. And you're telling me, I thought.

Well, out of decency I had to force me eyes away. I turned my full concentration on a heavy crate of books and wrestled it round the room ... but it was no good. Brigitte's delectable nether regions were simply not to be denied, and as though my eyeballs were attached to them by elastic they kept zinging back for another gawp.

Thing was – did she know she was showing them? Seemed impossible she didn't. Yes, I decided – she *had* to know, and if so – what was she trying to *do* to me?

I'll put it to the test, I thought. So, while she was at full stretch, I called out, 'What d'you fancy next?'

She didn't pull back into kneeling position but just stopped scrubbing and turned her head. 'Pardon?'

'I said ... what do you fancy next? What record?'

'Anysink you like – I leave it to you.'

'O.K. Erm ... how're your knees holding out?'

She grinned. 'My knees are just fine.'

I mean ... she just *had* to know what she was showing me!

'Good!' I gulped. 'I'll ... put another Nat Cole on.'

Oh, brother ...

She resumed scrubbing, the effort swinging her bottom from side to side, and I resumed ogling. Try as I might I could not drag my eyes away. She had me so flummoxed I shifted the same box of books fourteen times.

'Zere!' she said at last, chucking the scrubbing brush into the bucket. 'Now you can move the stuff back against ze wall.' She got to her feet. 'I give you a hand, non?'

I wondered where she had in mind.

'No, that's all right, Brigitte, you've done your bit.'

'No, no, zese trunks are 'eavy, I 'elp you.'

'Well, if you insist.'

We started with a metal-bound trunk, full of old office files. I took hold of a leather handle at one end, she took the other, having to bend down and blinding me with a full overhead shot of her charlies in the process.

'Right – on three,' I said. 'One ... two ... three ... up!'

She gave a mighty yank and the handle snapped. With a yelp of surprise she tottered back, the three buttons exploding on her uniform and the whole thing flying open to reveal her naked boobs and a tiny pair of virtually transparent panties.

'Oh!' I gasped, eyes like saucers.

'Oohh!' she cooed, gazing down as though she'd never seen it all before. 'Look what 'appened!'

By golly, I was looking.

Well, I expected her to take immediate and panicked action to cover them, but she didn't. She gazed down at herself for a moment longer then slowly raised smiling, completely unflustered eyes to me and said quietly, 'Per'aps you would like to fasten ze buttons, non?'

'Erm ...' Jeezus, my heart was thumping. 'Well ...'

'My 'ands are a leettle dirty ... do you sink you could ...'

'Well, I ...'

She advanced on me, smiling wickedly. 'Don't tell me ze great lover is actually shy ...?'

'Well, no ...'

'You did not sound too shy with madam last night.'

'Brigitte ...'

'Come – fasten ze dress for me ... I *dare* you.'

Well, put like that.

She came up very close, 'Please, cheri ... do it for Brigitte.' Her voice was low and throaty, as unsteady as mine.

'Brigitte, you're a very naughty girl ...'

'And you are a very naughty boy, non?'

'That's ... got nothing to do with it.'

'But it has *every*sink to do wiz it ...'

And then she was there and my hand was there, inside the dress, fondling her big, lush, plump, warm, juicy breasts, and she was leaning up against me with her eyes closed and her arms lightly around me, uttering little sounds of pleasure and really getting worked up, now working herself against my leg, hungry for it, her thighs parting around mine, and the heat was on and Herc was sitting up in bed like the alarm had just gone off, full of vim and vigour after a good night's sleep, wakey wakey rise and shine, boots and saddles, come to the cookhouse door boys, and now her arm was snaking up to lassoo my neck and down I went into a hot, moist limpid hungry mouth with an awful lot of grunting and grinding going on and now she was gasping, 'Come wiz me ... come!', taking my hand and pulling me out of the door and down the stairs and along the landing to a room next to madam's, a pretty little room with an enchanting floral bed and before you could say shoot we were ripping our clothes off and she was standing before me stark naked, a superb little specimen with wondrous legs and a heart of thick dark hair just where it ought to be and now she was up against me, hard, kissing my lips off and grinding into me, moaning and groaning, and scratching the skin off my back and doing all the things a red-hot lady does when she's got hold of a fella she fancies and suddenly we weren't there any more but lying on the bed, clasped in each other's arms, rolling and grinding, and stroking and squeezing and now she was flat on her back, legs akimbo, and I was in, in, clear through and up, and she was gasping and grunting, and bucking, and bouncing, and riving and thrashing, and gasping things in French I'd never heard and didn't understand and didn't need to understand because all that mattered was that she, we, us were having a fantastically beautiful, wonderful, incredible mutually whizzbangly stupendous time and she was coming ... oh, boy, was she coming! She let out a wail that started as a low, deep-down murmuring growl and suddenly erupted into a loud strident bellow that rattled the windows; and her arms and legs shot round me like barrel hoops, locking me in, driving me home, taking every last vestige of you-know-who who was surpassing his normally plentiful self and wondering how come he was getting so many birthdays in one week.

'Mon Dieux ... mon Dieux ... mon Dieux ...!' she was howling. 'C'est fantas*tique* ... fantastique ...! Aw, mon cher, vous êtes formidable ...! Oh ... Oh ... OHH!'

From which I gathered she was having rather a jolly time.

Suddenly she stopped, stared up at me, imploringly. 'You do somesink for Brigitte?' she gasped.

'Anything you like,' I grinned. 'It's all a very great pleasure.'

'You do it ... like ze stallion?'

I laughed. 'Oui – comme l'étalon.'

'Aw, mon petit, I love you!'

A quick scramble and she was on her knees, face buried in the pillow, ready for the off.

'Alors ...!' she cried, and 'OHHHH!' she gasped, 'Mon Dieux, that is ... fantas ... *tique*!'

'All right?'

'Ohhhh ... ohhhh ... you just don't *know*!'

And she was off again, out of the slips on greased heels, racing down the straight for a stupendous finish, me going neck and neck all the way with her, breasting the tape in a photo-finish with a mighty mutual roar, Brigitte clutching the pillow to shreds and yelling a running commentary in wild, hysterical French and finishing on a flurry of moaned, groaned, panted gasps and enough satisfaction to last her for at least an hour and a half.

'OooooohhhHHH!' She collapsed beneath me, taking me with her, to lie behind her, arms around her, to comfort and hold her. 'Aw ... mon cher, I sink you kill me.'

'I sink ... you kill me ... too,' I gasped.

'Better zan ... cleaning attics, non?' she chuckled.

'Better than anything else I can put a mind to,' I laughed. 'A truly lovely way to spend the day.'

'We have a leetle rest ... zen we do some more, hm?'

'Eh?'

'Work!' she laughed. 'Some more cleaning.'

'Oh! Oh, yes, we'll do some more of that.'

She took my hand to her breast and snuggled in. 'Merci beaucoup, monsieur.'

'And merci to you, too, love.'

'It is lovely to 'ave you 'ere. I wish you could stay always. Zen I could do my work in ze mornings and make love in ze afternoons, what do you sink of zat?'

'Fantastique,' I laughed. 'Only I don't think I'd get much work done for thinking about the afternoon. Also I don't think madam would go much on the idea.'

'Oh, I don't see why not – you would make love to her at night!'

'Help!' I laughed. 'Hey, hold on ...'

'I sink you could manage it.'

'And what d'you think madam would say if she knew I was doing this to you?'

She gave a shrug. 'She wouldn't mind.'

'You're kidding,' I laughed.

'Non, non, really ... she likes me to be 'appy. Anyway, why would she mind – provided you make her 'appy, too?'

'Well ...' There was no answer to that. 'You mean to say if she came in right now and saw us she wouldn't hit me with the nearest chair?'

'Of course not. Why should she? You are not 'er 'usband.'

'No, true, but ...'

'Madam is ver' broad-minded, believe me. She would not mind.'

Well, there was a turn up for the book. Tobin, I thought, what *have* you landed yourself this time? Ha! How very fitting that I should be working for Hire-A-Guy. Ah, Buzz, you just wouldn't believe it. Come to think of it I was having a bit of trouble believing it myself! Two lovely birds in one household, each not only fond of it, but downright *keen* on it! Unbelievable.

Lying there, all warm and cosy in Brigitte's bed, the snow driving against the window like it was jealous and wanted to get in, I did a bit of mental calculation, wondering if I could possibly stay the course for the next two weeks. Without doubt it would be a strain, but I reckoned that if I got a good night's sleep at the hotel and made sure the work wasn't too hard around the house I might just make it. Anyway, if it did get too much I could always beg a day off, say I had to get my hair cut or something, and rest up for twenty-four hours. Mm, it might just work at that.

Well, I started off as I intended to continue – by having an hour's kip right then and there, and when I woke up Brigitte was standing by the bed, fully dressed again (a mere figure of speech in that outfit) holding a tray. On it was a bowl of hot soup and a plate of chicken salad.

' 'ello, mon petit,' she grinned. ' 'ow are you feeling?'

'I'm feeling just lovely. How are *you*?'

'Merveilleux. I've brought you some lunch – we have to keep your strength up, non?'

'Absolutely imperative.'

'You eat zis all up – zen per'aps we do some more cleaning.'

'Certainly. But, Brigitte ...'

'Oui, mon cher?'

'I do not think it altogether wise that you continue wearing that tiny, tiny dress if we are to work in close co-operation.'

'Comment?' she cooed, all innocent.

'Come off it, you know precisely what it does to me.'

'You mean ... it disturbs you or somesink?'

'Ha!'

'O.K.,' she laughed, 'I change it.' She wiggled to the wardrobe and turned, giving me the eyes again. 'Though maybe I wear it again tomorrow, hm?'

'You do and see what you get.'

'I wear it tomorrow,' she nodded, opened the wardrobe, selected a pair of slacks and a thin white cotton shirt, threw them on the bed and in a flash was standing there in only a tiny pair of yellow panties.

'Brigitte . . .!' I gulped, spilling the soup.

'But you told me to take the dress off!' she protested, eyes like blue Dresden plates.

'Get dressed!'

Well, she did – and somehow managed to look even sexier in the trousers and shirt than she had in the dress!

'Zere – how is zat?'

'Brigitte ... you'll have to wear a bra, love, or I can *not* be held responsible for my actions.'

'Bra? But I have no bra.'

'No, that figures. Well, breathe out or something.'

She gave a giggle and headed for the door. 'Finish your lunch, I go to do some more work. I'll see you in ze attic.'

'I'll be there.'

I joined her half an hour later and despite the fact that we messed around an awful lot, playing the old records and teasing one another, we managed to get the floor scrubbed and all the old garbage piled at one end of the room.

It was about four o'clock and we were just finishing off when we saw the lights of a car sweep up the drive.

'That will be madam,' said Brigitte. 'She will be pleased wiz our work, no?'

'It certainly looks very nice.'

'Wait here, I call her.'

She went out on to the landing and shouted, 'We are up here, madam – in ze attic. Come up and see!'

My heart started thumping a bit as I heard Lucy's footsteps on the stairs and a moment later she entered, looking very dishy in a light fur coat, her hair done up in a neat chignon.

'Hi,' she smiled, puffing a bit. 'How'd it go?'

'Voila!' I said, presenting the room.

'I can hear Brigitte's been helping you,' she grinned. 'You'll be speaking fluent French in a week. Well ... you two did a marvellous job. You ... obviously work very well together.'

I coughed. 'Fine,' I said, avoiding Brigitte's twinkling eye.

'Well, I'm sure you need a shower and a drink, I know I do.'

'Rough day?' I enquired.

She laughed. 'Exhausting. You've no *idea* how much a massage takes out of you.'

'Oh, I wouldn't say that,' I grinned.

'Come on – you can use my shower.'

She went through the door. Brigitte, the devil, popped her head in and whispered, 'Bonne chance, monsieur! Now you begin the night shift!'

My God, what *had* I got in to!

Ten minutes later I was standing in Lucy's glassed-in shower, working up a good lather and pondering the wonderous vicissitudes of life, when I saw a squiggly figure approach the frosted-glass door. Lucy, I thought – and dropped the soap. I stooped to pick it up and the door opened. I rose – finding Brigitte there, grinning like a Parisian pussy-cat.

'Ah, mais vous etes *tres* prodigieux, mon chou.'

'Brigitte ...! What are you doing in here?'

'Looking at you, mon petit.'

'I know you're ... are you crazy, madam may come in!'

'Madam knows I'm in here wiz you,' she said snootily.

'She ... she does?'

'Mais, oui – she sent me here.'

'Eh?'

Oh, blimey – not the two of them together!

'Wiz zese!' she laughed, bringing two towels from behind her back and hanging them over the partition. 'Bonne toilette, monsieur! – See you downstairs!'

She closed the door and exited, singing. Mad bird.

She'd barely left the room when another shadowy figure approached the door. It was getting busier than Piccadilly Circus in there. The door opened and this time it was Lucy – naked as sin.

She game me a comical smile, a meaningful look up and down, then stepped in and closed the door. 'Hi,' she said, coming close for a big wet kiss, pressing herself against me, her face in the stream of water. 'Mmm, that's nice.'

'Which – me or the water?'

Her hand snaked down, making me jump. 'I've been thinking about you all day – while I was being massaged. I decided there's something about you I was missing, but I couldn't put my finger on it.'

'You're certainly making up for it now,' I murmured.

She broke away, took the soap from me and began lathering my shoulders. 'So – how was your day? How did you get on with Brigitte?'

'Oh ... fine,' I shrugged. 'She's a nice enough girl.'

'Hm hm ...' she went, covering my back. 'Do you ... find her attractive?'

'Mm ...? Yes, I suppose so ...'

'Sexy?'

I had to think about that one. Ha!

'Erm ... hadn't really thought about it to tell you the truth...'

'Liar!' she laughed, slapping me on the bottom. 'You've been in bed with her!'

I turned ... gaped. 'Wh ... who – me! Good God, Lucy, what d'you think I am!'

'We all *know* what you are,' she grinned. 'And even if you weren't, my darling maid certainly is. You'd be super-human to hold out more than an hour once she had her mind made up about you – which it was.' She laughed again and kissed me. 'I only hope she didn't exhaust you ... and *that's* an unnecessary observation because I can see she didn't. Did you have a sleep?'

'Well ...'

She kissed me on the nose. 'Good. Come on, let's get out of here before you dissolve. That ... would be a catastrophe.'

CHAPTER FOURTEEN

At ten sharp the next morning, dressed in my white coveralls for the benefit of Peeping Tom ... or George or whatever his sneaky name was, I hit the chimes on Lucy's door and was soon wallowing in Brigitte's radiant smile.

'Ah, bonjour Monsieur Odd Job Man, comment allez-vous?'

'I'm just lovely, Brigitte. Er ...' I paused in the doorway and pointed, for the benefit of our watcher, to the snow in the driveway, 'for the sake of appearances, how about me clearing the snow this morning?'

'What a good idea! Yes, you can clear it from there ... and there ... and over there ...'

'Hey, steady up, gal, I'm supposed to take things easy!'

She giggled and closed the door, flung her arms around me and kissed me. ' 'ello, 'ow did you sleep?'

'Like a babe – and, by golly, I needed to. Between you and madam you had me on my knees last night.'

'But today you are good as new, non?'

'Today I am better than new – and you are more naked than ever. You're going to catch your death running around like that.'

'But it is so, 'ot in ze 'ouse,' she protested, opening her neckline another button and starting my motor running.

'Then turn down the central heating, you sex pot. Madam has gone out, hm?'

'Oui – today she has gone for her sun-ray session. We are all alone. Would you like some coffee before you start ...' she laughed, '... to shovel ze snow?'

'No thanks, I'll get right to it, but I'll need something hot and strong when I'm finished.'

'Zen you shall have it,' she promised. 'But don't take too long, hm – I have work for you to do in ze 'ouse today.'

'Oh, you have, have you. What sort of work – as though I need to ask.'

'Well, I 'ad a dream about you last night. It was ver' beautiful ...'

'Was it? What was I doing?'

'La! All *sorts* of lovely things ... and today I wish you to do them for real.'

'You're a hussy, you know that?'

'Ah, oui,' she laughed, 'but it is so much more fun than being anysink else!'

'To change the subject – where do I find the snow shovel?'

'In the shed at the side of the 'ouse.'

'Right – I'll see you in half an hour.'

'And not a moment longer.'

'The way you look – it may be a whole lot shorter.'

And so, setting aside my overwhelming preference for internal employment, I collected the snow shovel from the shed and started on the front drive.

I'd been working on it about fifteen minutes, whistling away, my mind full of Lucy and Brigitte and Brigitte and Lucy and just occasionally, though not too often, on Buzz, bashing his balls around the indoor court in Victoria, when a middle-aged guy in blue coveralls, carrying a leather bag and a telephone handset, turned into the drive and crunched towards me.

'Hi, there!' he grinned, showing more space than teeth. 'Anyone in?'

'Er, yes, the maid's in.'

'Maid, eh ... that's the way to live. Got a complaint 'bout a faulty line, like to check it out.'

'Go right ahead.'

He nodded at the shovel. 'You're doin' a fine job ... sure makes ours easier. Last winter I was up to ma waist in some drives. No consideration, some folks.'

'Heartless,' I agreed.

He moved on, rang the chimes, got Brigitte, flashed an identity card at her and entered the house. She managed a little-wave and blew a kiss at me before closing the door. About ten minutes later, just as I was finishing the drive, he came out again.

'Yep, there's a fault all right. Kind of intermittent, though – sometimes she will, sometimes she won't – just like the wife!' He cackled a laugh. 'Snow, probably. I'll have to check a few things down the line. Don't worry 'bout it.'

I promised him I wouldn't.

'Well, I'll be seein' yuh ...' He started off, but came to a sudden halt, staring hard at the Cadillac, 'Say, now ain't *that* a whole lot of goodness! Sweet Mother, what I'd give to own that. Huh, fat chance you an' me ever got parking one of them in the garage – leastwise our *own* garage! Heck, I can just imagine the ole gal's face if I rolled home in one of them. Same goes for you, too, I reckon. You're gonna have to shovel a whole lot more snow for even a downpayment on the spare tyre of that baby!'

Up yours, I thought. Try as I might I did not like the idea of being taken for a professional snow-shoveller.

'It ... happens to *be* mine,' I said nonchalantly, enjoying his toothless gape.

'Well, by golly who'd a thought it!' he gasped. 'Appearances sure can be misleadin'. Are you ... one of the family, then?'

'Sort of,' I said, casually cleaning my nail with the tip of the shovel.

'Sure,' he nodded, 'shoulda knowed it. Close up you don't look like no labourin' fella – you ain't got the hands for it. Well, I surely do apologize ...'

I grinned at him. 'Think nothing of it. Thanks for calling.'

'Oh, you're welcome ... mighty welcome.'

Off he went, shaking his head. A couple more shovels and I was finished. I put away the shovel and rang the chimes.

'Ah, cheri,' smiled Brigitte, 'come in, you must be frozen steef.'

'To the marrow, beloved ... lead me to the coffee.'

Slipping on to a stool at the peninsula bar, I asked her, 'What did Toothless Dan, the Telephone Man have to say to you?'

'Aw, not much. He tested all ze extensions ... said zere was a leetle fault, zat is all.'

'He didn't try to get fresh, hm?'

'Fresh?' she laughed. 'Him! No, mon chou, but he was 'inting for a cup of coffee. "By golly, zat smells good!" he said. "Sorry," I said, "but it won't be ready for half an hour." Phee, what would I want with a toothless old fogey when I have you?'

She put down the cups and came round the unit, sat on my knee with a sexy wriggle, 'Now I tell you about my dream, hm?'

'Er ... hadn't you better go and sit over there, rabbit?

Her eyes popped. 'But you have done all ze work for today – you have cleared ze snow!'

'Oh, no, we've got to do more than that.'

'Mais, non! Madam left explicit instructions zat you were not to overtire yourself ...' she giggled, ' ... with ze 'ousework, zat is! Now – I tell you about my dream ...'

'You're *sure* there's not something we ought to be doing?'

'Yes, there is,' she laughed, 'but we shall not get to it unless you let me tell you about my dream!'

'Brigitte, I meant *housework*. What about this decorating that madam was talking about?'

'Decorating?' she shrugged. 'Zere is no decorating to do. I tell you, zere is absolutely no ...' She stopped, eyes narrowing cunningly as she pounced on something. 'Ah, no! I am wrong! Zere *is* somesink for you to do – zere is my lamp to fix in my bedroom!'

'Oho!' I laughed, 'you little ...'

'So – let us take our coffee upstairs ... and while you fix my lamp, I shall tell you about my dream. Let us go.'

You just can't win against that sort of determination, can you? Not that I was working very hard at it, mind you, but you have to make a bit of an effort for the sake of appearances.

'I'll need a screwdriver,' I said.

'But you already have a *beautiful* screwdriver,' she chuckled, kissing my ear.

'Brigitte, am I going to get *any* sense out of you today?'

'No! I don't *feel* like being sensible – I feel like being very 'appy. O.K. – I find you a screwdriver.'

'And a sharp knife.'

'Bien ... anysink else?'

'No, that should do it.'

'O.K.' She pecked me on the nose, skipped off my knee, found the tools and we were off upstairs, into her little floral room.

'Ah, home from home,' I sighed. 'Strange how familiar it all seems. Is that the lamp?'

'Huh huh ...'

I sat on the edge of the bed, clicked on the lamp and got nothing.

'You've checked the bulb?'

'Of course,' she replied, launching herself on to the bed and coming to rest almost in my lap, chin in her hands.

'Then it could be a loose wire. We'll take a look.'

'Ah, you are so clever.'

'Well, there's nothing *too* academic about checking for a loose wire ...'

'So very clever ... so 'andy wiz your 'ands ...'

'Brigitte, stop that. How can I check delicate wiring while you're stroking my leg.'

'Last night I dreamed about your legs.'

'You did?' How very odd.'

'Ah, oui, I dreamed ... non, I shall start at the beginning.

I dreamed I was all alone in zis big 'ouse. Aw, I was *so* lonely. Zen suddenly, came a ring at ze door. Dressed only in my tiny nylon nightie I went to answer it ...'

I grinned at her. 'Yes, that sounds like you.'

'Don't interrupt, zis is serious.'

'Sorry.'

'Dressed only in my tiny see-through nightie I went to answer it – and it was you! Aw, you were so handsome in your dark blue uniform ...'

'Ah, I was in the navy ...'

'Non, you 'ad come to read the electric meter. 'Ow your eyes caressed me ... undressed me. I felt so shy ...'

I couldn't suppress the laugh and she slapped me on the leg, taking advantage of the moment to leave her hand there, nestling in my lap.

'Contrary to what you may think, monsieur, it is not unknown for me to feel shy. Granted, it does not 'appen too often, but nevertheless ... where was I?'

'I was stripping you naked.'

'Ah, yes. So – I invited you in and you checked ze meter ... and zen – as you were leaving, I said to you, "I wonder if you could *pleeze* take a look at my bedroom lamp, it is broken." And do you know what your reply was?'

'Sorry, miss, I'm a married man and have to run home to my wife and six kids?'

'Idiot,' she laughed. 'Non, you were very gallant. Certainly, you said, if zere is one sing I cannot refuse it is a lady in distress.'

'You know, that sounds rather like me.'

'It was you. So – we came upstairs ... and you sat exactly where you are sitting now ... and I came and lay on ze bed exactly where I am lying now ... and I watched you mend ze lamp ...'

'And ... then what happened?' I said, lumpily, because her hand had slid down over Herc and she was now doing all sorts of sly, subtle little things to him and he, being the pushy bloke he is, was beginning to respond in his own very forthright manner which tickled her no end because I was now having considerable difficulty keeping the lamp in my lap.

'Zen ... you suddenly became aware of ze beautiful ... half-naked girl lying beside you and you put down ze lamp ... like zis and took her in your arms ... like zis ... and you kissed her most passionately ...'

'Like zis?'

About three minutes later she broke away, gasping, 'Mais, oui! *Exactly* like zat!'

'And ... then what?' I croaked, choked to the gills.

'Zen I pulled you on to ze bed ... like zis ... and took all your clothes off ... like zis!'

It took her about five seconds – with help.

'And ... then?' I squeaked.

'Zen you took off all my clothes ...'

'Like zis!'

'And zen I pushed you back on ze bed ... and did wonderful sings to you ... like zis!'

'Ohh, baby ... did you really do that?'

'Hm hm,' she nodded, unable to speak.

'By *golly*, I wish I'd been there ... ohhh ... wow ... by the heck, that's lovely ... what a pity it was only a dream ... but this could ... oh, boy ... never happen in real life, could it ... Brigitte, you'd better stop that ... now where are you going?'

'Up here!' she chuckled, swinging aboard and settling down. 'Oh, mon Dieu, zat is ... incroy*able*!'

I had to laugh, she was pulling such funny faces. 'All right up there?'

'Fantastique!'

'About that dream ...'

'Oui?'

'Did you really have it?'

She laughed and shook her head. 'Mon chou, I was so tired after yesterday I did not dream anysing all night.'

'No, I had a feeling it was a put-up job.'

'Ha! *You* can talk! However, if I *had* had a dream last night, I'm sure it would have been exactly like zis – otherwise I would not have had it!'

'Mmm, that sounds nicely femininely logical.'

'Ohhh ... zis is too wonderful,' she groaned, easing up ... then down ... then up ... down ... up ... down. 'Ohhh, you do it to me again, you beast ... you make me come again ... ohhhh ... ohhhh!' And she was away, bouncing like a road-thumper ... cher-pow ... cher-pow ... cher-pow and ... ohhhhhhh! falling forward on to my chest to beat on it like a tom-tom and cover my face with kisses.

'Ohhh, you ... you ...

She collapsed and lay there heaving like a Grand National winner.

Give the ladies one thing, they can take their lumps and recover a lot fitter and faster than us chaps. Barely a minute later she was sitting bolt upright again, eyes a-sparkle and with that smirk of self-satisfaction that tells you you've got to do a damn-sight better than *that* to finish 'em off.

'Well?' I grinned.

'Now what?' she beamed.

'Now, Miss Brigitte, I am going to tell you about a dream *I* had last night.'

'Ah, oui?'

'Oui. I dreamed I was travelling through the Sahara Desert and I came upon an old man who'd lost his camel. So I gave him a drink of water and lift to the nearest town – only to find when we got there that he wasn't a poor old bloke after all. He was none other than a fabulously wealthy oil sheik!'

'La!' she laughed, going along with this nonsense.

' "I must repay you for saving my life," said the old geezer. "Name your own reward and it shall be yours – a hundred camels ... jewels ... oil-well or two?" No, thanks, Sheik, I said, my reward shall be a two week stop over in your harem of fourteen fabulous fillies. And so – on the first night ...'

'Oh, mon Dieu,' she gasped, 'zere goes lunch!'

CHAPTER FIFTEEN

Well, Brigitte and I footled away the day in a most delightful way, taking a long, refreshing nap after the exercise, polishing a bit of silver and listening to some music in the afternoon and generally having a lovely time.

Then, at four o'clock, Lucy came home looking positively radiant from her sun-ray treatment and in very chipper mood, and I was very thankful I'd had that recuperative kip because I could tell right away she was feeling a mite frisky. And so it proved! We sat around chatting for a couple of hours over a few drinks and then she suggested we go upstairs and take a Turkish bath – a sexual euphemism, I knew, but at least we went through the motions.

By the time she'd got up a good head of steam in the Turk Room, however, she'd got an even better head of steam going in the bedroom, and as we rolled and wrestled on the bed it looked as though the Turkish Bath would be doing a solo all night until somebody switched it off the next morning – there seeming little point in sweating that much twice!

But that, alas, was not the way things worked out.

Around about eight o'clock (forgive the imprecision, I was not unduly concerned with time at the time), our voracious thrashings were brought to a sudden and shocked halt by an horrific female scream that echoed along the landing, emanating from a point immediately outside Lucy's bedroom door, and the next moment Brigitte was hammering on the door like a thing possessed and gasping, 'Madam ... madam ... it's your 'usband! 'E is *'ere*! In ze 'ouse! Quick ... quick ...!'

Lucy's mouth dropped open. She turned a whiter shade of pale, her eyes grew four times their normal size and she let out a terrorized bellow like she'd been kicked by a horse. 'Oh, my ... GOD!'

Speaking for myself, panic seized every fibre of my being and for three or four completely paralysed seconds I hung suspended above dear Lucy, rigid as a board, useless as a eunuch, and thoroughly ashamed of myself for being so.

In the fifth second, however, the screaming seriousness of the situation began to percolate through to my petrified brain and in the sixth I was off the bed and running around in demented circles grabbing up my clothes.

Lucy by now was sitting bolt upright, staring wildly into space and mouthing, 'Oh, my God ... oh, my God ...' until the disastrous potential of the moment finally penetrated *her* seized-up mind. 'Ohh ... Jeezus!' she finally gasped and she, too, shot off the bed. 'Two million ... *dollars*!'

'Now ... don't panic, Lucy! Think ... think ...!'

'Two ... million ... dollars!' she cried, almost in tears.

'Don't worry ... I'll save it!'

'How ... *how* ...!'

'Er ...'

Desperately I searched the room for somewhere to hide ... wardrobe ... cupboards ... far too obvious ... under the bed? ... ridiculous ... I ran to the window, peered through it, spotted a narrow ledge running below, covered in snow and ice, abandoned the thought and once more turned to the room, now *really* panicking as Brigitte's tearful, terrified warning came through the door. 'Oh, madam ... madam ... hurry! He's coming up the stairs!'

'Lucille!' A stentorian bellow from the hall that turned my blood to ice-water.

'Oh, dear God ... dear *God* ...!' cried Lucy, throwing on her gown and hurriedly straightening the bed. 'He's caught us ... he's caught us!'

'Not yet he hasn't!' I answered staunchly, breaking into a run, heading for the bathroom, not having a clue what I was going to do when I got there. I scanned it ... and abandoned it. There was just nowhere to hide!

Then it came to me ... the Turkish Bath! The steam!

I spun round to Lucy. 'The steam room!'

She gaped. 'You can't!'

'I must! Get him out of here as fast as you can!'

'But, Russ ...'

At that moment the bedroom door buckled under a deluge of heavy blows and a man's gruff, angry, triumphant voice rang out, 'Lucille! This is Karl! Let me in!'

Trembling terribly, poor Lucy cast tear-filled and tormented eyes at me, gasped, 'Go ...! Go ...!' and as I departed swiftly for the T.B., she was heading towards the door.

Yanking open the heavy door I plunged inside and thunked it behind me. My God, it was murder in there. Maybe in her preoccupation Lucy had turned the temperature to high-high, I wouldn't know, but it seemed two thousand degrees hotter in there than the first time.

Great billowing clouds of scalding steam enveloped me. I stumbled across to the lowest tier and up I went to the topmost, furthermost corner, lay on my stomach and flattened myself to the boards, realizing now that Lucy *must* have turned the temperature to high-high. It was a bleeding cauldron up there.

I don't know whether you've ever had the misfortune to fall asleep under an African sun at high noon, but even if you haven't the analogy might give you some idea of what it was like up there in the gods. The heat was a battering, oppressive weight, a moist, suffocating blanket that drove the breath from my lungs and brought me out in a torrential sweat.

After only a few seconds I'd had more than enough and

truly felt I was beginning to die. I lay there panting, gasping for air, my heart thumping so hard I knew I could not last more than a minute or two, and if Karl was not out of that bedroom within that time I'd either have to give myself up or I *would* die.

I lay motionless, fighting the panic that engulfed me, urged me to run out of there into the blessedly cool air of the bathroom ... and then suddenly their voices came to me, helping my fight to stay.

'Where is he!' demanded Karl, the deep-chested rumble of a very big man.

'Karl, how *dare* you force your way into this house!' Lucy, bless her, was fighting back, employing the old stratagem of attack as the best form of defence. 'Get out of my room ...!'

'This is still *my* house and *my* room, Lucille,' he thundered, his voice closer, perhaps at the bathroom door. 'Come on – where is he! I know he's in here.'

'Wh ... who the hell are you talking about! Get out of here ...!'

'Your lover-boy is who I'm talking about! The English guy who's pretending to be working in the house! Some work ...!'

'Him!' Lucy laughed scornfully. 'Karl, don't be ridiculous ...!'

'Lucille, you're wasting my time! No odd-job man drives a Cadillac convertible, f'chrissake! The white coveralls didn't fool us for a minute! The guy's your lover, pussycat – and he's up here right now!'

'Karl, don't be so bloody preposterous! The man *is* working on the house!'

'So – where is he right now? His car's still parked outside.'

'How should *I* know where he is! Ask Brigitte – maybe she knows!'

'I already asked her. She's scared out of her mind because she knows he's up here with you.'

'She knows nothing of the kind! Karl, there may be two months to go before the divorce, but you have no right to come barging into my ...'

'Correction, Lucille, I have every right. This guy's gonna save me two million bucks – that's how much right I've got.'

'And how do you *know* it's his Cadillac, anyway! He might have hired it ... borrowed it ...!'

'Oh, it's his all right ... he said so himself.'

'He ...?' she faltered.

Hey, what was this he was trying to pull!

Karl continued, triumphantly. 'You had a telephone engineer to the house today, did you know that?'

'I ... no, I didn't...'

'You were out, I made sure of that. Only the guy wasn't a legit engineer – he was working for me. He's the guy that's been keeping an eye on you for quite a while. He got talkin' to your lover-boy in the front drive and the dope admitted that it was his Caddy and that he was practically a member of the family! The guy's downstairs now – ask him to play the tape back to you. He had a recorder goin' in the handset he was carrying!'

'You ... bastard!' she seethed.

'All's fair in hate and alimony, honey. Now all I gotta do is find the bum ...'

His footsteps rang on the tiled bathroom floor.

'... and when I do, maybe I'll slip him a coupla G's for savin' me two million.'

Ohhh ... God! What a bloody, big-headed fool I'd been! There – just shows where false pride can get you. A little harmless swank about owning the Cadillac and it looked like costing Lucy a fortune.

I lay there dying, racked by the terrible heat and overwhelmed by guilt, willing to sacrifice my right arm twice over if I could restore the situation to what it had been this afternoon.

How did I *get* into these bloody messes?

How many times – while hiding under a bird's bed or in a cupboard – had I sworn that I'd never get into such a bleeding pickle again?

Well, this time I truly meant it. Please God make Karl Koeller-Jurling disappear and I will never ... *never* ...

'You're wasting your time Karl!' shouted Lucy, following him into the bathroom. 'That man is not here and if he's not downstairs I don't know *where* he is! Now kindly get the hell out of my bathroom and out of my home – yes, *my* home! You've got your nerve forcing your way in here, trying to trap me after all the goddam fornicating you've done! My God, you were making love to some Mexican bitch in Acapulco two nights after we were married ...!'

'True,' he laughed. 'But *my* philandering isn't in question –

yours is. Knowing your libidinous nature, honey, I knew you'd have to take a lover sometime – it was only a matter of waiting. And now ... I've caught you!'

On the word, the door opened.

Shutting my eyes, as if that helped, and flattening myself so hard to the boards I was in danger of going clean through them, I gritted my teeth and held my breath, knowing damn well it was all to no avail. He was going to climb right up to me, tap me on the shoulder and say, 'O.K., lover-boy, get your trousers on, the fun's over.'

But he didn't – at least not immediately. He gave a cough and gasped, 'Jesuskrist, Lucille, what you doin' in here – smoking hams?'

'I was just about to take a steam bath when you ... you violated my privacy!'

'The heat's too damned high.'

And don't I fucking well know it!

'Mind your own damn business,' she snapped. 'You gave up all rights to advise me on anything six months ago. Now, if you're satisfied my "lover" isn't hiding in here, will you please close the door and get the hell out of here!'

He gave a low, mean chuckle. 'Well, if he is in here there won't be anythin' left to grab hold of when he comes out.'

Too bleeding true, mate. The sweat was cascading off me in torrents and dripping down on to the tier below, my strength with it.

'Well, now, I guess he must be hiding in one of the other rooms,' sneered Karl. 'I heard Brigitte give you the warning ... maybe lover-boy had time to slip out.'

'I told you, Karl, I don't know where he is ...' Lucy's voice faded a little as the door, thank God, closed.

I released my stupefied breath and collapsed, shaking all over, now feeling quite ill, baked alive, dehydrated. I trembled to my knees, collected my sodden clothes, rolled off the tier on to the lower one, dropped down to the next and finally landed on my hands and knees, panting like a clapped-out gun-dog. God, I felt weak. I raised my head (an effort in itself), set my sights on the far distant door and then, gathering all my strength, crawled towards it, finally flopped against it and lay there for a full minute gulping steam.

Question was – what now? With that bloody Cadillac parked outside, Karl was not going to give up until he found me –

and find me he would, even if he had to tear the house apart to accomplish it. He had two million very good reasons for doing it.

Well, Tobin, are you going to sit there all night like a limp lily and let him find you? Or are you going to pull yourself together and get your steam-cooked brain working on a plan to save Lucy two million bananas? For after all, you great dick, you are very largely responsible for getting the lady into this mess!

Right – put like that ... come on, now, on with the shirt ... yerk! Ever tried getting into a wet shirt? I pulled it apart with a sucking sound and jammed it over my head, and after that it was uphill all the way. Lovely, you really ought to try it sometime. Next – the socks. Ha! Ever tried putting a pair of socks on underwater?

Well, I finally made it, stood up ... and promptly fell down again, legs like rubber sausages. A momentary breather and I tried again, propped against the door ... and made it. The shoes were no problem, but the trousers and jacket were lulus and the second I got them on I had to open the door or I'd have suffocated then and there.

Cool, unimaginably wonderful air, ice-cold at a mere seventy-five degrees, rushed over me. I clung to the doorpost, gulping down huge lungfuls of it, soon having to stop because I was over-oxygenating. A few moments more and I felt fit enough to travel – very slowly.

Closing the steam-room door behind me, I started off at a cautious wobble across the bathroom. Reaching the bedroom door, I heard voices out on the landing, the door to it standing wide open. Across the bedroom I went, hugged the wall and listened. They were on the landing to the right, searching every room, no doubt.

Very quietly I closed the door then crossed to Lucy's window, undid the centre catch and pushed the window wide open. Holy Mother, the wintry blast hit me. Icy knives sliced through my sodden clothes, bringing my thousand-degree temperature scuttling down to sub-zero in an instant. I started to shiver. God in heaven, was there no happy medium? Was I destined to spend the rest of my life either frying or fucking freezing!

I popped my head out, blinded by the driving snow, looked right, spotted Brigitte's window a mere fifteen feet away. I looked down. The ledge was suicidally narrow – perhaps six or seven inches – and covered in snow. I looked up – ah! the guttering! I could reach it!

Well, here goes, Lucy, love. If I fall and break my neck you'll be no worse off than you are now and neither will I. The salvation of your fortune lies only fifteen feet away and at 133,333 dollars and 33 cents a foot it's worth having a bash.

With a deep breath and a silent prayer, I cocked my leg over the sill, located the ledge, felt upwards and found the icy gutter, then swung my other leg out. A quick, tremulous shuffle to the left and I was able to close the window ... and there I was – committed.

I will not regale you with the unending horrors of that nightmare walk, add gruesome detail of the cold, slimy and unspeakable terrors that lay dead and dormant in that gutter, or over-tax your already strained imaginations with superlatives of freezing, shivering discomfort. Sufficient to say that when, many minutes later, I finally reached Brigitte's bedroom window I was closer to freezing finality than I had been to dehydrated death in the steam room.

Covered in snow, teeth chattering like machine-guns, hands turned into blue-black claws, I shuffled and clung the last blessed few inches to the left and stepped on to Brigitte's sill. And how, you may well be asking yourselves, did I plan to get in if the window was locked? Well, I'd long ago made up my mind that in the absence of any other solution I was going to fetch one of the small panes a swift kick, fairly certain her door would be closed and Karl would be making too much noise to hear the breaking glass.

Fortunately, though, such a drastic recourse was not necessary, for there was the little darling herself, peering through her partly opened door at the activity on the landing.

Shivering uncontrollably, I released one dark blue talon from the guttering and tapped on the window. She gave a jump and shot round, eyes like dinner plates, suddenly recognized me and with a quick clutch of despair at her bosom, came haring across to open the window.

'Mon pauvre ... mon pauvre ...!' she wailed. 'Oh, 'ow awful ... 'ow terrible! That dreadful man ... mon petit, you are frozen! You will catch your death!'

'Highly likely,' I nodded, teeth chattering like a road drill, everything shivering and blue and stiff and just bloody 'orrible.

'What can I do ... what can I *do*!' she cried, fluttering her hands like a couple of papillon.

I managed a grin – a creaky, lop-sided effort, but a grin, 'You really want to know?'

'But, of course ...!'

I told her.

Her mouth shot open. 'Russell Tobin, you are *impossible*! At a time like zis ... wiz madam in such terrible trouble ... all you can sink about is ... going to *bed*!'

Karl burst into the room about five minutes later and caught us at it – well, not quite *at* it, but locked stark naked in each other's arms and *looking* as though we were at it.

Brigitte shot up, let out a piercing shriek and threw her arms tight around me for protection, acting it up a treat.

I did my bit by staring wide-eyed at Karl ... then at Lucy ... then at the phoney telephone engineer who was standing behind, presumably as witness.

'Oh!' I gasped, opening my mouth and closing it a few times to simulate shock.

And Karl was doing much the same thing – except he wasn't pretending. 'Huh ...?' was all he could manage for a bit.

Lucy, bless her, recovered fast, put two and two together like lightning and got two million. She let go a couple of good outraged gasps then came on strong.

'What the *hell* is the meaning of this! Brigitte ... how *dare* you do this in my house! And *you* ...!' she swung on me, eyes blazing, 'what in God's name d'you think *you're* doing! I hired you to *work* in this house, not seduce my goddam maid!'

'I ... I ...' I gulped, then got mad. 'You've no right to come bursting into Brigitte's room without knocking!'

Lucy was on me like a collapsed roof. 'I've got a perfect right to do what the hell I *like* in my house, young man. Now you get dressed and get out of here as fast as you can before I call the cops! By God, Hire-A-Guy are gonna hear about this tomorrow!' She rounded on Karl, so flaming furious I couldn't believe she was acting. 'And as for you, you creep – you get the hell out of here, too – and take this ... this creature with you. Jesus, Karl, my attorney's going to hear about this – like right now! And if this doesn't cost you another million ...'

Away she strode, heading for the phone, with Karl right behind her, wailing, 'Now, Lucy, *honey* ... now, listen, will yuh ...'

Toothless Dan turned sheepishly from the door.

'Hey, you!' I shouted. 'Close that bloody door!'

'Jerk!' he scowled, slamming it hard.

We gave him a couple of seconds to clear then Brigitte and I fell about each other, silently laughing ourselves into hysterics.

'Oh, Russ ... Russ,' she chuckled, ' 'ow clever you are!'

'I couldn't have done it without you, love. You deserve an Oscar.'

She gave me another hug. 'Well, I tell you what ... instead of an Oscar, I'll have ...'

She slid her hand under the blankets.

'Brigitte ...! I've got to go! Karl will be watching to see if I really get kicked out.'

'Ah, oui,' she sighed. 'I suppose you are right.'

We got out of bed and once again I dragged on my soggy, miserable clothes. Nice, that.

'You will catch your death!' she protested.

'I won't have them on for long. I'll be in the hotel in fifteen minutes and into a good hot bath. A couple of brandies and a good night's sleep and I'll be as right as rain.'

She came to me, now in her dressing gown, and flung her arms around me. 'Zis is goodbye, isn't it, Russ?'

'I'm afraid so, chicken. I won't be able to set foot in this house again.'

'I shall miss you so much. It's been so much fun.'

'Angel, it's been wonderful.'

I gave her a big kiss and was about to give her an even bigger one when Lucy tapped on the door and came in. She stood there looking at me, then at Brigitte, shaking her head, tears in her eyes, then came to us and put her arms around both of us.

'What can I say ... what can I *say*? You were just wonderful, both of you.' She turned to me, shaking her head at the state of my clothes. 'And you, you big lunk ... I presume you climbed out of the window and walked along the ledge? God, you might have killed yourself.'

'Nah, only the good die young. I presume you got rid of ...'

'Fast,' she laughed. 'Karl was driving away before I'd finished dialling.'

'Did you call your attorney?'

She shook her head. 'No – I'll be very satisfied with two million. You realize, of course, that I'd have lost the lot if you hadn't done what you did?'

'Yes ... but I also figured it'd be my fault if you did. So – I lost it for you and then managed to get it back – and the relief is worth a lot more than two million, believe me. Lucy ... I'd better go. Karl will be watching to see if – and *how* I leave. So you'd better give me a good rousing send-off at the door.'

She nodded, sadly. 'Say goodbye to Brigitte then come into the bedroom, hm?'

'Yes.'

A few minutes later I entered the room. Lucy came to me and hugged me. 'What a terrible ...'

'Unbelievable,' I laughed.

She looked at me, smiling sadly. 'Thank you – for everything.'

'And I thank you.'

'You deserve a big reward.'

'I've had my reward.'

'Maybe ... when the divorce comes through, you could ...'

I smiled and nodded. 'That would be lovely. I don't know where I'll be in two months' time, but ...'

'I'll fly you back, wherever you are. Remember the address ... and keep in touch.'

'You think I could ever forget it?' I grinned. 'Come on – throw me out and make it good.'

'Hm,' she smiled. 'That will be the hardest piece of acting of all.'

A minute later I was flying out of the front door.

'You may as well leave town!' she shouted, as I headed for the Cadillac. 'You'll never work for Hire-A-Guy again!'

'Well, if it's for birds like you, missus, I wouldn't want to!'

And as the front door slammed, as though to punctuate the ignominy of my departure, I slipped on a patch of ice and fell on my arse in the flower bed.

CHAPTER SIXTEEN

In a day so chockful of surprises it seemed unreasonable, to say nothing of unreal, to expect still another, yet such is the erstwhileness of fate that before I was fifteen minutes older I was once more standing rooted with a shock of such total unexpectedness that, had I been prone to any ticker weakness, might well have finished me off on the spot.

Looking a right crumpled sight in my soggy, mud-stained clothes, I entered the hotel somewhat furtively, unanxious to attract any attention in case they chucked me back into the street, thinking I was a tramp.

Quickly collecting my key from a highly-suspicious porter, I made a bee-line for the elevator and the fourth floor, and there, with a sigh of relief and an overwhelming yearning for a hot bath and seven double brandies, I unlocked the door, entered the room, fumbled for the light-switch and damn near died of fright.

There was a body lying prone on Buzz's bed, the face averted!

I shot back, grabbed for the door and was about to turn tail when the body sat up, beamed a huge grin and cried, 'Hello, you old bastard, how are yuh?'

'Buzz ...!'

'Spot on, son, glad to see you haven't forgotten.'

He leapt off the bed, all six feet two and two hundred pounds of him and crushed all five fingers to powder with a hearty handshake.

'Buzz ...!' I gasped. 'What the heck ...'

He held up a hand, the size of his racquet. 'I know ...'

'But I wasn't expecting you for another ten days, man!'

He shrugged. 'Can I help it if I'm a lousy tennis-player?'

'You ... got knocked out?'

He grinned and shook his head. 'Nah, half the players didn't turn up – they've all got flu out there. They cancelled the tournament.'

'Oh, hell ...'

'But – nil desperandum. I've had a wire from home. I'm

flying back right aw ... ay ...' His voice tailed off as he saw me – or my condition – for the first time. 'What the *hell* have you been doing – wallowin' in a hippo pool!'

'Buzz ...' I shook my head, '... you're just not going to believe this ...'

'Jeezuschrist,' he grinned, 'You've been at it again, Tobin, haven't you? You've been in bother again!'

I nodded dumbly and he shook his head. 'Man, for a nice, quiet, clean-cut Pom you get into more trouble than any half dozen cowboys I know back home. Here – get this down you, you look as though you need it.'

He turned to the bedside table, sloshed about nineteen fingers of scotch into a glass and handed it to me. I took a good swallow, slumped down on the foot of his bed and lit the fag he gave me. 'Ah, that feels better.'

'Well, come on, what the hell have you been up to?'

I laughed. 'Got a couple of hours?'

'I've got the whole night. Cheers ...'

'Cheers ... and, by golly, it's nice to have you back. I reckon you arrived in the nick of time.'

'Bloody looks like it, too. I left a young, carefree lad at the airport a couple of days ago and come back to find a haggard, shagged-out old wreck. By God, you must have been doing some ... anyway, get on with it – from the top.'

'You shall have it from the top – and also from a deep, hot bath. I'm freezing. These clothes are wet.'

'Anyway you like, as long as I get it. This ... is gonna be good!'

About an hour and two fat scotches later, now dressed in clean, dry clothes and a spirit of supreme well-being, I was drawing to the end of my story, describing how I inched along the ledge to Brigitte's room, and Buzz was rocking with laughter and thumping the pillow. Come to think of it he hadn't stopped laughing or gasping or God-Almighty-ing since I'd started.

'And there I was – flat on my arse in the geraniums,' I said. 'Painful end of story.'

'You ...' he shook his head and sighed. 'By God, Tobin, some blokes have all the luck. A Cadillac yet!'

'It's down in the garage if you don't believe me.'

'Ho, I believe you. After what happened on the train and in New York, I'd believe any damn thing you told me! Dammit,

Tobin, after that I don't know whether I should invite you!'

'Invite me? Invite me where?'

'Home, mate – to Aussie.'

'Eh?'

'I've got a tournament lined up – Aussie–American. I'll have to leave tomorrow. Got to be back there in four days. Just . . .' he gave a shrug, 'thought you might like to tag along.'

'Well, I . . .' I exploded a laugh. 'Well, I . . .'

'Don't worry about the fare, if that's what you're thinking. You can cash your London flight and I can fix you up with the difference until we get home. You'll be able to transfer some loot out there.'

'Yes, sure. No, I wasn't thinking about that . . .'

'Well, what, then?'

I thought about it . . . then grinned at him and shrugged. 'Nothing!'

'Oh ho!' he laughed. 'Oh, we can have some fun out there. I'm on home ground . . . fix you up a treat. And . . .' he grinned, pulling his nose, 'you realize where we'll be touching down, don't you?'

'No. Where?'

He leapt to his feet and started doing a daft dance, hands undulating like snakes and hips wiggling while he made a noise like an Hawaiian guitar.

'Scotland?' I suggested.

'You daft sod . . . TAHITI!'

'No!'

'Too right! The island of dusky, snake-hipped lovelies whose only pleasure in life is giving pleasure . . .'

'Wow!'

'Well, son . . .' he dropped on the bed and helped us to another forty-seven fingers of happy water, '. . . what d'you say? You'll have the time of your life, I promise you. It'll make what you've done in the past week seem like a Baptist Bible meeting. Think you can stand the pace?'

I narrow-eyed him. 'Are you suggesting, Malone, that Tobin cannot cope with whatever Australia has to offer?'

'Well . . .' he said doubtfully, 'you haven't seen our sheilas, mate . . . they're big, strong, strapping, sun-tanned Amazons – not these lightweight pigeons you've been razzing. These are women! Still, I reckon if I sorted out one or two of the punier ones . . .'

'Malone – enough! You are trampling on the Tobin pride!'
'Then you'll come?' he beamed.
I raised my glass and gave him a grin. 'Try and flamin' well stop me!'

CHAPTER SEVENTEEN

I am writing this aboard a Qantas jumbo, heading west for Australia, next stop . . . Tahiti.

This may conceivably be my last communication. Ever.

Tarra.

'Tobin . . .?'

'Yes, Buzz?'

'Ever done it standing up on a surf board?'